SAVED BY THE DEMON PRINCE

LAUREN CROWNE

ENID BOOKS

1

VERA

"Vera. I'm taking you home."

Like hell he was.

Standing in front of us on the terrace, Leo was framed by his long black coat rustling in the light wind, the hood fallen back to reveal his face. The demon's silver eyes reflected the twinkling lights set up around the terrace for tonight's party, though the intensity of his gaze burned far brighter than any light around. As seconds passed, more and more fae rushed over to see what was happening, forming a circle around where we stood, but Leo ignored them all. His large black wings relaxed behind him, but he never took his eyes off me.

As I held Leo's stare and refused to look away, Laurie, clad in a white tux, wrapped his arm around my waist to hold me back. Was the fae prince trying to shield me from Leo or keep me from going to him? I wasn't sure, but I pushed Laurie away all the same.

I didn't need Laurie or any other fae's protection. Not from Leo. I didn't fear him.

At that moment, it was Leo who should fear me.

How did the demon have the gall to come here, to the capital fae city of Rowan, after what he'd done? After handing me over like a discarded toy to Laurie and his sister Mia, not bothering to care what I wanted, what I needed? And now he had the audacity to say he was taking me home?

Telling me he was taking me home, as if I had no choice yet again.

Leo stood completely still, waiting.

"Um..." For once, even Laurie was speechless. His dazzling blue wings, larger than any wings I'd seen other than the king's own, fluttered behind him. He ran a hand through his white hair but didn't seem able to decide what else to do. He touched my arm. "Vera, you should—"

That was enough for Leo's eyes to flick to the fae prince beside me. He let out a quick snort. "If you thought for even one second that she—"

"Get out of my sight."

At the sound of my voice, Leo and Laurie both snapped their heads in my direction. Trying to stand straighter, I gripped the railing of the terrace beside me for support. My silver ball gown suddenly felt tighter, too tight, suffocatingly tight. I squeezed the iron railing even harder.

To anyone else, it would have looked like Leo's expression didn't change, but I knew from the slight twitch of his tail that my words had the impact I'd hoped for. I knew they'd hurt. I wanted them to hurt.

He deserved all that pain and more for abandoning me. Much more.

"Vera...," Leo started, but no more words came.

"Don't" was all I said back, swallowing the lump forming in my throat.

"You know I had to—"

"We were a team," I shot back. "We were supposed to be a team."

The longer we stared at each other on the terrace, the more the emotions I'd worked so hard to shove down came rushing back up to the surface. The shock and pain I'd felt when I'd woken up with the fae prince and princess in a field somewhere, not snuggled against Leo in his bed. The hurt I'd felt knowing he'd purposely sent me away because I was too weak to stay with him. Too weak to be in the demon kingdom, where it seemed like all his relatives were intent on harming me or him or both.

There was another feeling there too, one I wasn't ready to fully acknowledge, one I forced myself to ignore. I didn't trust myself enough to know what I would do if I gave in and acknowledged that this demon—this demon that I had loved—had come all the way to the fae city for me no matter the consequences.

No. I couldn't think about that.

Leo opened his mouth as if he were about to say something else, but several of the royal fae guards grabbed his arms. He didn't try to stop them but stood firm on the terrace as the fae locked their hands around his forearms. More guards flew in by the second, and a larger crowd was now forming around us, wide-eyed fae with glittering wings dressed in their finest attire, all staring in shock at Leo. The murmurs were growing louder and louder.

How did a demon get inside the Gate?

Only fae can enter Rowan.

Did the veil fail?

I knew that Leo had been able to enter Rowan because he was part fae, but no one else knew that about him. It made sense that all the fae gathered here thought something must be wrong with the magical veil protecting the city.

Even the guards seemed confused and unsure of what to do next. "Your Highness." One looked to their prince for direction. "What would you like us to do?"

The murmurs of the crowd grew louder and more frantic at the sight of a demon at the fae castle. Guards started clearing away the onlookers, one of them trying to lead Laurie and me away from Leo, but then the rest of the royal family landed beside us.

"What is going on here?" the king demanded. He looked frantic as he tried to make sense of the sight in front of him. The king's blue wings, larger even than Laurie's, fluttered behind his back in agitation.

Laurie left my side to get his father's attention, but the king wasn't listening. He was too busy shouting orders and telling everyone to get back.

"Father, give me just a moment," Laurie said, but the king was barking commands at the guards to clear the terrace while his sister and the queen ushered the guests away.

"Who are you?" the king demanded of the demon before Leo could say anything to me.

Leo stared past the king, his eyes never leaving my own. "Vera, leave with me, and I'll tell you everything."

Mia was at my side, her hand on my arm. Unlike everyone else shuffling off as quickly as possible, Mia wasn't pulling me away, and when I glanced at her, she seemed more torn about what to do than concerned. "Maybe we should go," she whispered.

"I'm not the one who needs to leave," I told the princess, speaking loud enough that I knew Leo would hear.

The king whipped his head around, his brow wrinkling when he looked at me. "Vera, you know this demon?"

"Father, let me talk to him," Laurie said, but the king held up a hand to silence him.

"How did you get into our city, demon?" the king demanded.

"I don't plan on staying," Leo said through clenched teeth. Then he nodded in my direction. "But I'm taking her with me."

"You don't get to decide where I go anymore!" I shouted, starting to feel tears prick the corners of my eyes.

Don't cry. Don't cry. Please, I begged myself, *of all things right now, please don't cry*. This was not the moment to look pathetic. This was the moment to show him I didn't need him. That I was over his betrayal and could be on my own. I could cry when I got back to my room, but right then I needed to keep it together.

Don't let Leo see you cry.

I scrunched up my face, trying to hold back the tears.

Leo's face fell, his expression suddenly going slack, and he surged forward, but the fae guards held on to his arms, stopping him from coming closer to me.

The king was right in front of Leo, demanding answers, but I wasn't listening. From the looks of it, neither was Leo, his silver eyes staring over the king right at me.

"Laurie," Mia whispered to her brother, who was on the other side of me. "What do we do? Dad's going to do something stupid."

"I don't know." Laurie's hands clenched at his sides as he thought, but then he froze. "Holy shit," he said, louder this time. "Is that a Hellfire ruby on his hand?"

It was as if time stopped. I followed Laurie's eyes and saw it myself. On Leo's finger was a ring with the unmistakable glow of a deep red stone, a Hellfire ruby, a gem created by demon scientists using the hearts of fae. I'd last seen those the night Leo's father had announced that Leo was taking over the throne. The Hellfire Crown was adorned with them, and now Leo wore one on his hand.

How many fae had been killed to make that ruby? The blood-red glow was faint since the stone on the ring was so small, but it was there nonetheless, glowing like a beacon to draw our attention.

Did Leo really have the gall to come to the fae city with that on his finger?

I heard a sound. Without even realizing it, I had crushed the metal railing I'd been gripping, the pieces clanging together as they hit the floor of the terrace.

"Vera, did you just…?" As Laurie's voice trailed off, I looked from my hand to his blue eyes, which were wide with surprise. Mia was staring at me too, her mouth dropped open in shock.

"I didn't mean to," I mumbled, turning my hand over to make sure I wasn't hurt. In fact, I wasn't injured at all.

My hand seemed fine, but somehow I'd destroyed the iron railing with my grip alone. It was true I'd felt stronger the longer I stayed in Rowan, but I'd assumed that was due to my heart healing after Leo left me. I hadn't imagined my physical strength had increased as well.

"Give that back!" Leo's deep voice bellowed, distracting us from what I'd just done.

The guards held him tight as one handed the king the ring they had somehow wrestled away from him. Then another guard snapped metal cuffs onto Leo's wrists, and another put a clamp on each of his wings.

"What the hell?" he seethed, struggling against them, but it was no use. The fae here were simply stronger than him when those cuffs were on him, and he couldn't fly away.

I felt Laurie's hand on my elbow.

"Do you want to leave?" he asked.

"Not yet."

I took a hesitant step toward Leo, who had stopped struggling against the guards and instead was watching me, but again Laurie touched my arm. "Vera, we can sort this out later. Right now you don't have to say anything to him."

"I don't plan on it."

The fae prince sighed. "Then I'll buy you a couple of minutes." Laurie nodded to the guards that it was okay as I approached Leo slowly.

Out the corner of my eye, I saw Laurie pull his father to the side, the two of them arguing with each other about Leo's arrival and what they were going to do with him.

Their voices faded into the distance as I got closer to Leo. When was the last time we had seen each other? It had been weeks, maybe a month. Why then did my heart still want to jump out of my chest at the sight of him? Why did his mere presence, his body so much taller and bigger than my own, still make me want to leap into his arms, let him hold me and tell me everything was going to be okay?

It wasn't going to be okay.

It was never going to be okay.

Finally, I stood only a few inches away from him. I knew what I wanted to do.

Looking into Leo's silver eyes, I reached up to touch his face with the same hand I'd just used to crush the iron railing. I made sure my touch was soft, gently pressing against his cheek. Just as I remembered, his skin was warm, and I noticed his breathing start to increase the longer I held my hand there. His pupils dilated, and his chest started to rise and fall in quick succession.

Before, when we were together, Leo had learned how to absorb my magic without it causing the usual effects, but judging by this reaction, he must have forgotten how in the time we'd been apart. Or maybe now he didn't care to control the feelings anymore. The longer my skin stayed connected with his, the hotter the touch became, like it could burn us both if I let it.

He relaxed into the palm of my hand, closing his eyes. The simple movement, so familiar, was enough to make my insides twist. *Why, Leo?* I wanted to scream. I'd gone over that question in my head a million times since he sent me away. *Why didn't you trust me, trust us, enough to try to make it work?*

"Vera," Leo whispered, his eyes still closed.

I took my hand away, and the connection was lost, my skin that much colder in the absence of his warmth. Leo opened his eyes, his lips parting slightly as if he was about to say something.

I didn't give him the chance. I reared back and slapped him across the face. *Hard.*

Leo's head swung to the side as his jaw fell open. Without saying a word, I turned around, took a deep breath, and then walked steadily away.

"Vera!" I heard Leo call out.

I glanced over my shoulder one last time. "Enjoy your new bracelets."

2

LEO

I deserved that.

Actually, I deserved a lot more than a simple slap across the face from Vera. The jail cell they'd put me in didn't have a mirror, but when I touched my cheek, I could still feel the sting of her hot palm. That power was new. The slap had hurt more than it should have. After I got both of us the fuck out of there, I'd have to find out what was happening with her magic.

The shocked look on that fae bastard's face had made the whole trip worth it though. He must not have thought I'd really come for her. The way that white-haired prince had stared at me, mouth open in surprise, made getting thrown in fae jail worth it too.

Leaning against my cell's cold stone wall, I felt a burning in my chest when I thought of the way he'd tried to block Vera from me. As if he could do anything to stop her. Some of the remaining fae in Vestia had told me all about Laurie and how popular he was in their city. Popular or not, the fae prince didn't know Vera at all if he thought she was that easy to hold back.

Judging by the way he had tried to stand in front of her, he must really think she belonged to him now. Well, he was wrong. I knew the truth. I'd known it as soon as I saw her standing on the terrace.

For what felt like the hundredth time since those asshole fae guards put me down there, I got up and looked through my cell's bars. Like every other time, there was no one. No other prisoners. No guards. Just a long dark hallway of stone walls and floors, lined with empty cells, a few torches burning in the distance.

There was no use calling out; I knew how far below the palace surface we were by how long it had taken to fly down there. I'd been blindfolded, as if that would matter. The entire trip had been down one long column to the basement, the perfect jail for someone who couldn't fly.

I heard footsteps on the stone, coming closer by the second. I strained through the bars to see who it was, but at the first hint of blue, I sat back down.

Finally the footsteps stopped.

"Dude. You fucked up."

I didn't even have to look up to know the white-haired fae with his ridiculous blue wings was standing in front of my cell. "You came down here just to tell me that?"

"No. I came down here to enjoy the sight of a demon locked behind bars."

"The same demon who saved your ass on that rooftop, in case you forgot."

"You only had to save me because another demon shot me. In your demon kingdom."

"Judging by this dungeon, the hospitality of the fae of Rowan doesn't seem much better. Why don't you fix that since apparently you're the prince of the whole damn place?"

"That's right. I am. I'm the prince who rescued Vera and got her out of that cursed realm."

"Because I told you to. Don't act like you didn't want her to go with you."

When I finally looked up, the fae crossed his arms over his chest and nodded. "True. I did," he said. "That's one of the big differences between you and me, demon. I want Vera with me. Always."

"Why do you think I came here, idiot? She belongs with me. Get me out of here or leave me alone."

"Why *did* you come to Rowan? Lay it out for me. Prince to prince. Or is it king? What is your title now? We don't get much news here."

"It's complicated," I grumbled.

"Good stories usually are. Let's hear it. Entertain me. You've got the time, after all."

This fucking prick.

"I'm not your entertainment, fae. Unlock this cell so I can get my girl and go."

"Your girl? Did we see two different things tonight? Because I'm pretty sure I heard her tell you to get lost."

"Fuck you. You owe me your life, asshole. Act like it."

"No, you need to realize the position you're in. Right now I'm all that stands between you and my angry parents. Your stunt tonight revealed to every fae in Rowan, very publicly, that our main security system has flaws. A demon was able to get through our protective veil, the one thing that keeps Rowan invisible and safe. That's not exactly something they can let humans and demons outside this city know."

"And?"

"And your demons will want you back, but they won't be able to find you. I'm going to bet they didn't even know you were planning on coming here. I bet you kept that a secret."

He was right, but he didn't have to be so fucking smug about it. When I didn't answer, he kept going.

"No one knows you're here." The fae prince leaned against the cell across from me, comfortably, as if he had all the time in the world. "Since the veil blocks your demon tech, no one can get in touch with you. If you didn't have me to vouch for you, who knows what might happen? Aren't you wondering why there aren't any other prisoners here with you?"

"Because your city is just so perfect?"

"No. Rowan isn't perfect. It's not that we never have prisoners; we just don't keep them alive long. There's no one else down here because, to my parents, nothing's more important than peace."

"They keep the peace by getting rid of anyone who breaks their rules? How noble."

"More noble than deceiving the one person who cared about you the most. You sent her here, Leo, and this is where Vera is going to stay. Of her own choice."

I couldn't stop my tail from sharply tapping against the cold floor, but I did my best to keep my voice level and calm. "Keep talking, and when they finally do let me out, you're going to be the first fae I strangle."

"So much for caring about all the fae, huh?"

"I can make exceptions for arrogant assholes like you. Besides, judging by that fancy party I saw out there, it seems like all of you are doing just fine. I'm glad you're throwing parties while humans are still selling off your kind."

"You think I don't know that? That I'm not trying to do something about it?"

"All I see is a prince more worried about his dick than his fellow fae."

"Fuck you, Leo. As if you're doing anything for the fae yourself. What happened to all *your* noble ambitions?"

"Fine. I'll admit it. The only fae I care about right now is Vera."

Laurie pushed off the wall, coming closer to my cell. Blue eyes narrowed, he pointed a long finger at me. "But does she care about you? I was there, Leo. These past weeks, I was there when she cried herself to sleep every night. I was there when we had to force her to eat or when she was so sad that I had to hold her—"

I sucked in a breath, my eyes meeting his. "You held her?"

"Yeah. I did. And I'll do it every day of my life if it means that she never cries over you again."

I swallowed, a lump forming in my gut. The idea of Vera doing any of those things, because of me, was hard to stomach. "Why are you here? Did you just want to gloat?"

"Kind of. I wanted to see if you're here to torture Vera more or if maybe now you've come to your senses after seeing her. Vera belongs here. She should stay here. Every day her magic gets stronger here. She has friends here. Family."

"Her family is here?"

"No. *My* family. I'm going to marry her, Leo."

I was on my feet in an instant, my hands gripping the bars of my cell. "Like hell you are."

"She's happy here. Are you really going to get in the way of that?"

"Open up this cell and then say that again."

"I'm just asking you to think of what she wants. Let her go. For good this time. Let her be happy. Once you're out of here, leave her alone."

There was no universe in which I'd ever leave Vera again.

Seconds passed in silence.

Finally Laurie let out a loud breath. "I see," he said. "For saving me that night, I'll talk to my father about getting you released, but then you need to leave. You're in our territory now, demon. Don't forget that."

Without another word, he was flying down the hall.

I sat down and slumped against the wall of my cell.

Bastard.

Where was Vera right now? Was she somewhere upstairs, begging the king for mercy on my behalf? No. I shook my head; that fae prick was probably right. It was much more likely she was describing all the ways I had hurt her and telling the guards to keep the evil demon prince in jail even longer.

She had every right to feel that way, but I knew the truth. Vera was mine.

And she always would be.

Now I just needed her to remember that.

3

VERA

I didn't wait around to hear more from Leo.

Had I done the right thing?

Had he really expected me to jump into his arms and fly off into the sky?

The more annoying question was, *should I have?*

Pushing my way through the fae on the terrace, I started walking, not caring where I was going but knowing I had to be away from the party, from the fae, from everyone, from *him*.

The evening had been unbearable even before Leo crashed the party, and now, on top of fending off nosy questions about why I didn't have wings, I'd have to answer for the demon who decided to infiltrate their city.

The walk through the palace was a blur, and when I made it back to my room, I slammed my door shut behind me, the thud of the heavy wood mirroring the thumping of my heart. I leaned against it before sinking to the floor in a huge puddle of skirt.

Breathe.

After scrunching up the poufy silver fabric of my dress and getting to my feet, I took off my heels and threw them across the room as hard as I could.

Fuck him.

Fuck him and his stupid wings.

Fuck him and his stupid soft hair and stupid muscular arms and stupid silver eyes.

I wasn't sad. No, I wasn't. I was angry, so incredibly angry. Angry enough I could cry. I balled my hands into fists, tears rolling down my cheeks, but a knock at the door interrupted my thoughts.

"Go away!" I shouted over my shoulder to whoever was dumb enough to try to talk to me right then.

"I wanted to check on you," said the voice on the other side of the door.

I wiped away some of the tears with the back of my hand. I didn't know what to say to Mia. I didn't feel like saying anything. How could I? I hardly understood what I was feeling myself. The only thing I wanted to do right then was stew in my anger, not be comforted by someone.

"I brought you cake," she sang out, a little too enthusiastically for how I was feeling, her words slightly muffled by the thick wooden door. "I didn't know if you had a chance to try it at the party earlier, so I grabbed you a slice. Can I leave it with you?"

Cake? Really? Right now?

"Please?"

With a groan, I got to my feet and opened the door a crack, and Mia's eyes lit up at the sight of me, her bright blue wings fluttering behind her. She pushed the door open, and then her expression fell as she looked me over.

"Thanks," I mumbled as she held out a plate and fork.

"Food makes things better, right?"

I sighed. "I wish."

"Maybe I should have brought you the entire cake?"

"No, this is enough."

"You sure?"

"Yes." I forced a smile. "Thank you, but I think I need to be alone right now."

She nodded quickly, the soft curls of her white hair bouncing.

"Understood. We can figure out everything in the morning. I'll come find you, okay?"

I watched her fly down the hall, then looked down and saw something on the floor at my feet. A small black envelope. Had Mia meant to give it to me and dropped it? I tucked it under the plate and went back into my room.

I didn't want to get food on the beautiful ball gown. I spent a few minutes wrestling with the zipper and finally was able to shimmy out of it. The sparkling silver dress really was gorgeous, I thought as I ran my hand over the fabric. It was a shame I had worn it on such an awful night. It was also a shame the silver was such a close match to Leo's eyes.

Leo's eyes...

No. I needed to stop thinking about Leo.

Desperate for a distraction, I busied myself with changing into pajamas and getting ready for bed. When I first came to Rowan, the royal servants made sure to fill my dresser and closet with only the nicest clothing made from the most luxurious fabrics. I would have been happy sleeping in a simple T-shirt, but no, the drawers were filled instead with pretty silk nightgowns, all the same bright blue color of the royal family.

At first I had been suspicious that these dresses that looked like nothing more than a wisp of fabric held up by two tiny straps could be comfortable for sleeping, and on some level it scared me how used to these finer things I'd become as my time passed in Rowan.

Was this me now, a lady of the royal court, wearing pretty dresses and expensive gowns? It was a far cry from the brown, misshapen things the humans had us wear back in the dorms.

After I changed, I put the ball gown back on the hanger and laid the dress carefully over a chair. I sat down at the little table where I'd placed the cake and simply stared at it. A couple of hours had passed since I saw Leo, and I couldn't help but wonder where he was. Did they convince him to leave? Would the king put him in jail?

I thought of the way Leo had looked at me after I slapped him, how he looked like he had... understood?

I didn't understand it myself.

My whole body flinched when I heard another knock.

"Mia," I called out as she knocked again, "I appreciate the concern, really, but I promise"—I swung open the door—"I don't need any more—"

But it wasn't Mia on the other side. This time it was Laurie.

"—cake."

In the hours since I last saw him, he had changed for bed as well. Laurie's white linen shirt was unbuttoned down the front, exposing his toned chest, and he wore loose white pants hanging low on his hips. If guards had followed the prince, I didn't see them anywhere. All I saw was him.

"I don't have any cake." Laurie raked a hand through his white hair. "But maybe I could interest you in something else?"

4

LEO

If they'd just let me take Vera and leave, I would gladly fly away with her tucked safely under my arm. But no, they'd thrown me in this dark cell instead with no indication how long I'd be down here.

How long had it been since the fae bastard left?

It was hard to tell. It felt like hours had passed when the sound of something dragging against the floor interrupted my thoughts. I listened but didn't hear anything else, then finally decided it must have been my wings or tail scraping against the stone.

Leaning back, I tried spreading my wings again, but the cell was too small for me to even stretch my legs out. The fae guard had removed the cuffs and clamps that kept me from flying, but it seemed he only did that because there was no way to fly in the first place.

Would I get an audience with the king and queen to explain everything? They'd been in such a hurry to get me away from the eyes of the other fae that I hadn't been able to say much of anything at all.

A demon in the fae city. I chuckled. The fae palace, no less. Must have been a sight to see.

"Laughing while in jail. You are an interesting prisoner, Your Highness."

I jumped to my feet. In front of my cell was a woman in a black cloak that pooled on the floor around her. Her cloak and the long black dress she wore underneath seemed to blend into the shadows created by the distant light of the torches. It was as if she had appeared from the darkness itself. The fae woman's shoes softly touched the floor as her white wings stopped fluttering, but she stayed a few feet from my cell.

"Who the hell are you?" I asked her.

"I had heard that you were tall, but he didn't say how large your wings were. Very interesting, indeed."

"Is the king finally ready to listen to me?" I asked. "Unlock this cell and take me to him."

"That is not why I'm here," she said. The fae peered out from underneath the hood of her cloak, her dark eyes narrowing as she watched me. No, it was more like she was examining me with the same curiosity I felt when inspecting a sample in my lab back home.

"Then get lost."

Her dark red lips turned up in a grin. "You are the demon prince himself, correct?"

She reached up and pushed back the hood, revealing wavy brown hair that fell below her shoulders. The fae woman seemed to be around my age, but since fae could link and heal each other, some used that to hide their age, so it was hard to tell for certain. Her sleeve fell back slightly when she moved her hood, and I glimpsed a watch on her wrist—demon tech. *My* tech.

Why would she be wearing a holo-watch that wouldn't even work in Rowan? The veil disabled all modern technology, so what would be the point of having it in the first place? And where did she get it?

"If you know who I am, then you know I'm the last demon you should be keeping in jail. You fae should be throwing me a fucking parade for all I've done for your kind. Let me out so I can tell the king and queen myself."

"Let's not be too hasty, Your Highness. I want to have a look at you first."

"And I want a meal and a shower, but here we are. Who the fuck are you?"

"My name is Selena, and I am the Keeper."

"On second thought"—I sat down on the floor—"if you're not going to release me or bring me food, then I don't really care who you are or why you're here."

"Oh really?"

"Yes, really. Go find someone who can unlock this door, or leave me alone."

"Then I suppose I should unlock the door." She dug into her pocket and pulled out a long silver key. "But I'm not going to."

Rolling my eyes, I pulled my legs up to my chest and rested my elbows on my knees. I had zero desire to play whatever game this woman had in mind.

"Fine. If you aren't letting me out, I have nothing to say to you."

"I don't think that's true." Selena put the key back in the pocket of her long black dress but then took out something and twirled it in her hand. When the dim light caught the deep red of the stone, I knew exactly what she held. I shot up from the floor and lunged forward. My face slammed into the bars as my hand shot out for the ring, missing it by inches as she held it back.

"That's mine."

"Is it?" She held up the gold ring between her thumb and forefinger, tilting her head to look at it from several angles. "We've all heard of Hellfire rubies and how they're made from the hearts of fae. Wouldn't that make them the property of the fae?"

"No."

"I have heard about the power they contain too. But to hold one in your own hand is an entirely different thing. I can feel the power practically pulsing from the gem."

My blood was boiling as my fingers gripped the bars of my cell. If this fae thought she could play with that ring, my ring, containing the stone made from my mother's heart, she was mistaken. With every second that I wasn't wearing it, my skin was crawling, my blood itching as if it could explode from my veins at any moment.

"That's not yours. Give it back," I growled. "Now."

"It's certainly not yours either. I heard you were a slaver, but you don't own the fae hearts used to create this ruby. If anything, this ring belongs to Rowan."

"Bullshit. You have no idea what you're even talking about."

She had the audacity to smirk. "What happened to you not talking to me?"

I pulled against the bars, testing their strength as I'd done numerous times since they'd put me in there. As I was, I didn't have the strength to break the bars and get out on my own. If I had the power of that ring, however, I might be able to manage it.

"Fine," I said through clenched teeth. "You have my attention. What do you want, *Keeper*?"

She smoothed down her dress as if she had all the time in the fucking world.

"I want to know more about this ring," she said. "I want to know more about you. You see, from what I've heard, we're a lot alike, you and I."

"How would you have heard anything about me? I thought you fae stuck your heads in the sand and ignored the rest of the world."

"Some do. Some do not. Like you, I think about the future. Like you, I am not content with the status quo and never have been. When I was named Keeper—"

"I don't give a shit about you. Tell me what you want. I don't have time for your life story."

"You have nothing but time at the moment, Your Highness. I thought we could use *this* time to get to know each other better."

"I already know you're shady as fuck for showing off demon tech." I pointed to Selena's wrist. "That shouldn't work here, and you shouldn't have it."

"You caught me. As Keeper, I'm Rowan's expert on fae magic, but I'm also fascinated by the technology of your kingdom. I'm intrigued by the young inventors of Vestia, who continually push the limits of science. Young inventors like yourself. When the king agreed to let me experiment with this ring, I knew you would be the one to help me get what I want."

"And what do you want?"

All smiles were gone. Her expression twisted into one of determination, her eyes narrowed. "I want to destroy the veil."

A loud bark erupted from my chest that echoed down the dark hall. I couldn't help but laugh. The veil protected the fae city, keeping the thousands of fae who lived there invisible from anyone who wasn't fae. Its strong magic prevented technology from working inside the city, but that was a small price to pay for security. Supposedly created thousands of years ago by the original fae queen, the veil was their primary method of protection, and if it were to fail, they'd all be vulnerable. Hunters of all species would descend on Rowan to capture fae, and it would only be a matter of time before those here were all enslaved.

"That's treasonous. Why would you tell me that?" I asked her.

"Because you're going to help me."

"Hell no I'm not. I have enough of my own issues at the moment." I gestured to the cell around me.

She took the ring out of her pocket again and held it up. "The Hellfire rubies combine the hearts of fae to concentrate their power into one gemstone, correct? If I can replicate that process and combine fae power in a similar fashion at a level that's never been done before, I should be able to disable the veil. That's what I need help with."

"Let me get this straight. Your goal is to create a tool to get rid of the one safeguard protecting your entire city?"

"My goal is to bring Rowan to a new age. An age beyond the veil. An age where fae take back their rightful place as the gods of this world."

I snorted. "Gods? Yeah, right. Hard to see you as a divine species when outside this city fae wear handcuffs, not silken dresses."

"Together we will change that. Your reputation precedes you, Your Highness. Your genius is known the world over. I know about magic, but I lack the tools to make my dream a reality. If we work together, we should be able to undo the mechanisms creating the veil."

"And be responsible for exposing all the fae of Rowan? You're looking for a scapegoat when hunters descend on the city, as you know they will."

"We are strong enough to handle intruders."

"Fae will die."

"A small price to pay. Your Highness, we want the same things."

"Bullshit."

"The fae of Rowan will never help their enslaved brethren unless they're forced to. They will never be truly free until the veil is destroyed. Once the veil is gone, they'll be forced to confront the world they've abandoned. Didn't you create Syn in order to free fae from the blood trade? Don't you dream of free fae the world over? The fae of the demon kingdom are freed now thanks to you, aren't they?"

She had to have a contact outside Rowan if she knew that. The ink was hardly dry on the proclamation that had freed the fae slaves in Vestia. As Keeper, was she able to travel back and forth from Rowan to Vestia? There was no other explanation for the watch and the information she knew. Someone was either bringing her intelligence, or she was going to get it herself.

"Yes," I said. "The slaves in Vestia are free."

"Wonderful. But the fae owned by humans? What of them? Wasn't your lover once owned by humans? Vera. That's her name, isn't it? I've heard the young prince will soon ask her to be his bride."

My chest clenched, and my fingers tightened around the metal bars.

"I've also heard that her blood contains a magic far different from other fae," she continued. "Without your help, I suppose I'll be forced to study her blood on my own. I'll probably need quite a large sample if I want to try making a Hellfire stone."

That was enough.

"The second I'm free I will rip your throat out if you say her name again."

"No, I don't think you will, Your Highness, although I believe you'd be pleasantly surprised by the power of my blood if you were to do so. You probably haven't sampled the blood of the fae of Rowan yet. Do you know the sheer power present in the blood of a fae who has never spent a day in captivity?"

She pushed up one of her sleeves, pressed a button on her watch, and in a flash, a holo-knife was in her hand. Without hesitation she sliced her bare arm, blood forming on her skin where she'd cut. The blade vanished back into the watch, but Selena held her arm out toward me. I backed up, my heart already starting to thump against my chest.

"You're reacting to my blood already. I can tell," she said, and damn, I wished she was wrong.

But just as she suspected, I was breathing a little faster, beads of sweat forming on my neck. Even though she was standing a few feet away, I could smell her blood and feel my body screaming at me to go closer.

"They say our ancestors' blood was even more potent," she said.

"You're insane," I said, but without realizing it, I stepped closer to the bars, my eyes locked on the blood dotting her skin.

Before I knew it, she grabbed my shirt and pulled me closer, pressing me against the bars. Her strength was unreal. Was it aided by the power of the ring? Her face hovered inches from my own.

"Help me, and you'll be free," she whispered, her lips barely brushing my ear. "Help me, and I'll give back the ring. Help me, and you can be reunited with your lover."

It was a trap. A very obvious trap. But what else was there to do? Once I was out of jail, I could get Vera and leave, forgetting about this stupid plan. I just needed to get Vera alone, and then I could explain everything. I could tell Vera what I'd done in Vestia to make it safer. How I'd eliminated the threat of the Ignitors. If I had time, I might even tell that white-haired bastard he had a crazy fae on the loose wanting to take down the veil.

I shook out of her hold and took a step back.

"I want my girl, and I want my ring. Open the door, and we have a deal."

The key was already in her hand, red lips turned up in a sickly-sweet smile on her pale face.

"As you wish, Your Highness."

5

———

VERA

Laurie leaned against my bedroom doorframe, one hand slotted into the back pocket of his white linen pants. Like me, he'd changed for bed, and his loose clothes looked just as perfect on him as his tux had earlier. Did he know that the way he leaned caused his loose button-down shirt to fall slightly open, exposing even more of his bare chest and stomach?

Oh, he knew. There was no doubt that he knew. The way his lips quirked up in a smile told me that he knew exactly what he was doing. Any thought I had of cake or mysterious letters seemed to fly out the window. It was true that a distraction might have been just what I needed, but was letting the half-dressed prince into my room at night the right decision? I wasn't sure.

"Aren't you going to let me in?" he asked.

"Well..." Gripping the door as if my life depended on it, I poked my head out into the hallway.

It wasn't only the sight of Laurie at my door making my hands sweat. It was the prince standing there, looking like *that*, all smiles and charm, in loose clothes like he was ready to climb into bed—into *my* bed? Laurie's playful smirk didn't at all match the sinking feeling that had been gnawing at me ever since I saw Leo. If I let him in, where would it lead?

"Where are your guards?" I looked both ways down the hall but didn't see any of the usual grumpy-looking fae who followed the prince everywhere lately.

No sign of them meant Laurie was alone. And I was alone. We would be alone. In my bedroom. Alone.

"They think I'm in my room." Laurie smiled and shrugged like this late-night visit was no big deal at all, his bright blue eyes twinkling with even more than their normal mischief. "It's their fault for not guarding the window. Besides, everyone's too busy figuring out what to do after tonight's drama."

A demon entering the fae city, where no demon should have ever been able to go, was dramatic indeed.

"I thought you might want a friend right now. Was I wrong?" he asked.

I hesitated, my hand still on the door. "I was going to bed."

"Then I'm glad I got here when I did," he said. And then as if I wasn't even standing there, his blue wings brushed against me as he flew past me into the room.

With a sigh, I shut the door, but when I turned around, I gasped. Laurie was right there, no more than a few feet away, blue eyes staring down at me. "Vera."

"Yeah?"

He took a step closer, his hand reaching out toward me. I took a step back to put some distance between us, but my back hit the wooden door.

"Your strap... It fell." He pointed at my arm where the thin strap of the silk nightgown had slipped down my shoulder. Oh gods, I was still only wearing this flimsy nightgown. The plan had been to drown my feelings in cake and then go to bed, not chat with the fae prince in nothing more than a thin piece of blue silk that barely came down to cover my thighs.

"Must be a bad design," I mumbled. I could feel heat blooming in my cheeks as I rushed past him, across the room over to the closet, hunting desperately for a robe or jacket or literally anything that might cover me up and make this less awkward.

"Wasn't one of mine," I heard Laurie say behind me. "You don't have to change, you know. It's really fine."

"It's not fine," I called over my shoulder. I couldn't stand around wearing practically nothing while I was alone with Laurie. In my bedroom of all places. I reached up to look on the top shelf but immediately realized that made the nightgown slide up even higher on my thighs, exposing the bottom of my butt.

Great. Just great. The prince of all the fae just saw my butt.

I'd resigned myself to dying of embarrassment right there in the closet when suddenly a blanket was thrown over my shoulders.

Spinning around, I saw Laurie standing a few feet away, leaning against my bedpost, nodding to the bed where he'd stolen the blanket.

"That work?" he asked.

I tugged it closer around me, the fluffy fabric soft on my skin. "Yeah. This works. Look, it's really late, and I'm not so sure—"

"I'm sorry I showed up unannounced. I said I thought you might need a friend, but the truth is I needed to talk to you again." Laurie's glittering blue wings fluttered behind him as he stared down at the floor.

When he ran a hand through his messy white hair, his earlier confidence seemed to vanish. Was he nervous? Had I *ever* seen Laurie nervous? The more he fidgeted, the more anxious it was making me as well.

"We didn't get a chance to finish our conversation earlier," he said.

Our conversation. In the chaos of Leo's arrival, how could I have forgotten that Laurie had confessed his feelings only moments before? Not only had he confessed, but he'd asked me to stay with him in Rowan and be part of the effort to free the enslaved fae outside the city.

"We were interrupted," I said, toying with the edge of the blanket wrapped around me. This kind, passionate, handsome prince had promised me everything I'd ever wanted, and I had been on the verge of answering him when Leo had shown up.

"That's an understatement. Vera," he said, his voice low and soft. The look in Laurie's bright blue eyes changed, the nervousness gone, and in its place was something else entirely.

I held my breath, unsure what I was going to say if he brought up his feelings again. I could barely process the fact that I'd seen Leo tonight, that I'd slapped him, that Leo had told me he was taking me home with him. There was simply no way that I could also figure out how I was feeling about this gorgeous prince who acted like it was the most normal thing in the world to be standing in my bedroom with his shirt half-unbuttoned, showing off his insane chest muscles.

And those abs.

I had to stop thinking about his abs.

With the way he was looking at me right then, I knew it was a mistake even allowing him in into my room. He needed to leave—that much I knew for sure—before this whole evening got even more awkward.

"Laurie, look—"

Laurie's gaze shifted past me. Was he avoiding my eyes because he knew what I was about to say? Did I know what I was about to say? Shit, did I even know what I was about to say?

I wrapped the blanket around me tighter and took a deep breath to prepare myself. "Laurie," I said again. "The thing is—"

"I didn't get to have any cake."

"Huh?"

"Cake. I didn't have any." He pointed toward the little table and the plate Mia had brought me. "Mind if we share?"

"What?" I asked, louder than I had intended. "I mean yes, I mind," I tried to calm my voice. If he stayed for cake, that meant he was going to stay and talk about his feelings toward me, and that simply couldn't happen tonight when everything was so mixed up in my head. "So no. We can't share the cake."

"Why not?"

"Because..."

Laurie stood patiently by the bed, white eyebrows raised as he waited for me to finish, a slow smile spreading across his lips. "Because why?"

"Because..." *Because right now you look like you want to eat me instead of the cake,* I could have said. *Because if you keep standing there with your shirt unbuttoned, smirking at me, I'm going to want to lick the icing from your abs instead of my plate.*

"Because I only have one fork."

I groaned internally at how dumb that sounded.

Laurie barked a laugh. "Is that all? I'm sure we'll figure something out." He glided right past me and plopped down at the little table. It appeared there was no stopping him, so I draped the blanket around me like a shawl and sat with him.

I was thankful Laurie seemed to have a never-ending list of things to say. He told me how he'd heard one lady had fainted from fear when she saw a demon for the first time and how the captain of his father's guard had tried to resign for his failure to protect the city. According to Laurie, the younger fae weren't scared of Leo as much as they were interested in the mysterious, handsome demon.

I felt my shoulders tighten at that last part.

"You're making me feel bad," Laurie said. "I'm doing all the talking and the eating."

"I'm enjoying listening to you."

"But you aren't eating."

I grabbed the fork from the table and scooped up a piece, shoving it into my mouth quickly. "Yeth aye mmm." I swallowed and proudly placed the fork down. "See?"

"Okay, but now you've got something." Laurie tilted his head to look at me, eyes narrowing.

"Got what?"

"A little bit of frosting. Right..." Before I could do it myself, Laurie reached toward me, his thumb gently brushing the tiniest bit of cake icing off the corner of my mouth. "There."

I felt a small jolt from his touch as his hand lingered, as if the sugary frosting had been injected straight into my veins. He must have felt it too, because Laurie chuckled as he took away his hand and sat back in his chair.

"My magic seems to have trouble controlling itself when it comes to you. Speaking of magic, tonight on the terrace, the railing..."

I sank down into the blanket still wrapped around me. "You saw."

"I saw you crumble it under your hand like a badass. For once I was glad you were holding on to it and not me."

"I'm so sorry. I'll fix it!" I insisted as I sat up, letting the blanket fall behind me. "I don't know how to fix iron, but maybe there's a book where I can learn—"

"Vera." Smiling, Laurie reached over and took my hand in his, that spark returning but now simply heat radiating from his skin onto my own. "No one expects you to fix the railing. We have master iron-workers who specialize in that sort of thing. I was surprised that you were able to break it, that's all."

I pulled my hand from his, turning it over and inspecting my palm. I picked up the fork and tried bending it to no avail.

"I didn't know I could. I knew that I've improved in speed, but without wings, I assumed I'd never be as strong as regular fae. But ever since I've been here, everything seems more..." I glanced around the room, struggling to find the right word. My eyes landed on Laurie, his blue eyes focused right on me as he leaned closer.

"Intense?"

"Yeah. Intense."

Laurie leaned even closer, and I held my breath, but he reached behind me and grabbed my blanket, pulling it back around my shoulders to cover me. Then he sat back and tapped his chin with one finger.

"I wouldn't be surprised if the combined magic of Rowan is increasing your own. Maybe it's finally time you met the Keeper so we can ask her a few questions. If you want to talk about intense..." Laurie shook his head and whistled.

"I met so many fae tonight," I said, thinking of the dozens of beautiful fae women who had crowded me all evening at the party, each one peppering me with questions about my relationship with the prince. "I'm not even sure who they all were."

"The Keeper wasn't there, and believe me, we're all thankful for that. She is not the party type. It would be more likely for her to cast a spell on the champagne than drink it. But with all the research she's done, no one knows how fae magic works better than her."

I wasn't so sure about that. I picked up the fork again, twirling it in my hand as I thought of a certain demon I knew who had been researching fae blood for years.

"Vera. There's something I need to tell you. Something that concerns your safety. I need you to be honest with me."

"I am honest." I pointed the fork at Laurie. "I am not the one who hid the fact that I was royalty for months."

Laurie raised one white eyebrow. "Fair, but you are keeping secrets now."

"I am not! I am an open book. Zero secrets."

"Let me rephrase that. You might not have secrets of your own, but you definitely keep secrets about a demon we both know. This is what I wanted to tell you. You need to be careful going forward."

"Me?"

"Yes. Everyone who was there tonight saw you and a big bad demon together. Word is going to spread fast. It was obvious that you knew each other, so I know my parents are going to want to question you. I can explain your relationship to him as best I can, but that won't stop the rumors. Rumors will spread that a demon infiltrated Rowan to take back his fae. This will only add another layer of mystery to you in the eyes of the public. I would never tell you what to do, but it might be safer for you if you stay here, in your room, for the next few days. I can post extra guards outside."

"No. I'm not doing that. I'm not going to hide in here. I'll tell anyone who asks the truth."

"Will you? Will you really?"

"What is that supposed to mean?"

"Will you tell them the truth that Leo is part fae?"

I dropped the fork, the metal tongs clattering against the plate. "That's... That's not..."

"Please don't lie to me. I'm guessing that it was his fae genes that allowed him to get through Rowan's veil."

"Why would you assume that? Maybe he used some kind of device that he invented, or maybe it was magic? It could have been anything. You don't know."

"Those ideas are possible," he admitted, "but we both know the real reason."

Was he bluffing? Or did Laurie really know that Leo was half-fae? If he did know, how had he found out?

"Fae are going to find out the truth. Vera, if fae start to think that you're the reason the veil was breached, it could be dangerous for you. You'll be called in and questioned. There could be a tribunal. There are fae with the ability to pull the truth from you. I would never let anything happen to you, but even I can't stop them from asking questions."

"So? Hypothetically, what if they do find out about this hypothetical secret?"

"All I know is that once I start pulling on a thread, the whole garment comes undone. We could discuss sharing his identity with my parents first, but once it's out, it's out. If you want to keep Leo's secret, the best way is to lie low."

Damn it.

He was right.

I'd seen firsthand the animosity some fae in Rowan felt toward me, a perceived outsider, when I first came here, and it wasn't like those feelings had vanished overnight. Now I was also connected to the demon who had shattered their sense of security in one night. Maybe I did need to stay by myself for a while.

"Let's say, for argument's sake, you're right. Then what? I should just stay out of sight?"

"It's your decision, but I think it would be wise for you to stay here. In this room."

"For how long?"

"Maybe a few days. Let everything quiet down first. I was so close to convincing my parents to send out teams to free fae slaves. I might be able to use all this to help push that along, but a full investigation into Leo's appearance is not a distraction we need right now."

I sighed. So much for the brief days of freedom I'd felt in this city. "If I'm going to be stuck in here, I want you to tell me what you think you know about Leo."

"I don't know anything. It's just a hunch I had."

"I don't believe you. Tell me why you think he's fae."

"Like I said, it's a hunch. A hunch I developed the night we left Vestia."

"Oh." The night Leo used a suppression device to knock me unconscious and then give me away. "That still doesn't explain it. What happened that night that made you think that?"

"Nothing in particular."

"That's a lie."

"There's no reason to rehash that night, okay? How about some cake?" He reached for my fork, but I knocked his hand away.

"Trust me, I don't want to talk about that night any more than you do. But if you're going to make some outlandish claim about Leo, then at least explain why you are so convinced."

"It's nothing. Let's talk about something else."

"You brought it up!"

"I said it was a hunch." Laurie shrugged. "I don't know anything for certain."

"Then I don't know if I agree to stay in my room any longer."

"Vera. Come on."

I continued staring at him, not willing to let it go.

"Fine. That night, the night we left, I was shot."

"What?" The whole time we'd traveled together, neither Laurie nor Mia had mentioned anything about him being injured. "You were shot? By whom? Where?"

"Here." Before I could stop him, Laurie peeled his shirt off over his head. I was about to tell him to not be ridiculous when I saw it. All words left me as I gasped at the sight of the mark on his stomach. The scar was pink and hadn't healed completely.

"An arrow was lodged in there. And another was in my wing," he said.

I leaned in to see it closer, reaching out to touch the scar until my finger grazed his skin. I flinched, realizing what I'd just done.

"I'm sorry, I didn't mean to..."

Laurie didn't seem bothered in the slightest. "You can touch me, Vera. I don't mind."

I opened my mouth to speak, but no words came out. My face felt hot, but Laurie only smiled and leaned back in his chair.

"You should put your shirt back on," I told him.

"I don't want to."

"Are you trying to distract me from asking more questions?"

"Maybe. Is it working?"

"Not at all."

"Uh-huh."

"That still doesn't explain your so-called hunch."

"After I was struck by the arrows, I fell," he continued. "I lost consciousness, so it's really all a blur. Leo was there when I woke up. That's all." He shrugged, his earlier confidence gone. Now he just seemed annoyed. There was definitely something he wasn't telling me.

I narrowed my gaze as I stared at Laurie, keeping my eyes pointedly on his face only. "That's all? That's why you think he's part fae?"

"Yep."

"What am I missing? The fact that Leo was there made you think he's fae?"

"Something like that." Laurie shifted in his seat. Yep. No doubt about it. Laurie was totally hiding something from me.

"Now you're the one keeping secrets. If you won't tell me the whole story, for whatever reason, then I'll ask Mia. She knows what happened, right?" I stood up, leaving the blanket on the chair. I headed back to my closet to find some clothes, but Laurie jumped out of his chair and came after me.

"Vera, wait." He reached forward, grabbing my wrist. I spun around at the contact, and he softened his grip but didn't let go.

Then it clicked. I knew what Laurie was hiding.

"What you're telling me"—I weighed each word carefully—"is that demons tried to kill you that night, you were shot by multiple arrows, and then Leo actually saved you."

"When you put it like that... I guess that's true."

"You think he linked with you."

"I guess..."

"Laurie."

"Okay, fine! That bastard saved my life. So he took a few arrows out of me. What's the big deal? He's the one who has been lying to everyone about who he is."

"As if you can talk, Mr. Prince Who Posed As a Slave! All of that to hide that Leo did something nice for you? Do you know how ridiculous you sound right now?"

"Then you admit that I'm right. Is it his mother who's fae?" Laurie asked, bright blue eyes wide and twinkling. "I've seen his father, and there's no doubt that he's related to the demon king."

I held up a hand to stop him. "I have admitted nothing. Why didn't you say something sooner? Do your parents know what happened to you?"

"No."

"Why not? Why didn't you tell them?"

"At first I didn't want to give them another reason to be mad at me for leaving Rowan. If they heard that I was almost killed, I'd be on lockdown even more than I already am. They don't need any more reasons to keep fae in Rowan when we should be out there fighting to end slavery. Really though," he said, his voice softer, "I didn't say anything because I'm selfish."

"That doesn't make any sense. You're not selfish, Laurie. A prince who wants to end the enslavement of his people is not selfish."

He shifted his eyes away from me and exhaled loudly. "That's where you're wrong." Laurie abruptly stood up from the table and started walking toward the door.

"You're leaving?" I called after him.

For a brief second, Laurie glanced over his shoulder before nodding. "You'll stay here until things settle down?"

"For now I agree with you that it's the right decision. Before you go... What's going to happen to... him?"

"There's a meeting in the morning. The veil is how my parents justify keeping everyone inside Rowan and never venturing out, but if it's true that outsiders can get through, then my parents will have to admit that the veil isn't foolproof, or—"

"Or what?"

"Or they'll have to come up with some other excuse and make sure that Leo never leaves."

I didn't like the way that last part sounded. No matter how angry I was at him over what he'd done, I didn't want Leo to be used as an example to prove the strength of Rowan.

Just then there was a banging on the door and shouts from the hallway, and both of us turned our heads in that direction.

"Excuse us, miss," a guard called from the hall. "But we are looking for His Highness. Have you... uh... Would you know where he... We thought maybe... Is it possible that you have seen him?"

"Their guesses were right," Laurie whispered as he looked around my room, his eyes landing on my bed. "Think I could hide under your blankets until they go away?"

"Absolutely not."

"The closet?"

"Laurie!"

"Come on. I'll just stay the night and sneak out tomorrow."

The look on my face must have told him everything he needed to know. Laurie smirked as he walked backward toward the door. "Oh well, it was worth a shot."

"At least put your shirt back on!" I hissed, grabbing his shirt from where he'd left it on the chair.

"Why should I?"

"It is the demon, miss!" the guard called out again.

We both froze. Our eyes met in surprise, and then Laurie spun and flew to the door, swinging it open, with me close behind.

There stood two guards with mouths open in shock at the sight of their prince, shirtless, standing in my doorway with me beside him in only my nightgown. They both quickly averted their eyes and bowed. "Your Highness, we didn't realize. We apologize, but we have to tell you—"

"What is it?" Laurie demanded. "What's happened with the demon?"

"Your Highness, he's... he's *gone.*"

6

LEO

There was no way in hell that I was going to help Selena.

But she didn't need to know that.

"How far below the surface are we exactly?" I called out as I followed behind her through the dark halls of the dungeon. I had to hand it to the fae. By building their jail far below ground at the bottom of one large stone shaft, they had created the perfect setup to keep humans in jail; without wings, there was no way in or out. Add in more tunnels than it would ever be possible to keep track of, and they'd set up the perfect labyrinth to trap any would-be escapees.

Guided by the light of her holo-watch, I walked a few steps behind Selena and forced myself to ignore the pain creeping up my body. The longer I was without my ring, the more it felt like a fire was running through my veins, threatening to burn me from the inside out. Clenching my hands at my side, my fingernails digging into my palms hard enough to draw blood, I could feel myself losing control. Ever since my father injected me with the anti-fae serum, I hadn't felt completely whole unless I was wearing that Hellfire ruby.

Right then I only cared about three things: getting my ring, getting Vera, and getting the hell out of the fae city. But if this crazy fae woman had a plan to destroy the veil protecting the city, I was at least going to stick around long enough to hear it so I'd know how to stop it. That blue-winged prince could think of it as a consolation gift, as my one and only thank-you for protecting Vera.

I hadn't worked this hard to create Syn only for Selena to bring the fae right back into slavery.

I tried to keep track of where we were going, but eventually we had taken too many turns down too many different tunnels, and I knew it would be impossible to retrace our steps. How old were these passageways? Judging by the rough cuts in the rock walls, it seemed likely they had been created many, many years ago.

When we came to a large chamber with several passages leading off in different directions, I stopped. I could hear the echo of voices in the distance.

"Who else is down here?" I asked Selena.

She kept walking, heading through the center passage, her watch lighting the way. How was she able to make the holo-watch work down here? I was the one who had invented the damn thing, so it would follow that I should have been able to figure this out. It had also worked in the dungeon, which had also been below ground. Was it possible that demon tech, which didn't work on the surface in Rowan, only worked underneath the city? Did that mean the protective veil that blocked technology didn't go below the surface?

As I watched her black cloak disappear into the dark hall, I weighed my options and tried to resist the urge to claw at my skin. I wasn't sure how many hours had passed since I'd last had the ring on, the ring containing the Hellfire stone made from my mother's heart, but it felt like an eternity. Without it, my skin itched, every nerve twitching just under my skin. It was as if every part of me was seeking that ring, that stone.

I flew up to her side, my wings twitching in irritation behind me. "I need to know what I'm walking into."

"We are walking toward destiny," she said without stopping.

"I don't give a shit about destiny. I'm only here because it gets me one step closer to Vera. If you think I have other motivations for helping you, you're wrong."

"I too would like you to reunite with your lover. If the young prince is distracted by a wedding—"

"Wait, what?"

"—he might not be as motivated to take action against the outside world as he once was. Then once he becomes a father, his priorities might change even more and his children—"

"Hold the fuck up." I flew to stand in front of her, stopping her from going any farther.

Selena's red lips turned up in a smile. "I'm simply making conversation, Your Highness."

"Making conversation my ass. What did you mean by a wedding? Is there something already planned? Tell me what you know."

"We are almost to our destination. We can discuss this more—"

"Now. We can discuss it now. What wedding?"

"It is only rumors. For now. If you cooperate, I could assist in making sure that the rumors do not become reality."

"I'm here, aren't I?"

"Indeed."

Cursing under my breath, I had no choice but to follow behind Selena as we walked through the dark cave. I felt like a pet dog on a leash and hated every second of it.

There was no way Vera would marry that white-haired bastard. No way at all. I needed to figure out how to get away from Selena and back to the palace.

The path turned into a long set of stairs carved into the rock, each step getting darker by the second as we descended. The air around us was hot and thick as we reached the landing at the bottom. Then I followed her down a wide hall carved into the stone. There were other paths that branched off our own, and I could hear the crackle of fire and the faint sounds of voices in the distance. We weren't alone, I realized, but I still wasn't sure how many other fae were in the cave.

"Who else is in here?" I asked her again.

"Believers."

Great. It was one thing to deal with one crazy fae, but apparently now there were others like her.

"How many?" I asked her.

"Enough."

"And what do these 'believers' believe in, exactly?"

At that she stopped walking. "Do you know the story of Queen Morgana, Your Highness?"

"I don't keep up with fae royalty."

"The queen was one of the founders of Rowan," Selena said, her voice strong with pride. "A goddess herself, some say, who descended from the heavens to infuse her magic into the city. By her blessing, all trees grow, all flowers blossom, all fae fly."

Not all fae fly, I mused, the image of Vera appearing in my head.

"The queen protects us all," Selena continued. "She will be by our side when we take back what is rightfully ours."

"And what is that?"

"The world."

Selena's eyes blinked up at me, showing no hint of understanding how entirely fucked up what she'd just said was.

With each step through the cave, I felt less and less sure about what we were doing. I thought back on the voices I'd heard earlier. How far away were they, and how quickly could I take back the ring and get the fuck out of this cave before someone came to help her? Selena was much smaller than me, and though I assumed her magic was powerful as the fae Keeper, her strength couldn't be that much greater than mine. If I managed to ingest some of her blood, I could power up and then... No, I didn't need to take it that far.

"Free fae is one thing," I told her. "Your people have a right to live peaceful lives and not be enslaved, but that doesn't mean you have the right—"

"Do not dare to tell me what is right." For the first time that night, Selena's calm facade seemed to crack, just slightly, the edges of her mouth twitching. "The world bows before the fae, not the other way around."

"Listen, Keeper, I don't bow to anyone. Certainly not to you."

That's when I heard the shuffling of feet. From the darkness on either side of the path, shadows shifted and fae in black cloaks moved closer. Had they been standing there all along? How long had they been listening to us?

"He is not a threat." Selena spoke loudly into the air, to seemingly no one at all, and the movement in the shadows immediately ceased. "You may return to your duties."

Their heads bowed as they passed us. Ten, twenty, thirty, no, at least fifty fae—all women from what I could tell—walked by us with a slow, measured cadence, and each one wore a long cloak like Selena's. Unlike her, however, their wings were beneath the black fabric, only visible by their shape.

Black Guard.

I'd seen black cloaks like these on fae before, but it had been a long time. There was a contingency of these fae in Vestia, and some of them always seemed to hover around the auction houses. Fae who willingly died to hurt slave owners, fae who committed violent assassinations and ruthless massacres, all in the name of revenge. If these women were connected to *that* group, I had more problems than I thought.

I would have continued staring at their somber march down the stone hallway in front of us, but Selena was already turning down a separate hall.

For the first time, despite being so far underground, I could see a light ahead of us. The air was thick and hot with steam, and I could hear water running. Moonlight shone down into the cavern through an opening several stories high above us, illuminating a small pool of water. Against the far wall of the pool, about halfway up the side of the wall, was a carving.

It was far away, but the light hit the carving just enough that we could see it. Cut into the stone wall was the shape of a fae, a woman around the same size as the fae beside me. However, unlike Selena, the carved fae's wings were larger than any I'd ever seen, easily visible from where we were down below. The wings of fae who lived in Rowan were already larger, and the colors more vivid, than fae who had lived in captivity, but these... these were insane. Massive. Spread out wide on either side and draping down toward the ground, the wings were easily three times as large as the fae herself.

While only flecks of color remained on the body of the carving, there were still remnants of paint on the wings, multiple colors, visible in the moonlight. Fae wings today were only one color, never anything like this.

While the wings were striking, they weren't the most striking part of the statue. Nestled into the stone where the fae's heart would be was a shining gem. No bigger than a fist, it would have been hardly visible from where we stood except that the stone glowed, like the fae's wings, a rainbow of colors.

My instincts kicked into overdrive to analyze what I was seeing. What kind of stone was this? What was the source of the glow surrounding it? Was there a light source somewhere behind it? How had this been created, and how old exactly was it?

But the longer I stared at it, the less I thought and the more I *felt*.

I didn't know how I knew it, but I knew nonetheless.

That stone was alive.

And I couldn't take my eyes off it.

Just as I could sometimes feel the Hellfire stone on my ring pulsing against my finger, I could feel a power emanating from this stone. It felt similar to the way the crown in Vestia had made me feel when I put it on, like this rock was silently calling to me.

"What is this?" I gestured to the carving. "Who is this?"

"It is as I told you. She is our queen. Morgana. One of the founders of Rowan." When I looked beside me, Selena was peering out from her black hood, her eyes narrow as she watched me. "Can you feel it, Your Highness? Are you able to sense its power?"

Of fucking course I was. I wasn't sure if it was my fae genes allowing me to tap into whatever energy this was, but the electricity in the air was palpable.

"They say this stone was created by the original fae queen. Her magic is infused within it, protecting the city of Rowan. There were others like it, I have heard, but the last of them were lost or destroyed during the Blood War. Only this one remains."

"And?"

"The magic of this stone is what sustains the veil. We call it the Keeper Stone."

"And you want to destroy it."

She nodded.

Something wasn't adding up. "So do it. It's right in front of you. What's taken you so long? There has to be a reason you haven't smashed it to pieces by now."

"If only it were that easy." She extended a hand toward the carving on the other side of the pool. "Give it a try yourself."

Crossing my arms over my chest, I snorted. "No way. You just said that the veil would fall if the stone was destroyed. I'm not going to be responsible for that. Do it yourself."

"As you wish. Then I will try to break it and show you what happens. Numbers seven through eleven," she called out.

Five fae women I hadn't seen standing there stepped forward from the shadows, each wearing that same long black cloak like Selena's.

"Reveal your wrists."

Each fae dutifully pushed back her sleeve and held out her bare arm. The holo-blade was in Selena's hand in an instant. Standing in front of the first fae, she took the woman's wrist in her hand, then sliced it. She brought the wrist to her mouth and sucked the blood. When she released the wrist, Selena's hands went over the wound as she linked with the fae and healed the cut.

"Thank you, Keeper," the fae said, her head bowed.

These women were crazy. Totally and completely crazy.

"What the fuck are you doing?" I was horrified as I looked around at the bowed heads and bare wrists. My own body felt even more on edge than normal. "What is this?"

"I'm not doing anything that demons haven't been doing for years."

Selena's skin was shining, her lips and chin dotted with dark red blood as she repeated the process with the four other fae, each one thanking her when it was over.

I heard footsteps behind me, and suddenly the cavern was filled with fae, all wearing that same black cloak. There were at least fifty— no, maybe more—and each had pushed up one sleeve, all holding out their arms as an offering to Selena.

I thought of a day many months before when I cut Vera's arm when we were training. The sensation I'd felt from tasting her blood had been intoxicating, overwhelming, invigorating; I'd almost lost my mind from the feeling. I'd only tasted a little of Vera's blood, but Selena had just finished healing a fifth woman whose blood she'd drank. Selena's body was now surrounded by a pulsing glow, as if a soft, golden light was shining down on her.

"It is taboo for fae to drink each other's blood, but if we had done it during the war, might we have won?" she asked.

As Selena flew over the water and made her way up toward the Keeper Stone, I mentally calculated how fast I could fly out of the cavern before they'd catch me. With Selena powered up like that, I doubted that I could get far at all, and the opening at the top was simply too distant to make a break for it. And she still had my ring.

With that much power coursing through her, I thought it likely that she would simply smash the entire thing, stone included. I'd seen powerful fae on the numerous hunts Rand and I had been on over the years but never one with this much power. I sucked in a breath as I watched her from across the pool. Once near the carving, Selena reached out, touching the stone with her hand.

Here we go.

I held my breath, but nothing happened.

Hovering in the air, Selena stayed still with the exception of her beating wings, as if she were a statue herself, her hand covering the glowing stone. But there was still no change. No earthquake, no lightning strike, no big explosion.

Nothing.

She pulled back her hand, and I could see her wings working

underneath her long cloak as she flew back to me. After landing, she adjusted the hood over her head as she studied my expression.

"You see now, don't you? The stone will not allow me to destroy it," she said.

"And you think I can?"

"Perhaps."

I felt some small comfort that even as strong as she was in that moment, with more fae magic than I could imagine coursing through her, she still couldn't break the damn thing.

"I need your mind," Selena said. "I've exhausted all the magical routes I know to destroy it."

"Hard pass."

"Are you sure?" Selena moved closer, her hands touching my shirt. I flinched at the close contact. I didn't want her anywhere near me. She tilted her head to look up at me with hooded eyes. "What if you were aided by my own magic?"

I grabbed her wrists and pulled, surprised by how hard it was to get her off me.

"No," I told her.

"Don't you want some of this power yourself? If I am not your taste, I have many girls who will willingly give themselves to you."

Fae were crowding all around me, and even as I batted them away, their hands reached for me and began stroking my arms, my chest, my back. "Stop it," I shouted, and my wings shot out to push them away and give me space. "Back the fuck up."

"Don't be so hasty." Selena reached into her pocket and took out the small gold band. "Tell me about this first."

"Tell them to get away from me, and then I will."

The fae women had moved closer again. Several had cuts on their wrists from earlier, the blood still dotting their skin. I didn't want to shove women who were so much smaller than me, but I also didn't want them anywhere near me. If some of their blood got on me, I didn't know how I would react, but I didn't want to find out. I flicked my tail to encourage them to move, but one woman grabbed it in her hand. In an instant, other fae were there too, petting it and stroking it.

I tried to yank it back, but the fae held on, a disturbing smile on her face.

"Call them off!" I yelled, trying to pull my tail from her grasp.

"Does the ring enhance your power?" Selena asked, ignoring me completely. She held up the ring so that the moonlight shone down on it. "Or is it something else?"

With a firm whip of my tail, the fae finally let go and I leaped into the air. The push of my wings sent me straight up and away, and I snatched the ring from where Selena held it aloft, slipping it on as I kept flying. Instantly I felt that calm that always came over me when wore it. I breathed deep, feeling the ring's comforting warmth, like a thick blanket, like Vera tucked tightly against me on a cold night.

But unlike how it felt normally, this time was different. This time felt very different.

This feeling was new.

I landed and realized that I was on the other side of the pool, underneath the carving. The waterfall was close by, water rushing down and crashing into the pool, but I hardly heard it.

My brain was telling me to get the hell out of there, to fly up and away and leave these crazy cultists behind, but I couldn't. I'd meant to fly out of there, but now that I was nearer to it, I was transfixed by the glowing stone.

I knew I shouldn't go closer. My body was trembling, my ring finger throbbing at a steady beat, and no matter how much I fought it, my feet moved forward on their own. I flew up slowly, deliberately, the pulsing in my hand growing stronger until finally I was there. Right in front of the glowing stone. The blood in my ring hand seemed to beat in time with my heart, growing louder and louder until I watched as that hand rose as if it wasn't mine anymore.

My fingers grazed the stone. There was a flash of light, and then—

Darkness.

My eyes blinked open, and I wasn't in the cave. It was still night, and I was still outside, but I no longer heard the roar of the waterfall. In fact, it was silent. Too silent.

As my eyes adjusted to my surroundings, I knew where I was.

I was in Vestia, in the back gardens, far from the palace. This was the out-of-the-way corner where Aurora—where my mother—grew roses. The rose bushes were still there, as wild and beautiful as they had been when I was a child, along with the stone bench where we'd sit in the afternoons.

Reaching out, I gently touched one of the plump red flowers in front of me, the petals soft to the touch. Was I actually there, or was this a dream? Could this be some kind of vision brought on by the Keeper Stone, or had its magic somehow transported me here?

"Leo."

My eyes flashed open wide, my hand dropping from the flower. That voice. I knew that voice.

No way. There was no way.

Heart thumping in my chest, I forced myself to turn around. Seconds passed like hours, and when I saw her, moonlight reflecting on her silver wings, I thought my whole body might crumble then and there.

"Mother?"

7

LEO

"You have no idea how long I've waited to hear you call me that, Leo."

It was illogical. It was irrational. It didn't make even an ounce of sense no matter how my brain tried to rationalize it, but there she was.

With moonlight shining down on her like a halo, like an angel, my mother stood a few feet away. She wore a long white dress, the fabric pooling in the grass at her bare feet. Her silver wings glittered behind her as if wet with the morning's dew. She looked very much the same as when I last saw her when she was alive, but now that I was a grown man, she looked younger than me, as if she hadn't aged at all in the over twenty years that had passed since her death.

Was this a trick of Selena's? Some kind of fae magic that caused hallucinations? Had the magic of the Keeper Stone interacted with my brain somehow?

"Is that really you?" I asked her. It was an odd thing to have her eyes looking up at mine instead of the other way around.

"It's part of me."

"What does that mean? Is this real? Are you really here? What is this?"

She wrinkled her nose and looked around at the empty garden. "I'm not completely sure myself."

I thought back through what had happened, trying to make sense of it. "I touched a stone in Rowan. The Keeper Stone, they call it. Next thing I knew, I was here. With you."

"Ah." She nodded and took a step back, her soft features eyeing me up and down. A small smile formed on her lips. "You look so much like him."

Clenching my teeth, I looked away, my jaw set tight at the mention of my father. "I am nothing like him."

"I see." She hummed as she came close again, touching one of my cheeks and then the other.

Relaxing a little, I closed my eyes. I couldn't help but lean into the warmth of her touch.

"A better version of him then. Luckier in love, I hope."

I opened my eyes to see her still smiling up at me. How could she smile when talking about that monster? Even the mere thought of him was starting to make my skin itch and pulse race.

"That bastard doesn't know what love is."

She raised an eyebrow. "Oh?"

"You know that. Even now he's out there lurking somewhere. I got rid of his councilors, but he snuck away like the rat he is. If it wasn't for him..." I was unable to continue as rage started to consume me.

"Leo." She pressed her hand against my face, and I placed my own over hers, surprised at how small it was compared to my own. Her touch was soft, soothing, and I relaxed into it, the storm within me temporarily calmed.

Was this even real? Was she really here? Was this some dream and I was going to wake up soon, or was this my chance to finally get the answer I'd wanted for so long?

Dream or not, I had to know.

"All that time..." I struggled to keep my voice even and calm. "All that time you knew I was your son, but you never said anything. Why? Why didn't you tell me? Why did I have to live for so long not knowing?"

Her smile faded, and she frowned. "Your father and I both agreed to keep that secret for your benefit."

"Then it was my fault?"

"No! Darling, if your identity as half-fae had been exposed, it would have publicly humiliated the queen, and she wouldn't have stopped until you paid the price."

"Instead, you paid that price for me. It cost you everything. I couldn't protect you, so you..." I could hardly choke out the words. "You died."

"Any mother would die for her child."

"So it *was* my fault. I knew it." I turned back around to the roses, unable to look at her in case she saw my shame. I sat down on the bench and stared at my hands, my fingers moving in small tremors I couldn't stop. "You died because of me."

"Leo." Coming up behind me, her small hand touched my shoulder.

I reached back and laced her fingers with my own, and the shaking stopped.

"It wasn't your fault. My choices were all made out of love, and I don't regret any of them."

"How can you say that? You didn't choose to die."

"I chose to stay with you and your father."

"And look at what happened!"

"Without him, I wouldn't have had you. Leo, I loved your father."

"What? No. You were his slave; he married that awful demon and made you be a nanny to your own son."

"Because that kept you safe. Love is messy and complicated, but never doubt that I loved you, and I loved your father. He loved us too in his way."

I couldn't hide my shock. "He doesn't know the meaning of that word."

"That's not true." Her hand unlocked from mine, but her tiny fingers touched the ring I wore. "Your father made this stone with love, not hate, Leo. As a memory, not a trophy."

"I can't say that I understand what the two of you had in the past."

"And that's okay," she said. "The past is past. You're rebuilding the future, aren't you?"

"I'm trying."

She nodded once. "Then that's enough. You're not responsible for the sins of the past. All I've ever wanted for you was for you to be happy."

"Happy? After what happened to you? After what has been done to the fae? How could I be happy?"

"I still hoped that you would be. Every parent wants their child's life to be better than their own."

"Then that part will be easy since I don't have to live with that monster. He said he wanted to rid the world of fae. He wants to eliminate their powers, eliminate them."

"I don't know the demon he is today, but the Calladan that I knew was proud and fierce in all things, love included. Maybe a little like someone else I know?"

"Never. I would never do anything like what he's done. Everything I've done is to protect her, not hurt her," I insisted. I couldn't bring myself to tell her what had happened with Vera, how I'd sent away the love of my life against her will.

"Her?"

"Yes." Some of my anger faded when I looked behind me to where she stood, a curious smile on her face. "I'm seeing someone. I think."

"You think?"

"I think. No, I am. I... I love her, but, well, it's complicated."

"Tell me about her."

"Vera is fae." I looked up for my mother's reaction. Her eyes opened a little wider, but otherwise she didn't seem surprised. "You'd like her. Stubborn, brave, wears her heart on her sleeve. She's trouble too though. Good trouble, at least most of the time. I can't turn my back on her for five minutes without her getting into trouble."

"Keeps life interesting, I'm sure."

"More like frustrating."

I felt a hand touch my head, just like she'd done when I was a child. I leaned back on the bench, letting her run her hands through my hair.

"The most frustrating part is how much I need her. When she's not with me, it's like a part of me is missing. We separated, and when I saw her again, she was angry, just like I knew she would be. I can't explain it, but seeing her again in the fae city, she seemed so... powerful."

My mother gave a small clump of my hair a little tug. "Of course she did. I wouldn't expect the woman my son chose to be anything else."

I groaned. "There's just so much going on. There's so much I need to do. I have to—"

"Leo. You're not alone. You don't have to do everything by yourself."

Aurora—no, my mother—continued to massage my scalp, and as I relaxed into her touch, a stream of words came tumbling out.

"But who else is going to do it? All this time I thought that I would make Syn, end the Dust trade, and then everything would be okay. Then I met Vera, but now she won't speak to me, and I don't blame her, and these fae are insane, especially this one lady, and I left Vestia in a mess with Rand trying to clean it up."

"That little troublemaker grew up into a responsible young man, did he?"

"Debatable. I'm doing all this to protect Vera, but she makes it so damn difficult."

"If she's like what you say, maybe she doesn't need as much protecting as you think."

She took her tiny hands from my hair and came around to sit next to me.

"Did you know that I was a spy?" she asked.

"What?"

"A good one too. The entire time I was in Vestia, I sent everything I learned back to Rowan, hoping it would stop the war. I truly believed that when the war was over, once fae and demons were on the same side again, your father and I could be together in the open.

When he told me that he was being forced to get married as part of some deal, he gave me the choice to stay or leave. I was already pregnant, and I didn't want you to grow up without your father. He protected me until the queen intercepted some of my letters home. You know the rest."

"I didn't know any of that."

"I'm telling you this because we both tried to tackle problems on our own." She stared off into the garden. "What if I had told him about the letters from the beginning? What if he had refused the arranged marriage? What if he had helped sneak out information himself? Or collaborated with the fae with me? So many what-ifs."

My father had never told me any of this. He never spoke of her at all actually. Suddenly it felt like everything I knew was wrong. I had my own share of what-ifs, for sure.

I rubbed at both my eyes, dragging my hands down my cheeks in frustration. "I don't know what I'm doing."

"It sounds like you're already doing quite a bit."

"And failing at all of it."

I watched her stand up and walk over to the rose bushes where she snapped off a rose and brought it back to me. "I'm so proud of you, Leo, but no man can do everything on his own. Besides, it sounds like you already have someone who can help you. Talk to her and share this burden you've put on yourself."

She sat next to me again, and I took the rose from her. The moment the stem touched my hand, it seemed like the world around me flickered. Instinctively, I knew our time together was coming to an end.

"You are the one who said Vera was powerful," she said. "It might be time to stop trying to protect her and instead see how you can be better together."

Everything flickered again, as if someone had turned the lights on and off in whatever dream world this was. "Is this it?" I asked, looking around.

"I think so."

"Will we ever see each other again?"

"I don't know, but Leo, can I ask a favor of you?"

"Of course. Anything."

She smiled and reached for my hand, squeezing it tight. "Have some babies."

"Mom."

Her mouth opened in surprise at the word, but then her lips turned up in a smile again.

Then suddenly she was gone.

And just as suddenly I was underwater.

I opened my mouth in shock, and water flooded into my mouth. The water was dark and cold, and I knew that I had to swim—now, or else I was dead. Kicking my legs as hard as I could, my wings heavy in the water, I forced myself to swim up, up, *up*. With a final heave, I threw myself out of the water and onto the rocks.

Completely drenched, water dripping from my wings and clothes, I pulled myself to my feet beside the waterfall. Coughing up water onto the rocks below me, I caught my breath. I had almost drowned, but for some reason I felt fine. Great, even.

Normal.

The most normal I'd felt since my father injected me with that serum that should have erased my fae genes.

Had the stone done that?

Had it all been in my mind, or had that moment with my mother been real?

What I knew for sure was that something felt different. I felt different. Calmer.

What the hell had just happened?

My clothes were soaked, the fabric sticking to me and dripping onto the rocks below my feet. Water from my wings pitter-pattered into the pool as I flew to where Selena stood on the other side.

"How long was I out?"

"You touched the stone and then fell into the water."

"Just like that? How long was I under?"

"Less than a minute."

It had felt like so much longer. I stared up at the stone, the glowing rock still nestled in the heart of the carving. Maybe it was my imagination, but it seemed to have a slightly fainter glow than it had before.

"What did you do to that stone?" she asked.

"I don't know. It was like... we had a connection."

"During the war, only fae with abilities similar to the stone could connect to it and wield its full power. The closer the fae's power matched to the original fae who created the stone, the more of the power they could use."

"Then if we can find someone with an affinity for this power, that fae could, theoretically, harness the power of the veil and manipulate it in some way."

"Perhaps."

Judging by the look on Selena's face, she knew more than she was telling me. As she walked away to join the other fae, I thought about calling Marcus to brainstorm, but then I remembered that phones didn't work in Rowan.

Or did they?

I had an idea.

"Hey!" I called out to her. "I need my phone. It will work down here, won't it?"

Selena stayed silent.

Damn it. I was exhausted, and the last thing I needed was for her to draw this whole thing out with her dramatic silence.

"Your holo-watch worked down in the dungeon, and it's been working the entire time we've been down here. I'm guessing that the veil doesn't extend this far below the surface, and that's why we're so far underground. Am I right?"

When she still didn't say anything, I sighed. I didn't have time for this kind of bullshit. "It's not like I'm going to figure out this stone by just staring at it. I need my phone if you have it. I need whatever records you have on this thing. It will take weeks, maybe months, to study this. I'll need access to a lab. I'll need books, I'll need your notes, I'll need —"

"Why is your ring glowing?"

I unbuttoned my wet cuffs and rolled them up, and that's when I saw my ring. The gold band looked exactly the same but not the ruby. The red gem seemed brighter than it had before. It must have been affected by the stone, but how?

I had my suspicions, but the last thing I wanted to do was tell them to her. If she could ignore my questions, I could ignore hers. I glanced around at the fae surrounding us. "It's late. Do these fae live down here?"

"Yes, and you will as well for the duration of this arrangement." Selena snapped her fingers, and a fae woman in a black cloak appeared at her side. "Please show His Highness to his quarters."

She turned to leave, so I started to follow her back down the passage.

"One last thing, Your Highness...," Selena said.

"What?"

"When you touched the stone, what did you see?"

My thumb touched the gold band of the ring. "Nothing."

8

VERA

Had I heard the guard right? Had he really just told us that after Leo showed up uninvited, caused a huge scene, wrecked my emotions, and got thrown in prison, now, after all that, he had the audacity to *leave*?

No.

He couldn't leave. I wouldn't allow Leo to leave until I…

I didn't know what I needed to do, exactly, but I knew I needed to find him.

While Laurie stayed in the hall outside my room talking with the guard, I changed out of my flimsy nightgown as quickly as possible and scrambled to find some normal clothes in my dresser. The attendants had stocked the drawers with pretty much everything except plain pants and shirts, but I didn't have time to be picky. I found some pants and a long shirt in the dresser and grabbed a jacket from my closet. Laurie was back in my room just as I finished putting on my shoes.

He squinted at me from the doorway. "What are you doing?"

"Leaving."

"Why?"

"To go look for him. Obviously."

"Vera."

"What?" Not waiting for an answer, I was already moving toward the door. I was going to go find Leo whether he wanted me to or not. I wasn't going to let him leave that easily, not after his little performance this evening. I was going to find him and put him back in that dungeon if I had to do it myself.

Laurie put his hand out across the doorframe, stopping me from going any farther. Staring down, his blue eyes studied me. "Don't you think that maybe this is for the best?"

"What do you mean?"

"I mean, wouldn't it be a good thing if Leo left and went back to Vestia? Think about it. Wouldn't that be the best outcome?"

I watched Laurie's expression, trying to understand what he was thinking. "Best outcome for whom?"

"For... you."

For me? Why would Leo leaving be what's best for me? How could Laurie think that? Of course it wasn't what was best for me. Best for me would be me getting the chance to drag Leo back by his wings and tell him exactly how angry I was. Then he'd be here with me, and—

Oh.

The realization of what I was doing hit me like I'd been smacked across the head by a demon's tail. I'd rushed to put on clothes to do what? Run after Leo? When he'd left me yet again?

"Wow." I closed my eyes and exhaled loudly, feeling incredibly foolish. I kept my eyes closed, knowing that if I opened them I'd have to see Laurie, and I couldn't handle the look of pity that I was sure was coming from him.

"I was really about to run after the guy who left me, wasn't I? Who left me, then showed up out of nowhere and demanded I go with him, and then left me again." I let out a small, pitiful laugh. "You must think I'm pathetic."

When I finally did open my eyes, Laurie had taken a step closer to me, his expression softer. "Vera, you're not pathetic."

"I *feel* pathetic."

Laurie's voice was low, almost a whisper. "It's never pathetic to go after what your heart wants."

"Laurie, I slapped him. You saw me."

"I saw." The corner of his mouth turned up in a half grin. "I was jealous that it wasn't my fist hitting him instead. But here's the thing," he said, his grin gone in an instant. "If you didn't still care about him, you wouldn't have hit him at all."

"That doesn't make any sense."

"Yes. It does. You're angry, but you care. He doesn't deserve it at all, but you still care about that bastard."

Squinting up at Laurie, I crossed my arms over my chest. "I'm not saying you're right, but why are you standing up for him? Especially when I know…"

"Because I want you to want me, not him, Vera. Me alone. I don't want to be your second choice. I'm going to wait until you realize it, and when you do, I'll be here." Laurie took his arm down, opened the door, and stepped out into the hallway. He turned back for just a second, his hand still on my door. "There's nothing you can do right now that the palace guards can't."

"I suppose you're right."

Laurie's grin was back. "Of course I am. Get some sleep. I'll see what I can find out tonight and come by in the morning, okay?"

I nodded, and Laurie closed the door behind him.

I was angry with Leo, yes, but Laurie was right. I cared.

I cared so much it hurt.

A DAY PASSED.

Then another.

When the sun set on the third day after Leo's disappearance, I knew I had to face facts. He really wasn't coming back. Somehow he must have slipped out of Rowan the same way he'd snuck in. I was the one who told him to leave, after all, so why did I feel a lump in the pit of my stomach that seemed to grow larger by the hour?

What was I even doing in Rowan? Was this my home for forever?

With each passing day, it felt like I was moving further and further away from my original goals, and I felt more and more guilty about living in this amazing palace when I knew what was happening to fae elsewhere.

Watching the yard below my window, I could see how easy it was for the fae of Rowan to stay inside their happy bubble of comfort and ignore everything happening in the world outside. Here, especially here in this palace, I could quickly forget that fae were living much different lives not too far away from where fae strolled in a manicured garden and wore luxurious clothes.

Laurie and Mia weren't making any progress convincing their parents to send fae outside the gates, and now, after Leo's dramatic arrival, the entire city was on high alert for intruders. Guards practiced in the yard outside my window each day, and I frequently heard the hurried rush of wings passing by my door. Not that anyone ever stopped to tell me what was going on. This place had started to feel like home, but now it was starting to feel like a prison.

In some ways, Rowan seemed more isolated than ever.

On the third day since Leo disappeared, I heard keys unlocking my door. I jolted up in bed to see Mia flying through.

"I thought I locked it."

Mia grinned that same mischievous grin I'd seen so many times from her brother and held up her hand. "Did you think the princess didn't have a key?" Her grin faded as she glanced around my room. "So, uh, you've just been hanging out in here all day or what?"

"I guess."

"And now you've concluded your packed schedule by going to bed?"

"That's what people in beds normally are doing."

"I don't know about that. They do other things too, Vera."

"Oh? Do tell me more, Princess, especially if they involve you and your purple-winged lieutenant."

"We are talking about you, not me!" she said, but I didn't miss her small smile. "Seriously, how long are you going to mope around in here?"

"Laurie said it's important to lie low until everything settles down."

"Yeah, yeah, yeah. He says a lot of things. All I hear from that is he's keeping you to himself."

"That's not it. I promise."

"Then you're going to bed before the sun has hardly set because you want to?"

"No. I... It's been three days, Mia, and I thought for sure that... I don't know what I thought. No, I thought I was part of a team, and now half my team is just... gone. And I told him to go! I did this. But then I think, no, *he* did this, and then I think about how he came back, but did I want him to? Surely not. But what if I did? And then—"

"Girl." Mia's blue eyes were wide as she stared at me. "You need to get out of this room and out of your own head. Come on. Get up, lazy bones."

"Get up and do what?" I flopped back onto my pillow.

"Whatever we want." Mia pounced onto my bed, grabbing my blankets and ripping them off me. "I don't know who this is right now, but it's not the Vera I know. Get your ass up and let's go do something."

I reached forward and pulled the covers back to me even as Mia held on. "I told you, I'm not supposed to."

"Says who? My idiot brother? I don't take orders from him, and neither do you." She tried yanking the blankets back again, but I held firm. "Right?"

"Well. Yeah, you're right. I don't. It's just that Laurie said it's possible fae will blame me for a demon breaking through the veil."

"A demon."

"Yeah, a demon."

"Just any old demon."

"I mean..."

"We're not even using his name anymore? He's not the boogeyman who is going to jump out from under your bed when you say his name." She eyed me suspiciously. "You're not hiding Leo under your bed, are you? Is that why you're spending all your time in here?"

"Mia! I'm not avoiding using his name." I let go of the blankets and stared at my hands. "I'm just worried that if I say it, I won't be able to breathe again."

We sat in silence for a long moment, both of us seemingly unsure of what to say.

"That's it." With a final tug, Mia pulled the blankets off me completely and tossed them onto the floor. "We're going out."

"To where?"

"I wasn't entirely sure, but now that I've seen this tragedy"—she gestured at me—"I know the perfect place. I went a few times before we came to Vestia, and tonight we are going back."

"What is this perfect place?"

"A club. No, not like Elise's," she added when she saw the look on my face. "Way nicer. A lot of the guys on the guard go there to indulge in life's finer pleasures."

"So it's a bar."

"Okay, yeah, fine! It's a bar but, like, a nice one. Victor says he goes sometimes and might even go tonight or something." Mia muttered the last part.

Oh. Now I understood. I had no doubt that Mia wanted to cheer me up, but now that I knew her handsome, purple-winged lieutenant that she no way, no how, definitely didn't have a crush on might be there, her insistence made more sense.

"I can see how Victor might go to a place like this, but can the princess of Rowan just show up at a bar?"

"When there is an emergency," she said, pointing to me again, "the princess of Rowan does whatever she wants."

"An emergency, huh?"

"Yep. This is a Class 1 High Priority Friendship Mission. I declare that Operation Help Vera Get Over the Big Hot Demon Dude must commence immediately. By my orders."

"I'm not sure I can disobey the princess then."

"Damn right."

"And you're sure this is safe?"

"Vera! Since when do you care about safe? Where's your adventurous spirit?"

"It flew away about three days ago, I think."

"Hey." Mia sat down on the bed beside me and took one of my hands in hers. "It's going to be okay. You think anyone is going to try anything when you're with me? You're not giving me enough credit. If they do, they're in for a world of hurt."

She was right. I'd decided to stay in my room to avoid prying eyes, but it had been three days. Three long, boring days. A fun adventure would be the perfect way to start fresh.

I hadn't agreed to anything, but Mia was already rummaging in my closet.

"Where is it?" I heard her mumble. Then she took a step back and held up a dress she'd found. It was one that had been in the bag I'd had from Vestia. One of the dresses I'd worn when I worked for Elise. Short. Tight. Revealing. She tossed it at me, and I caught it.

"Put that on. The Vera I know doesn't lie around in bed waiting for the storm to blow over. The Vera I know *causes* the storm."

9
_____

VERA

"Let Operation Girl's Night Out commence!"

"I thought this was Operation Help Vera Forget Hot Demon Dude?"

"That too!"

Mia led the way through the crowded club. The building itself was more like a house than the large warehouse I'd worked in with Elise. The downstairs had a bar and tables, and the room was full, with fae filling the space, their beautiful wings creating a rainbow of colors. If the fae in the club recognized Mia, they did a good job hiding it; most of them stayed engaged in their own conversations and hardly glanced our way. If any of her soldiers were there, they were doing a great job avoiding us.

We got drinks and found an unoccupied corner where we could talk and fae watch. Being in the corner allowed us to hide Mia's wings against the wall, in case someone might recognize her and bother us, as well as hide the fact that I didn't have any wings at all.

As I watched the crowd laughing and drinking, I was struck by how everyone seemed so... happy. They made it look easy, but if it was so easy, why couldn't I feel the same?

"Where's your lieutenant?" I asked Mia, since I could tell she was looking around the room for him.

"Can you please not call him that if we see him? It reminds me that we work together."

"You're his boss actually. So scandalous." I grinned.

"I'm everyone's boss, so it's not like I have a lot of options. Keep an eye out and let me know if you see him."

I knew he was going to be pretty easy to see. Victor was built like a tank with purple wings. He towered over Mia. Actually, he towered over almost everyone. He'd easily be able to maneuver through this crowd. One look at the tall lieutenant, and I was sure anyone in front of him would be moving out of his way fast.

I'd just set my drink down when something shiny caught my eye. The lights in the room were muted but reflected off a silver tray right at me. Finding the source, it took me a second to figure out what I was seeing, and then I was shocked.

"Mia. Look over there."

"Is it Victor?"

"No. Look about four tables over. The one with the two guys."

"Why? Do you think they're cute?"

"That's not the point. Do you see what's on their table?"

She studied them for a minute. "I know them. They work for me. Wait, are they...?" She sounded as shocked as I felt. "Are they doing Dust? What the hell?"

Without waiting for me, Mia set her drink down too and stomped over to their table and snatched one of the boxes off it. The two fae men at the table were already on their feet, apologizing as Mia shook the box in front of them.

"Where did you get this? Do you have any idea what you're doing?" she asked.

"It's synthetic, Your Highness! It's not made from blood!"

What?

Racing over to join Mia by the table, I took the small box from her hand so I could see for myself. It was just as I'd suspected. I'd seen the label more times than I could count. I'd even helped Leo choose the font for the logo.

From what I remembered, Leo wasn't selling Syn to Rowan. Dust was illegal in Rowan, so how had these fae gotten their hands on this?

"This is the packaging for Syn," I told her.

"So they're not actually snorting Dust? It's not made from fae blood?"

"Well..." I had to think about how to answer that while I studied the two guys. Really seeing them for the first time, I took note of their movements. The box said Syn, but blown pupils and accelerated breathing were the only outward signs that anything was different. I'd never been around fae taking Dust or Syn, so I wasn't entirely sure how they would react, but demons typically glowed. There was no glow here, not even a faint one.

"Where did you get this?" I asked them.

"Um, well, you see..." The fae with the green wings scratched his neck, and his eyes darted around the room. "I know a guy who knows this other guy and..."

"How does it make you feel?"

"I feel great," the other one, a guy with the brightest yellow wings I'd ever seen said, his eyes glossy. "Honestly, I thought it was going to be better than this from what I'd heard."

Seriously? From everything I'd heard from Leo, Syn was much more potent than regular Dust. It should have increased their strength, agility, and libido. These two seemed fairly normal at the moment.

"We aren't the only ones," the green insisted. "Upstairs everyone is doing it!" He pointed to the staircase.

Mia didn't wait to hear more. She immediately headed for the stairs, and I followed her, the sounds of conversations fading as we walked up the stairs.

"Are you sure this is a good idea, Princess? I don't know if you should be up here if there's a bunch of people doing Dust."

Mia opened the first door we passed. "What could I possibly be— Oh."

The guys had been telling the truth; the room was full of fae snorting Syn, adding it on the rims of drinks or pouring it straight into their mouths. That by itself wasn't necessarily shocking; no, instead it was the sight of bodies writhing on couches, fae sloppily kissing and touching, moaning in pleasure as if they were alone in the room. The air was thick with the smell of sweat and booze.

"I've been somewhere like this before," I whispered, mostly to myself.

The crowded room. The drinks. The Dust. It was all too familiar, too much like the auction-night party I'd attended with Henry. I'd been so excited to do something different that night, to see firsthand what life was like for those who had the money and power to buy fae slaves. That night I got confirmation that humans were just as disgusting as I thought they were.

"This place has really gone downhill," Mia muttered beside me.

I walked past her into the room, going over to one of the small tables in front of a couch. They didn't even notice I was there as I picked up the silver box. It had the same packaging and the same colored Dust as we saw downstairs.

"This stuff is real," I said.

"How do you know?"

"Look at the color. Syn isn't this red. Someone is selling real Dust and pretending it's synthetic."

"Who would do that? Who would have access to real Dust?"

"Humans. Demons. It's pretty fucked up to sell fae blood to fae though."

"And this is where my guards hang out? They're all going to get an earful from me at our next training, especially Victor. Wait. Vera. Do you think Victor does stuff like..."

"Like hook up with girls in an upstairs room at a bar? No, I can say with confidence that he does not. Look, Mia, he's not even here. I think maybe we should go home," I told her. "I appreciate what you're trying to do, but we need to tell someone about this. As much as I hate to say it, we should find a way to contact someone in Vestia. I know some demons—"

"Victor! Hey!" Mia waved an arm in the air. "There he is. I'll tell him what we found and see what he thinks," she said before zipping over to him.

Real Dust. Here. Did Leo know? Not that I could tell him. I could try getting in touch with Rand, but what if he told Leo I'd called him? There wasn't time to worry about my love life, or Mia's, because even though I was happy for her, we had more important things to worry about now. We needed to leave. We needed to see if there was anyone at the palace who could take a look at what we'd found. We needed—

"You're cute," a voice said, and when I looked to my side, I saw a purple-winged fae with brown hair leaning against the bar next to me.

He was tall, probably about the same height as—

Nope.

I was not going to think about him tonight.

"Thanks?" I moved to go around him to head toward Mia, but he stepped in front of me.

"You're too young to be in a place like this, don't you think?" he asked.

He was talking about me not having wings, which meant he thought I was simply a young fae who hadn't gotten her wings yet. Not that I owed this guy an explanation.

I leaned around him and could see Mia and Victor still talking not too far off.

"No," I said.

He didn't say anything, as if he was expecting me to continue that thought. When I didn't, he leaned down closer to me.

"Don't worry. I'll stick with you to keep the creeps away."

"I wasn't worried."

"What's your name?"

"Vera, but I'm going to go and—"

"I'm Thomas."

I didn't like the way he stood so close to me, the way whatever cologne he was wearing seemed to invade my nose no matter how I turned my head, the way his smile looked like he knew something I didn't.

"I've been watching you all night," he said.

"Uh, what?"

"You should smile more. You'd be a lot prettier if you smiled."

I was starting to think that the universe hated me after all. It was beyond time to go home.

I tried again to walk around him to go get Mia, but he stayed close, blocking my path.

"I'm a chef." As if I had asked.

"Good for you. I can't cook. If you wouldn't mind moving—"

"Maybe I could teach you."

"Probably not. I tried once, but after that, Leo—" I clamped my mouth shut. I hadn't meant to even think about Leo, much less talk about him, and here I was, talking about him to a total stranger.

"You okay?" he asked.

"Yeah. It's kind of crowded in here, so can you move?"

"Do you want to go somewhere quieter? I think your friend over there is going to be busy for a while." He gestured to where Mia and Victor were still talking.

I wrinkled my nose at the suggestion. "No." I shook my head. "I don't think so."

"I don't live too far from here. You know, I've never been with a girl without wings."

Gross.

He reached forward as if he was going to pat my head, but I flinched and dodged his hand. My back hit someone standing behind me, and when I looked up, a hand was wrapped firmly around Thomas's wrist, stopping him from touching me.

"She isn't interested," said a familiar voice.

Hardly able to contain my excitement, I spun around. "Rob?"

The green-winged fae let go of the guy's wrist and smiled down at me, that adorable, goofy smile I hadn't seen in months. "Hey, Vera. Didn't expect to see you here."

"Likewise. What are you doing here?"

"Hey, buddy," Thomas said. "Me and her were just leaving."

The goofy smile was gone and Rob eyed him and up down with a look of obvious disgust. "I'm not your buddy. And it's you who should be going."

"Yeah, what he said. Bye!" I grabbed Rob's arm and pulled him as fast as I could away from the bar. I let Mia know that I'd found a friend as we passed by her, and then the two of us went outside where we could talk without all the noise.

"I never expected to see you here," Rob said.

"Same! I thought you left for the colony. Didn't you go with Teddy?"

"Oh yeah, that. I did, for a while. But then I heard what Leo did, and a bunch of us decided to see for ourselves if it was true."

"You heard that he left me?" I asked. How the hell had that kind of gossip made it all the way to Leo's fae colony? Leo had been buying fae for years and sending them there, with Teddy serving as a guide between the two. She must have found out what had happened in Vestia. "Damn, news travels fast."

"Huh?"

"Huh?"

"What are you talking about? Leo left you? Left you where?"

"That's what Leo did. Unless you're not talking about that? What exactly are *you* talking about?"

"I'm talking about what is happening in Vestia. The new laws. Everything was drawn up so quickly that it's kind of a mess. The nobility hates all the changes, and they're struggling with everyone leaving. I hear that dumb guy in charge is doing his best, but..."

"The king?" I asked, not understanding how Rob could be smiling at the mention of that monster. I shivered at the thought of my last run-in with the demon king. If Zell hadn't stepped in that night, I might not have made it out alive.

"The old guy? No. No one's seen him. I heard that he left Vestia, but there are also rumors that he's dead."

Dead? Could Leo's father really be dead? The last time I saw him, he'd been terrifying, threatening to kill me with the coldness of a glacier and a voice like sharp ice. The demon himself was so physically imposing that I couldn't imagine someone ever being able to kill him.

"After Leo killed the king's councilors—"

"Hold up. What?" I grabbed Rob's arm in shock. "No way."

"Yes! Don't you know any of this? This place really is a bubble, isn't it?"

"Tell me everything."

"Vera. Leo killed the old demons who were the king's right-hand men. Poisoned them, according to what I heard, with some famous lord or another giving him some kind of tainted Dust. Then his father fled, and then Leo freed all the slaves."

Holy shit.

Leo did what?

My breath seemed to catch in my throat, and I couldn't do anything other than squeeze Rob's arm as I tried to process my feelings. Disbelief. Happiness. Pride. All mixed up in the blender of my heart and threatening to jump out of my chest at any second.

I had stood on the balcony watching from a distance when the king announced that Leo was going to ascend the throne, but then I'd left town before the ceremony actually took place. I had had no idea that things would happen that quickly.

It was amazing. It was everything Leo wanted to accomplish there. Leo was a king now, and he'd realized one of his dreams by freeing Vestia's slaves. Then another realization sank in.

Leo was a king now, and he'd come all this way... for me?

But then I'd told him to leave.

And he'd left.

"I guess when you're the king, you get to do what you want," I said quietly.

"No." Rob shook his head. "Leo isn't the king. At least not yet. With everything that happened, they never had the coronation. The important thing is that more fae are coming here, Vera. From the colony, from Vestia. They're coming home."

It was all too much. Seeing Rob here felt like my family had returned, like I was seeing my brother after a long time apart. He was family, and he always would be. Combined with the news of the fae being freed, all of it was just too much. I let go of his arm and flung my arms around Rob's neck. He hugged me back, and I couldn't stop the tears welling in the corner of my eyes.

"It's okay to cry, Vera." Rob chuckled, patting my back affectionately. "But I can't tell if these are happy tears or sad tears."

I wiped away a tear and leaned my face into Rob's shirt. "I can't tell either!"

"Hey!" a voice shouted down the alley. "What do you think you're doing?"

Rob and I stepped apart just as a blur of blue and white zoomed toward us. Laurie landed between us, his blue eyes intensely staring into my own.

"Vera, are you okay? You're crying. What happened? Did he hurt you?"

Behind Laurie, Rob eyed him suspiciously. "Vera, you know this guy?"

"Yeah. He's no threat," I said.

Laurie spun around to face Rob. "You. Why is she crying? What were you trying to do, getting her alone in an abandoned alley?"

"Okay, you need to calm down. Rob, this is Laurie. Laurie, this is Rob. Rob is a friend of mine. We grew up together."

"A friend." Laurie didn't relax, even with that information. "Then why are you crying?"

"I think these are happy tears."

"*He* made you happy?"

"All right, that's enough. Rob, can you give us a second?"

"I don't think I want to. Vera, is this another guy that's been bothering you tonight? I don't know what it is with the fae in this city, but you guys need to learn some manners."

"Wait, Rob!"

Rob didn't wait. He got closer to Laurie, puffing out his wide shoulders and muscles gained from countless hours in the gym. Rob lifted weights like it was his job, and it seemed he was determined to show off.

"I don't know who you think you are," Rob said, "but Vera is like my little sister, and I won't hesitate to—"

"Rob! Stop this! Laurie is the prince!"

Rob froze. His green wings froze. His everything froze in place, and as if in slow motion, he turned to me.

"What?"

"Prince. Him." I pointed at Laurie, who had a smug smile on his handsome face.

"I heard that part, but I thought the prince's name was Lawrence."

"I go by Laurie."

"Shit." Completely deflated, Rob hurriedly attempted a small, awkward bow, but Laurie told him to stand up. "I'm so sorry, man. Sir? Your Majesty? I had no idea. I'm not from around here."

"I can tell."

"Seriously, I feel terrible. I'm going to go inside and die of embarrassment. You guys take all the time you need. I'll be right inside if you need anything," he said to me before doing another little weird bow and hurrying inside.

"Damn. Maybe we need to hire that guy as a bodyguard," Laurie said once we were alone.

"He'd be a good one. I've known Rob since we were kids, and if Rob is anything, he's protective."

"Protective or possessive of you?"

"Rob isn't interested in me like that, I promise. You actually know the guy he was involved with. He's—"

"He?"

"Yeah, he."

Laurie visibly relaxed. "Ah. Okay. Maybe I should go apologize to him then. I don't really want to though. He was kind of intimidating back there."

I chuckled. "Rob is such a softie. He's just big."

Now that we were alone, Laurie's blue wings spread out at his sides, essentially blocking anyone from coming near us, forming a protective cocoon for just the two of us. I'd forgotten how much taller than me Laurie was. We were standing in an alley by ourselves, but now that we were this close, it felt comforting and safe to have him here.

"Laurie, what are you doing here?"

"I was in the neighborhood."

"Lies. Were you following me?"

"You weren't in your room. I went to check on you, but you didn't answer the door, and then by chance I saw you and my sneaky sister leaving the palace. You guys left me out. I followed just in case something bad happened."

"Like me running into an old friend?"

"Yeah. Like that. It's just..."

"What?"

He moved closer until he wasn't more than a few inches from me. "It's just that you make me crazy. I do impulsive things all the time, but with you, it's ten times worse. I get jealous when someone talks to you, and a smile from you can make or break my entire day. When I'm with you, my heart takes over my brain and I do stupid shit."

"Yes, you do."

"Just... Let me be impulsive, okay?"

In a seamless movement, Laurie's hands gently cupped my face, and before I could react, his lips were pressed against mine.

There was an immediate shock, both from the sudden kiss and from our magic sparking to life with the touch of our lips. His hands left my face, and one wrapped around my waist, roughly pulling me against him. With one hand on the small of my back, Laurie held me firmly against his chest as if he could keep kissing me long enough to convince me to kiss him back. Maybe he could.

It made logical sense to give in to Laurie's kisses. It made sense to let my body melt against the handsome prince and let him help me forget about everything that wasn't him. He was willing, I knew. I'd known that for a while. And it made sense to give him what he wanted when he'd been nothing but kind and patient.

But the heart isn't logical at all. The entire time he was kissing me,

I couldn't shake the feeling that this wasn't right. I wasn't supposed to be kissing Laurie. I was supposed to be kissing someone else.

I'd never wanted to be wrong as much as I did right then.

I leaned back slightly, just enough to break the kiss.

"You have no idea how long I've wanted to do that," Laurie said between breaths. "Come here." His arms drawing me in, Laurie engulfed me in a hug, and I let my head rest against his chest. I was going to have to ruin this moment, but I let myself have this for a second. His shirt was soft against my face, and I could hear the beating of his heart.

I had to say something. I didn't want to say anything, but I knew I had to. This was the moment to be clear with him about my feelings, and it wasn't fair to him to stay silent any longer. I curled my fingers into his shirt, dreading what was going to come next.

When his hand started to rub on my back, I stiffened. Immediately his hand dropped, and he stepped back from me. A look of concern flashed across his face, but then his expression fell. Still only inches apart, I caught my breath as we stared into each other's eyes, and it seemed like whole paragraphs were spoken between us without either of us saying a word.

Immediately he brought me back into a hug.

"Laurie..."

"I already know what you're going to say." Laurie didn't move, his arms still around me, his head leaning against my own. "Can we just stay like this a minute longer before you say it?"

I nodded against his shirt and did as he asked, the two of us quiet and still except for the sounds of our breaths and the beating of our hearts.

"It's because of that demon, isn't it?" he finally asked.

"Yeah."

"Fuck."

Laurie sighed and leaned back, his blue eyes looking into my own. "I knew I wasn't the man you wanted to be with tonight. I thought I could convince you to be with me, to stay here in Rowan forever, but then that bastard had to show up, didn't he?"

Before I could respond, we heard voices and broke apart. When I looked over at Laurie, he had turned away, his hands in his pockets.

Mia came flying up first, Victor close behind. "There you guys are!" she shouted.

I glanced over at Laurie. "I think we should go back."

"Sounds good to me," Mia said. "Vera, why don't you go back with Laurie, and then we—"

"She should go with you," Laurie said.

Mia tilted her head, her brow wrinkling as she stared at her brother. "Are you sure? Wouldn't it be better if the two of you—"

"I'm going back by myself." Laurie started walking away from us. "We can talk tomorrow." He didn't look back.

I wasn't sure if those words were meant for me or Mia, and Laurie wasn't sticking around to explain.

"Laurie! What's wrong with you?" His sister started after him.

"Mia" came that deep rumble that belonged to her lieutenant.

Mia looked up at Victor, who shook his head, and she stopped where she was.

The three of us watched in silence as Laurie flew away into the night, his blue wings growing more and more distant as he ascended into the dark sky.

"Vera, what was that all about?" Mia asked. "Did something happen between the two of you?"

"Yeah. I think we both realized the same thing at the same time."

"And what was that?"

"That I'm still in love with Leo."

10

VERA

"Why is the sun this bright?" I groaned. "Is it this bright every morning? Can somebody's magic do something about that?"

Mia pulled one of my blankets over her head. "I wish."

After Laurie left us, we'd flown back and the two of us had crashed in my room for the night, deciding it was better to stay there than risk being seen going back to Mia's.

We needed to find someone in the palace to tell them about the Dust we'd found, but I was contemplating whether I'd be able to nap later when there was a loud, hard knock on my door followed by someone calling my name and announcing that they were the palace guard.

I was already dreading this. "Now in addition to explaining why the prince was in my room the other night, I'm going to have to explain why the princess slept in my room last night as well."

Mia's head popped out from under the blankets. "My brother slept over?"

"No. That wasn't at all what happened. After you brought that cake, he came by and—" I was interrupted by more knocking.

"She's coming. Calm down!" Mia yelled toward the door, but the knocking became so insistent that I eventually got up. Standing in my doorway were two palace guards in full uniform despite the early morning.

"Can I help you?" I asked them.

Mia was at my side before they had a chance to answer.

"Do you need something?" Mia asked.

They blinked in surprise, but instead of answering Mia, the younger of the two pushed the door open farther and walked straight through. Before I knew what was happening, she'd snapped a pair of silver cuffs on to my wrists. Instantly my arms felt like rocks, the feeling quickly spreading up to the rest of me.

"What the hell?" I tried jerking away from her, but the guard latched on to my arm and held firm.

Suppression cuffs? Seriously?

I made a meager attempt to shimmy out of the cuffs but only succeeded in scraping my wrists against the metal.

Mia was by my side in an instant, one finger pointed directly at the guard. "What is the meaning of this? Take those off her right now."

But the guard still did not answer. There was something in her eyes that I recognized, a stoic glare that reminded me of the way the humans had stared at fae back on Alliance Island. Why would a fellow fae look at me like that?

I could still stand, but it was like a blanket of fatigue had settled over me. The cuffs were suppressing my magic. Were they the same type of cuffs they had used on Leo? Had he felt like this too?

The other guard, who was older with graying hair and hard features, bowed her head to Mia. "Our apologies, Princess, but we are under orders—"

"Whose orders?" Mia demanded while I tried to shrug the guard's hand off my arm. "You are under my orders now. Take those off her."

"His Majesty ordered us to bring the lady to him in his study."

"My father? Why does my father need to see Vera? The two of you could have just asked instead of grabbing her and trying to walk away. An escort would be normal protocol, not slapping suppression cuffs on her. This is barbaric. Vera is our guest here, not some criminal. Unlock them right now."

"We were told to leave no room for argument."

The guard holding onto my arm was walking again, pulling me with her, and I felt helpless to do anything other than follow along.

"I didn't do anything wrong."

She acted as if I wasn't speaking at all. They weren't listening to Mia either.

I had to do something.

Summoning every ounce of strength I still had, I yanked my shoulder back as hard as I could and succeeded in knocking the guard's hand off me.

She froze, staring back at me with wide eyes. "You shouldn't have been able to do that."

In the confusion, Mia moved between us. "I will personally escort Vera to see my father. Leave. Now."

The two guards shifted anxiously in front of us. "We cannot, Your Highness."

"You can and you will. Let me remind you that I create the schedule and assignments for the royal guard. It would be a shame if the two of you were transferred to one of the eastern towns, wouldn't it?"

I leaned around Mia to look at them. "Yeah, what she said!"

Mia's eyes narrowed as she examined the two guards. "You both know I will keep my word, but I will not have Vera marched through the palace like a criminal. Take these cuffs off her immediately, and I will bring her to the king's study myself. That should be more than enough for my father. You can meet us there if you doubt me."

"We will let you take her, but the cuffs stay on."

"This is ridiculous. We need time to change and make ourselves presentable. She can't do that with those stupid cuffs on. If you won't do it, I'll get my own keys and this will be the last day you work in this palace."

The guards exchanged a glance, and then one came over and unlocked the cuffs. "Your Highness, we will wait outside the doors to

His Majesty's study. If she is not there soon, we will come looking for you both."

They turned on their heels and left my room.

"Those jerks," Mia said as we leaned out my door to watch them fly down the hallway. "Questioning me? As if I wouldn't keep my word and just disappear?"

"Well, not to defend them, but you and Laurie did kind of do that once."

"Okay, maybe!" Mia huffed as she put her hands on my wrists, linking with me just enough to take away the soreness. My skin tingled from her touch, but I felt instantly better.

"We also left last night without telling anyone."

"Fine! I get it. But they had no right to be such jerks to you. My father better have a good explanation for this."

"Do you think he wants to talk to me about Leo?"

"Possibly. We can tell him what we saw last night at least. Something isn't right here. Let's get dressed, and then we'll find out."

The guards kept their word and were waiting for us at the large wooden door to the king's study. I'd never been in this room before, and the first thing I noticed was there were no books, unlike what I'd expect of a king's royal office. The guard had said it was the king's study, but what exactly was he studying if there weren't any books? There were shelves lining one of the walls, painted white like the rest of the room, but they contained an assortment of little plants and statues. Not a book in sight.

Reading hadn't been allowed when I was growing up on the island, and once I was sold to Leo, I spent hours looking through the books in his study. The dark wood of his bookcases always made the space feel cozy and warm and welcoming. Some nights he had to drag me out of there after I'd get lost for hours in a book, sitting in one of his armchairs, lured by the smell of old pages and leather, my mind greedily absorbing all the stories I'd been denied before.

And here, where fae lived in luxury and freedom, they chose not to read?

There was no doubt the king's study was beautiful; the tall ceiling and floor-to-ceiling windows on the far wall let in the sunlight, giving the room a bright and airy feel. A crystal chandelier hung in the middle of the room, the delicate crystals casting tiny sparkles on the white furniture. Everything was clean and elegant but also a little empty and cold. It made me sad to think they were missing out on stories of adventure and faraway places and star-crossed lovers separated by oceans or war.

There, in a chair at the other end of the room near the windows, his blue wings sparkling in the sunlight, sat Mia's father, the king of the fae.

And beside him stood his son.

Laurie leaned against the tall window and didn't make any effort to acknowledge our presence. After last night, I wasn't going to be the first one to say anything. I took a deep breath as Mia and I shuffled in.

The king, dressed in a white suit with a gold vest, leaned forward in his chair as Mia and I came closer. He looked so much like Laurie and Mia, the same white hair, the same striking blue eyes and dazzling blue wings, but at this moment he had none of his children's usual happiness and charm. The king looked troubled, and after the guards showing up at my room earlier, I was dreading the reason why.

Beside me, Mia cursed under her breath. "Why is she here?"

Standing beside the king's chair was a fae woman I'd never seen before. She wore a black cloak that covered her dress, the hood pulled up over her head to hide her hair. The darkness of her cloak stood in an odd contrast to the light and sparkle of the study. She stood calmly beside the king, her dark eyes trained on the two of us. When I glanced over to Mia beside me, her face was scrunched, eyebrows knit together.

We stopped directly in front of the king, Mia and I both bowing. The king stood up, putting his hands on Mia's shoulders. He tilted his head, examining her for a moment.

"You seem tired. Did my daughter have a late night?"

"I'm probably just working too hard."

"I see." He patted her shoulders. "Then you should go get some rest. You're not needed here. I wish to speak to Vera alone."

Alone? Then why were Laurie and this other lady here?

"Forgive me, Father, but I'd rather stay, especially after those two guards outside tried to drag Vera here a few minutes ago. Did you know that they were going to bring her here in cuffs? Besides, it doesn't look like you're alone right now." Mia turned toward the fae in the black cloak. "Keeper."

So that's who she was. Laurie had mentioned her in passing, but this was the first time I'd seen her face-to-face. From what I'd heard, she was the resident expert in fae magic. I'd heard she was smart, capable, and kind of scary. The way she stared at me was certainly unnerving.

The fae woman didn't bow to Mia. "Your Highness."

"Cuffs?" The king looked back to her.

"I wanted them to make sure she came here quickly."

The king sighed, but then he turned to me with a smile. "Vera. This is all a misunderstanding. I did ask the guards to bring you here quickly, but our Keeper must have misinterpreted my instructions. Mia, we will discuss later." He gave his daughter a look that said his word was final.

"Fine," Mia said. "Come on, Laurie, let's go."

"He stays."

"Oh." Mia seemed surprised. She reached over and gave my hand a squeeze before leaving, then shut the door behind her.

"Now that we're alone," the king said, though we definitely were not with this chick in a black cloak and Laurie standing right behind him. "I need your help, Vera."

"Certainly, Your Majesty," I said, my spirits rising. Was he finally ready to really listen to me about what life was like outside this city? If Laurie was in this meeting, then maybe he had finally convinced his father of the necessity of sending fae out of the city to rescue the enslaved fae. But if that were the case, Laurie should be excited. At the moment he wouldn't even look at me. Not that I blamed him after last night. "How can I help, Your Majesty?"

"As you know, the demon escaped the palace dungeon."

Great. The only person we were going to talk about leaving Rowan was Leo.

"Leo," I said. I was struck by how strange his name sounded when spoken aloud. I didn't want to talk about Leo, especially not with Laurie standing right there.

"Yes. We have spent the past three days trying to find him."

"And?" I hated how eager my voice sounded, but I had to know the answer. "Did Your Majesty find him?"

"No." The king shook his head. "No one has. Is there anything you can tell us that might help our search?"

While I'd assumed that Leo had left Rowan completely, hearing that he really was gone without a trace made my heart sink. The king paused, waiting for my reply.

"He probably went back to Vestia, Your Majesty," I said.

"I'm not so sure, but we also don't know how he got in through the Willow Gate in the first place. If he has some other means of getting in and out of the city, we need to know it, Vera. Can you help us? The safety of the city is at stake."

It really wasn't, but I also didn't want to reveal Leo's secrets, even if this was the fae king.

The Keeper's eyes raked me up and down. "It takes two linked fae to open the Gate."

"That's not true."

The king looked at me sharply. "What? Of course it's true."

"No, I was able to open it myself when I came here."

"You must be mistaken. You were with my son and daughter, and they were able to open the Gate with you."

I looked to Laurie for help, but he was still staring out the window. "I must be mistaken, Your Majesty. I apologize."

"Also, it would not have been easy for the demon to get out of the cells below the palace," the king added. "Not without help. We don't think he acted alone. Is it possible he was traveling with someone? A fae?"

I thought about seeing Rob last night at the club. He hadn't mentioned seeing Leo at all, but was it possible they came here together? No, that seemed unlikely. I wasn't sure what Laurie had told his father, but I decided to keep that to myself.

"I'm really not sure, Your Majesty."

"I believe you were with my son when the demon first arrived."

After last night, the mention of Laurie made a knot form in the pit of my stomach. He still wouldn't look at me.

"At that particular moment, yes, Your Majesty." I weighed my words carefully. "We were on the back terrace."

"Alone?" asked the Keeper.

"Well, yes."

"So you didn't know the demon was coming?"

"You weren't there that night, were you, Keeper? If you had been, you would have seen that his arrival was a shock to me just like it was to everyone else."

"Of course it was." A broad smile broke out on the king's face. When he smiled he looked so much like Mia and Laurie.

The Keeper still didn't seem satisfied with my answers. "How long were you and the prince alone?"

"I don't know. Maybe ten minutes? Fifteen at most?"

"Doing what?" the Keeper asked.

The intent behind her questions was clear. If demanding my presence here hadn't been enough of a hint that she suspected me of something, now I knew for sure. I'd had enough of her questions and was about to tell her exactly that when Laurie spoke instead.

"We were dancing." Laurie stayed where he was by the window, still not meeting my eyes. "Vera was with me when we heard noises, and when we rushed over to find out what was going on, the demon was there. The rest of these questions are irrelevant, as I told you they would be."

"And afterward, once the demon was imprisoned, where were you, Vera?" the Keeper persisted.

"Are you accusing her of something?" Laurie asked.

"I was in my room."

"Alone?"

"Not the entire time. The guards can vouch for that. Laurie was in my room when the guards told us that Leo had disappeared."

"Vera, you don't have to answer her."

Ignoring Laurie, the Keeper turned her attention back to me. "What is your relationship with this demon?"

Well, shit. Wasn't that a great question? What *was* my relationship with Leo now? Was there any relationship at all? And on top of that, why was it any of her business?

The king seemed to sense my hesitation. "The past is the past, Vera. I know this might be awkward with my son here, but he insisted on being part of this. You can tell the truth."

I glanced behind him at Laurie, who was still looking everywhere except at me.

"Unlike the Keeper, I was there that night, so I know the demon was there to see you, Vera," the king said. "Somehow he was able to get past the city's veil that should have kept out anyone who wasn't fae. Then he was able to escape our jail, which should not have been possible. In order to protect this city, I have to understand how and why this happened." His face softened. "The jail is one thing, but the veil is something else entirely. The security of Rowan is my top priority. If one demon can get in and out of Rowan, can others? The veil is our entire safety net. If it no longer keeps out demons or humans, we are all in danger."

"Your Majesty, aren't fae stronger than all of them?" I asked. "Isn't that why demons developed suppression tech during the war?"

"We may be stronger in terms of raw power, but we've lived for years now without the organization or logistics needed for full-on combat. If I start organizing an army now, it will give the impression that we *need* an army, and then that feeling of safety will be lost."

"Maybe that's not a bad thing, Your Majesty. A fully formed fae army might be exactly what it takes to threaten the humans into letting their fae slaves go free."

"That again?" The king smiled down at me, much like someone might smile at a silly child. "I appreciate your passion, Vera. I see now why my son knows that you are a good match for him, but"—the king kept speaking even as I opened my mouth to correct him—"it is my job as king to protect the fae of Rowan."

"While thousands of fae are enslaved across the ocean."

The king shook his head. "But here in Rowan—"

"She is wise beyond her years," the Keeper said.

I flinched when I realized she was standing right beside me. I hadn't heard or seen her fly to us. Now that we were closer to each other, I could see her pale face, dark lipstick, and brown hair underneath her hood. She didn't seem much older than me, but there was something strange in the way she looked at me, and her stare gave me an uncomfortable feeling as if she was studying me. Call it a hunch or gut feeling or instinct, but I knew right away there was no way in hell I was going to tell this lady anything about Leo.

"How did the demon know you were here in Rowan?" She took a step toward me.

"He knew I came here with the prince and princess."

"And why did they bring you?"

"We were leaving a bad situation in Vestia."

"Do you know how the demon's ring works?" She took another step closer with each question.

"You mean the Hellfire ruby?" I asked.

"Yes."

"I know what it is, but beyond that, no. I don't know much about it."

"The more we know, the better we can protect the fae here, Vera." Her voice was eerily calm. "I understand you might want to protect him, but what about your own kind? I know you care about us as well."

"Of course I do."

"Then tell me, do you know how he was able to get through the veil?"

Did I know for certain? No. Did I assume it was because he was half-fae? Yes. Was I going to tell her? Not a chance.

"That's enough, Keeper." The commanding tone of Laurie's voice cut through the air.

"I have one last thing," she said.

Then, without warning, instead of taking another step, she leaped toward me, a dagger drawn. At such close range, she was sure to stab me; all I could do was hold up a hand in defense.

It was over in the blink of an eye.

"What the hell?" Laurie rushed to my side while I flipped my hand over to make sure I hadn't been cut.

Before I could even process what had just happened, the Keeper had already stepped away. My hand still up in front of me, I was frozen in shock as the Keeper calmly put away her knife underneath her black cloak. As if nothing had happened at all. As if she hadn't just tried to stab me.

My heart thumping against my chest, I stared down at my palm. Her knife had been so close. She had moved so fast. An image flashed in my head of another time, of lying on the ground, of blood.

Staring down at my palm, I realized my fingers were trembling. Somehow I was fine; she hadn't cut me at all. I must have used my magic without thinking about it. I balled my hand into a fist to try to stop from shaking, but all that did was make my arm start to tremble.

"Why did you do that?" My voice shook as well.

"Your Majesty." She ignored me completely. "It's obvious she does not have any information that will help us with the demon. I would, however, like to find out more about her magic."

Laurie stayed close, one hand protectively on my back. "Father, this is absurd. When you told me you were bringing her here, you never mentioned wanting to test her, and you certainly didn't say anything about stabbing her!"

"Yes, that's appropriate," the king answered the Keeper. "That demonstration was impressive. We may need help with securing barriers in the city in the wake of everything that's happened."

"You..." I couldn't believe what I was hearing. "You just attacked me, and now you're acting like nothing happened?"

The Keeper turned her attention to me, dark eyes blinking once as if suddenly remembering that I was there. "I've heard that you had been training with the princess."

"What does that have to do with anything? I demand an answer for what you just did."

"You do not have wings, but you seem to have manifested an interesting magical ability that helps you block attacks. That knife should have cut you, yet it didn't. I'd like to learn more about the barrier power you just demonstrated."

"And I'd like you to stay away from me."

"Vera," the king said, his voice smooth and calm, "our Keeper is the expert on fae magic. There is a lot you can learn from her. It's a position passed down through the generations to a fae who keeps and guards the history of our kind. Selena is the youngest Keeper ever appointed, but I had full confidence when I picked her that she was the right choice."

"You are too kind, Your Majesty," the Keeper said.

"But Father—"

The king kept talking over Laurie. "There's so much you could learn from Selena, Vera. So much that could be valuable for our city. I'd like you to spend some time with her over the next few days."

"I think I know enough already."

She smiled at me, a smile that held not an ounce of warmth. "We shall see."

The king patted his legs and then stood up. "Ladies, you may leave to work that out. Son, stay if you would; there are several things I'd like to discuss with you."

The meeting, or whatever the hell that had been, was over.

The Keeper and I shuffled out into the hallway, and I had zero intention of being anywhere near her. I started to walk away from her, as fast as I could, but she flew to catch up with me.

"He's suspicious of you."

"I'm not speaking to you," I told her. "I don't want anything to do with you."

"I'm talking about the king. The young prince wants to marry you, but the king is worried that you are somehow aiding demons."

"I didn't help Leo."

"I know."

"You know? Then what was with all the questions? You made me look like a criminal, not to mention making me share all the details about my time with Laurie."

"I was giving you a chance to tell your side of the story."

"Bullshit. You were making me look even more guilty, and then you tried to stab me. Leave me alone." I started walking away again. I didn't want to look at her.

She caught up to me in seconds. "I can help you clear your name. I know you didn't help the demon."

"Oh yeah? And how do you know that?"

"Because I know where he is. I can take you to him."

I paused before turning to look her in the eye. We'd just spent all that time discussing Leo's disappearance, with her basically accusing me of helping a fugitive in front of the king, and she knew where he was the whole time? What the hell?

"I could take you there tonight," she said.

"Why would I go anywhere with you? You've just proven that you're a liar. What makes you think I won't go to the king right now and tell him that you know?"

"Do that, and you'll never see your demon. It is up to you. Meet me in the back gardens at sundown tonight if you decide to come."

I had no idea what game she was playing, but I didn't want any part of it.

But if Leo was still here, and if she knew where he was...

Once the sun had fallen completely behind the horizon and the sky was shaded with the pretty pinks of sunset, I waited near a rose bush in the palace's back gardens. I shifted back and forth on my feet anxiously, knowing this could end up being the worst decision I'd ever made—or the best.

When the Keeper emerged from the shadows and held out her hand, I accepted it.

11

VERA

In the distance I could hear the steady sound of water splashing. We were underground, the air growing thicker and more humid the farther we walked. Everything felt sticky and sweaty, and my shirt clung to my chest and arms.

As the sounds of the water got louder, steam wafted down the path, circling around both of us and gliding past. The closer we came, the more the steam grew thicker and thicker until it was as if we were wading through a cloud, and I had to fan my face to be able to see through it.

Finally we came to a clearing, and I saw the source of the steam. Surrounded by tall stone walls was a large grotto, a pool with a waterfall pouring over the farthest wall. Hot, dense air rose from the water, filling the grotto and spilling into the passageways and up through the opening far above our heads.

Now that we had some light, I realized how far below ground we truly were. Due to the position of the moon, the moonlight made the water sparkle on one side of the pool but shrouded the other half in darkness. The bubbles, the steam, the moonlight—no matter where I looked, everything seemed to be the same color.

Silver.

As breathtaking as the grotto was, its beauty wasn't what made me gasp. No, it was something else entirely. As if by magic, the steam parted for the briefest of seconds, and there I saw him, standing waist-deep in the water. Shirtless, with his back to me, he ran his hands through his dark, wet hair.

Leo.

He was as far away from me as he could be on the other side of the pool, the side that was illuminated by the moonlight. Like a ghost shrouded in steam, Leo stood under the waterfall, the water running down his muscular back and dripping off his wings. The water traced his tattoos like little streams, trickling down into the pool below him. When he spread his wings, letting the water splash off them, I could see the dip of his waist and the hint of his hips.

Watching Leo there in the water, it felt as if a piece of myself existed outside my body, as if a chunk of my heart was waist-deep in the pool in front of me.

That was when I knew. Right then I knew that it didn't matter how far apart we were. I wanted him. But could I trust him? He'd left me once, now twice, and here I was running back to him anyway. Maybe it was myself that I shouldn't trust.

"We can talk later. I'll leave the two of you alone for now," the Keeper said.

Alone.

When was the last time I had been alone with Leo? My mind flashed back to that night, the night we made love and he used the suppression bracelet to knock me out before handing me to Mia and Laurie.

Unsure what to say, unsure what I even wanted to say at this point, I took off my shoes and tiptoed several cautious steps toward the pool. A small pile of clothes that I recognized as belonging to Leo sat on a rock beside the water, and my own clothes joined them there. The crashing water of the waterfall masked any sound I was making, and somehow Leo didn't turn around as I came closer.

The water was hot against my cool, bare skin, and steam rolled across the surface of the pool and over my body. I wasn't sure how deep the water was going to be, but at the middle of the pool it came up to my shoulders, so that's where I stopped.

At any moment Leo could turn around, and then I'd have to say something. I waited, watching him, watching the water droplets sparkle in the moonlight on his black wings. Every single one of my nerves and veins seemed to scream at me to say something to him, to call out to him, but *what would I say?* Everything I'd thought about for the past few weeks seemed to vanish, leaving my brain empty of everything except the sight of him.

Shoulder-deep in the water, I said nothing, waiting, shrouded in the steam of the pool. Leo's bulky black wings expanded to full size, and then he shook them, water flinging off the silver tips in every direction.

As if in slow motion, Leo slowly turned, and I held my breath. The light reflecting off the water made his eyes seem even more silver than normal as they met mine.

Neither of us said a word.

Instead, Leo was out of the water in a flash, heavy wings propelling him toward me. I didn't have time to blink before he splashed down in front of me, his arms around me, wings wrapping around us. Leo's hold was tight, pressing our bare chests against each other. His skin felt like fire, my fingers feeling tiny jolts of electricity everywhere I touched, both thrilling and reminding me that electricity in water can be dangerous and deadly. I had to be careful so that everything about this moment, about Leo, didn't do me in for good.

As I leaned into him, water dripping down my face and traveling between our bodies, I wondered if I could forget everything that had happened, forget how he'd sent me away, if I could pretend like none of that had ever happened and trust him again.

Love him again.

"Vera," he whispered into my ear as he held me against him, and I felt myself melting against him at the familiar, gravely purr of his voice. "You're here..."

I pushed back against his chest, gently at first, but then more firmly when he didn't let go. His hair was soaked, dark strands stuck against his forehead. His face fell as I turned and swam toward the shore, covering my body with water again.

I had to get away. At least for a second. There was no way that I'd be able to have a real conversation with him when he was standing there, looking like *that*.

I hadn't swum very far away before I felt his hand on my shoulder.

"Wait."

I tried to ignore the way his voice sent shivers up my spine. I shook my head and moved to swim back to our clothes. "Let's get dressed first."

"Vera. Stop running away."

That made me stop. I spun around in the water to face him. "Do you really want to talk about running away?"

"Can you at least listen for a second? I will tell you everything."

"Oh, now you want to tell me everything? Now you want to be honest?" I could hear my tone becoming more shrill with each word, but I couldn't stop myself. "I believed in you, Leo. I believed that you and I were going to change the world, together. But you never truly believed that, did you?"

"Vera—"

"No. I am speaking, and for once you're going to listen to me. You couldn't possibly imagine a world where I could be strong, where I could be your equal. Well, guess what? Here, in Rowan, I am strong. And I'm getting stronger. The magic that protects this city is growing within me as well. Every day I feel something changing within me, growing stronger."

"Really?" he asked, his eyes perking up with interest. "How does that work? Have you tried testing—"

I held up a hand to stop him. "I'm not your science experiment. Not anymore."

"You stopped being an experiment a long time ago, Vera."

"Then what was I? What was I that you could give me away so easily?"

"Easy? You think giving you to that fae bastard was easy? Wait just a second before you start to—"

"Wait? Leo, all I've done is wait! Wait for you to come back from business trips for Syn, wait for you to deal with your father, wait for you to come find me and tell me that this wasn't all a mistake, that you didn't mean to let me go. How dare you show up now, Leo? How dare you show up here, of all places, and say you're taking me home? You didn't even ask, Leo! You didn't even consider that maybe I'd want to stay here, that maybe I was trying to start over, that maybe I'd finally gotten to the point where I wouldn't cry myself to sleep thinking about you."

"You..." Leo moved closer to me in the water. "Vera—"

"Don't say my name like that, like you have any idea what I've been through. Like you know what you put me through. Like you still love me."

"I do love you. Everything I did, I did because I love you."

"Then what does love mean to you, Leo? Does it mean hurting the people who care about you? Does it mean hurting yourself?"

"I'm not sure. I'm not sure about much of anything right now, except for you."

"Leo..."

"Vera, stop."

"What?" I asked.

"You've talked enough tonight. You're going to listen to me now."

I was taken aback by this new demanding tone.

"I killed my father's councilors."

"I heard."

"They murdered my mother, and now they're gone. With the backing of the general, I appointed new councilors, and I freed all the slaves in Vestia. All of them. No more Dust will come from the demon kingdom. Everything is in place now. Everything so that I can be with you."

I searched his face, looking for any signs that he wasn't telling the truth. I found none.

"You're serious."

"Yes."

"It's only been a few weeks. You did all that?"

A wry smile broke out across his face. "I was sort of in a hurry. You see, there was this beautiful woman I needed to get back to."

"Leo..."

"Since I knew you were safe, I could let myself focus on what needed to be done."

"I see. Are you now going to become the king officially?"

"No." Leo's eyes dropped. "Not yet. There was no coronation. I made rules as regent, but we didn't proceed with the ceremony to officially make me king. If I go back, then yes, that's the logical step, but I don't want to go back."

"You don't?"

"There's only one thing not in place. And that's you." Leo came closer in the water, and my heart started beating faster. "I'm sorry I sent you away. I'm so sorry. You'll never know how much I regretted that decision. Every night I dreamed about you. Every day I thought about you. Everything I did," he said, taking slow, deliberate movements toward me, "I did to get one step closer to you."

He hesitated just a moment before taking the final step to be right in front of me.

I wanted to run from him and run to him. Unable to decide on either, I stayed still as Leo reached for me. His fingers grazed against my cheek, that familiar spark setting my skin on fire as he tilted my head toward him. Everything in me tightened, my heart beating wildly.

In my head I could lie and say that I'd missed this connection; I could tell myself that it had nothing to do with Leo himself, that he only made me angry and confused. I could lie and think that this was just lust, that I wasn't letting myself be open with him again, that I wasn't letting myself trust him again.

It would all be a lie.

"Can I kiss you?" he asked.

"Yes," I whispered.

There was just a brief pause, a flicker of a moment where his breath was on my lips and I wasn't sure if he was going to actually kiss me or not. But then his lips were against mine, and all thoughts vanished except for the ones including him.

His kiss was hungry, greedy even, needing and taking more of me with each passing second, but I didn't care. I was greedy too, giving in to his mouth and lips and melting against him. His body was fire, and I wanted to burn.

Maybe I would. Maybe I was stepping into flames of my own creation by letting him kiss me again. Lips crashing, tongues dancing, both of us tasting each other and touching anywhere our hands could go, letting the fire consume us both. One of his hands gripped my wet hair and pulled me against him, hard, as if he couldn't stand to be physically apart for another moment.

How long? How long had it been since I'd felt comfortable and at home like I did in his arms? How long had it been since I'd felt this needed?

How long would it last?

And then there were tears stinging the corner of my eyes. I blinked and swallowed, trying to hold them back as they started to trickle down my cheeks, but it was no use.

Leo immediately broke away from our kiss.

"Are you hurt?" His silver eyes scanned my face and body as more tears flowed. "Did I hurt you?"

I couldn't make myself form the right words. Even if I could have spoken through the tears, I didn't know the words I would have said. Everything was *right*, but everything had been wrong, and I wanted to kiss him, but I wanted to scream at him at the same time.

How dare he make me feel like this again?

How dare he still love me?

Tugging me against his chest, Leo's hands smoothed down my damp hair, his hushed voice whispering sweet words I hadn't heard in so long that only made me cry harder.

"Vera, what is it?"

"I..."

I didn't even know myself.

"I'm just so scared," I finally said. "What if..." I couldn't look at him, so I buried my face against his chest. "What if you leave me again?"

When we pulled back, I expected to see soft silver eyes to match the soft words he'd whispered, but instead Leo's face was hard, determined.

"I will never leave you again," he said, his voice strained.

"But you did. I wasn't strong enough, and you did."

Leo gripped both my shoulders, his silver eyes burning as he stared at me with a ferocity I hadn't seen before. I forced myself to match his intense stare, and I watched as he pursed his lips.

"Never again," he said. "I'm not letting you get away again."

Leo let go of my shoulders and tipped my chin up to him, his mouth again meeting my own. I was trembling, but with his arm around my waist, I was secure. If the other kiss was greedy, this one was careful, as if he was making sure that I was safe in his arms.

When we broke away from the kiss, Leo's stunning silver eyes were staring down at me, a new brightness shining in them that wasn't there before.

Maybe this could work.

Maybe we really could go back to how it used to be.

Missing his warmth, I leaned forward and closed my eyes, ready to feel his lips against my own again.

But that didn't happen.

"Okay, now it's your turn," he said instead of kissing me.

"What?" I blinked my eyes open. Leo was still staring at me, but now he smirked.

"Well, I apologized," he said.

"Yeah, and?"

"Now it's your turn."

"To do what?"

"To apologize to me."

"For what?"

Leo raised one eyebrow skeptically. "First, you slapped me."

"Seriously?"

"You seemed serious at the time."

I watched Leo, my expression blank. If it wasn't for the playful smirk on his face, I would have dunked him under the water right then.

"No." I splashed a little water at him. "Not apologizing for that. You deserved it."

"I have to admit that it was a lot harder than the last time you hit me. Second, you need to apologize for stringing that white-haired boy along."

Rearing my arm back in the water, I splashed water at him harder. "I'm doing no such thing."

"He's in love with you. Has been for a while. I even heard gossip that you're marrying him."

"Oh come on, I'm not marrying anyone. That's ridiculous." I moved to splash Leo again. This time he caught my wrist and held it tight.

"You're not?"

"Nope."

"Not even if someone asked?"

A long moment of silence passed between us before I finally spoke.

"It would depend on who is asking."

"I see."

His hand still around my wrist, he pulled me to him, his other hand going securely around my waist in the water.

"You have no idea how hard it is to stand here with you dripping wet in front of me." His gravelly voice made me want to melt right then and there.

"Then you should do something about it."

"If you insist."

His hands went under the water, grabbing around my ass and lifting me up. Instinctively I wrapped my legs around his waist and let him carry me over to the side of the pool. Even in the steam of the pool, the air was cold on my wet skin, and I pressed my chest against his to get back that warmth.

He was so hot. When Leo finally let me go, letting me slide down his body into the water, I relished each second that our skin connected. Leo swam over to the side and leaned back, resting his elbows on the rocks on either side of him. He tilted his head to the side.

"Well?"

Missing his body heat, I sank down in the water, letting it cover my shoulders. "Well what?"

"Vera." Gods, did he know how the deep rumble of his voice could send shivers down my spine? That it was ten times worse when he said my name? He had to know. "How long are you going to make me wait for you?"

I pretended to contemplate an answer as I swam back a few feet. His silver eyes narrowed as he watched me back away from him. "Hm. I think you deserve at least a little teasing, don't you?"

"I think the fuck not."

Leo pushed himself off the rocks and treaded through the water toward me. I tried to swim away, but he caught me easily before I got very far. I let out a loud squeal when his big hands went around my bare waist, and I half-heartedly splashed and kicked, but his hold only became firmer, dragging me back to him. Even in the water, his touch felt electric, each finger digging into my flesh a tiny flame that lit something inside me.

As he hugged me from behind, it must have lit something inside him too. We'd gone too long without this kind of touch, without this kind of skin-on-skin closeness. My magic had grown stronger since I came to Rowan, and I could tell from the way his bare chest heaved against me with each breath he took that he felt the effects of my magic, of me, of *us*.

He spun me around in his arms as if I was light as a feather, and lifted me up so I could wrap my legs around his waist to get closer. His fingers dug into my flesh, his nails surely leaving red indents that would later blossom into lovely purples and blues to mark this moment. Latching my arms around his neck, I leaned into him, dotting kisses down his jawline.

A guttural sound rolled from his chest as he freed a hand to cup my chin. "Hold on."

I let out a whine. "I don't want to." I slid my hands down onto his chest and started to grind against him. "I want more."

"Oh, if you think you're getting away without me fucking you, you are very, very wrong. But that's not what I meant."

"Then what did you—"

"I said hold on."

We were suddenly out of the water, Leo's wings pushing us up into the steam hovering over the pool.

"Our clothes!" I squealed, clinging to him even as he held me tight.

"Fuck our clothes."

"I'll get them later," I told him.

"What if I want you naked instead?"

I didn't have time to comment on the fact that we were flying completely naked down a dark hallway or ask a question about the small, strange bedroom he took me to. I didn't care about any of that, not when his hot mouth was pressing against my skin, trailing messy kisses down my chest.

There was a small bed—comically small for someone of Leo's size—and he put me down on it before climbing onto it himself. He told me to lie back and then spread my knees with his hands. My body obeyed him like a servant, opening up for him to see everything.

"You're beautiful," he whispered.

Desperate for his touch, for him, I reached out for Leo, wanting him closer. He obliged, slotting himself between my legs.

"Can you be careful with me?" I'd asked before, but now it meant more than ever.

"I will. You're mine, Vera. You have always been mine."

I cried out at the stretch as he entered me, that perfect stretch that I'd missed as my body worked to accommodate his size.

Leo muttered a string of praises as he pushed forward. "I've got you, little one," he said, encouraging me as his hips began with small, shallow thrusts, each one taking him deeper and deeper inside.

"You're almost—*fuck*—you're almost there. You're doing so good for me."

His praise, his hands, the way his chest rose and fell with heavy breaths—it all felt so perfect, so *right*, as if everything in the world was the way it should be now that we were together.

With a final thrust of his hips, he was fully sheathed inside me, our bodies completely connected. His wings spread out over us, Leo closed his eyes and groaned as he held me there. "I'm so fucking addicted to you. To your touch. Your skin. Your smell. To you."

I let one of my hands tangle in his dark, damp hair. "Had you forgotten how my magic feels?"

"This isn't just your magic, Vera. This is you. It's all you."

We were making up for lost time, but no matter how much we wanted to rush, Leo took his time. Just like he promised, he was careful until neither of us wanted him to be, and hours later, when he finally buried himself deep inside me, he came with my name on his lips.

I was pretty sure that I'd never heard a better sound.

Once Leo was asleep, I wrapped one of his blankets around me and went to look for our clothes. Thankfully the hall was empty as I tiptoed back to the grotto. I shrugged on Leo's shirt and gathered the few things we had left behind. But when I went to fold up the blanket, something caught my eye. It was high up, nestled in the rock. I hadn't noticed it before when I'd been there with Leo, but I had been a little preoccupied.

Now that I could focus on it, I had to wonder. Was that rock glowing?

"Would you like a closer look?"

I spun around and saw the Keeper standing a few feet away, wearing a black cloak. Did this lady ever sleep? It had to be the middle of the night.

"What is that?" I asked her, pointing up at the glowing rock.

"Legend has it that it helps you become more in-tune with your magic."

"It's weird. When I was in here earlier, I didn't even notice it, but now…"

"What do you feel now?" the Keeper asked, coming closer.

"I'm not sure. I do feel something though."

"Oh? I can fly you closer, if you'd like."

The Keeper extended her hand. I'd taken her hand once today already, and it had ended positively. After a moment's hesitation, I took her hand for the second time.

If I had only known.

12

LEO

My eyes shot open when a small rock hit my forehead.

What the fuck? Did Vera throw something at me?

Then I felt it.

The ground was shaking. The walls were shaking. Tiny rocks scattered all around me as they fell from the ceiling. I didn't know how or why or what was happening, but I knew we needed to get out of this cave. I reached next to me to wake Vera. We needed to get out—

Where the hell was she?

I stared at the empty bed for a second before jumping up and quickly pulling on my pants. I rushed out of the cave and shouted her name, searching for her in every dark passageway. Her name echoed off the stone walls, but I didn't hear any answer. Other than my own yelling and my bare feet slapping against the floor as I ran, the only other sound was the occasional scattering of rock or the distant sound of rock breaking.

Was this place about to collapse? Would it collapse before I found her?

I raced to the grotto, where we had last been together, and there she was.

Wearing only my shirt, the fabric falling just below her thighs,

Vera stood on the far side of the pool with her back to me, her long brown hair wavy in the humid air. Somehow she had made it all the way up to where the carving was, and she stood on the small ledge right in front of it.

How the hell had she gotten up there? Had she climbed?

No.

That wasn't it.

The relief I first felt at seeing her faded in an instant as I realized what was going on. Through the steam blanketing the pool, I saw fae standing in the water and on the surrounding rocks, all of them wearing that same black cloak I'd seen the Keeper's followers wear. They had done this. They had flown her up there.

"Vera!" I shouted, but no one turned. No one gave any indication they'd heard me. I didn't have time to yell again because a quake shook everything. I had to stop to hold on to the wall in order to stay standing.

Rocks cracked and tumbled down into the water below, and the whole place was getting hotter and hotter. We had to get out of there quickly; the cave was going to crumble in on itself.

I leaped into the air to fly to Vera, but I'd barely made it halfway across the pool when two fae in black cloaks flew right into my path, blocking me over the water.

"Get out of my way!" I bellowed, darting to the side, but they did the same, mimicking my movements. They were fast, and I noticed how their eyes glowed like Selena's had when she'd drank the fae blood.

"I said get out of my way!"

The two fae didn't answer; they continued to mirror each move I made as I tried to get past them, keeping me from getting any closer. Around them I could see Vera standing just as she'd been when I first saw her. Why wasn't she moving?

That's when I saw her hand. Her arm was extended out in front of her, and Vera's hand was covering that damned stone. Hovering in the air a few feet away from her was another fae in a black cloak. I could see enough to know this one was the Keeper herself. She must have dragged Vera in here to see what effect the stone had on her.

"Vera!" I shouted again over the two fae blocking my path, hoping I was close enough that she'd hear me. Instead of flying directly toward Vera, which I knew they'd try to block, I flew up, fast, as if I were flying out of the grotto completely.

Just as I'd hoped, the two fae stopped following me as I flew higher. They seemed content that I was no longer a threat and flew back down closer to where Vera stood.

Once out of the grotto, I was able to fly around the opening to get to the side near her. Just as I landed above Vera, I heard a loud crack, and a rock broke off from the wall below me. It fell dangerously close to where Vera was standing, but as another quake shook the cavern, she seemed unfazed, her body still and her hand never leaving the stone. This must have been how I looked when I had the vision of my mother.

Was she having a vision as well?

Damn it. Vera had come here to find me, and now she was caught up in the Keeper's plot with no way for me to protect her. I needed to think fast. How could I fly down there, grab her, and get out without the fae stopping me?

The ground shook below my feet, reminding me that time was running out.

I jumped in, flying down about halfway toward Vera, and landed on a small rock jutting out from the side of the wall. I grabbed on to the stones, steadying myself as best I could with my wings and tail; there was barely enough room to balance on one foot.

Then someone called my name.

When I looked up, I saw three faces peering down into the cave. Two I recognized as the prince and princess, and the third was a guy with purple wings who I didn't know. How had they found us here?

"Get out of there!" the prince yelled. "We'll deal with this!"

Damn it.

The last thing I needed was for one those dumbasses to jump

down here and end up needing to be saved as well. I didn't have time for their bullshit when Vera needed me.

"Stay up there!" I shouted at them, unsure if my voice would carry over the crashing rocks. Not that they listened. A flash of blue and white swished by as rocks continued to rain down into the water below.

That idiot.

Leaping into the air, I flew down to the bottom of the cavern right behind the white-haired fae.

Rocks continued to fall, but now the fae in black coats had two to chase. Still, even with the help, they refused to let either of us get close to Vera. The whole cave was shaking, but these damn fae wanted to play keep-away.

Mia and the other guy joined in, and since the others had their hands full, I decided it was time to bully my way to Vera. But just before I got to her, a giant chunk of the cave broke off right above her head, and then it was like everything happened in slow motion.

That rock kept falling, and it hit Vera, knocking her off the small ledge she'd been standing on.

The stone stopped glowing.

The cave stopped shaking.

My heart felt like it stopped beating.

I darted toward her, hoping I could be there in time to catch her, but the last face I wanted to see flew in front of me.

The Keeper.

"Get the fuck away!" I shouted, but she blocked me no matter how I twisted and dodged. I didn't have time for this. I needed to get to Vera.

"Looks like she fell," the Keeper said with mock sincerity.

My eyes scanned the floor of the cave, but all I saw was piles of rocks.

"You can have her now," the Keeper said. "Her job is done."

"And so are you!" Right then blue and purple zoomed by me, and the purple-winged fae grabbed the Keeper, holding her tight as she shouted and thrashed.

"You were all too late," she yelled down to us as he pulled her up and out of the cave.

I flew down to where I'd seen her fall, but the ground was a mess of debris and chucks of rock that had piled up, making it difficult to move the larger ones out of the way. She was under those rocks somewhere, and I had to get to her before it was too late.

Laurie landed next to me and pointed a finger at my chest. "Back up. You're not strong enough to move these rocks, so we'll do it."

I'd never felt more helpless, but there was no denying the strength of these fae. The twin fae moved rocks double their size with ease, flinging huge pieces of the cave away from where they'd fallen.

As I watched, a terrible powerlessness took over all my senses.

After everything, had I lost her?

When they finally moved the last big chunk of rock, and I saw the first glimpse of her hair, I swooped past them and straight to where she leaned back against the wall of the cave.

"Leo?" One of the fae behind me said, but I wasn't paying attention to them. "Do you see..."

Breathing, check.

Only minor visible injuries, check.

Alive.

"Leo," I heard them say, more insistently this time.

I didn't care about them. I only cared about her. Somehow, all those rocks hadn't touched Vera at all. Instead, she was tucked into a small enclosure created by the falling rocks, like they had made a protective wall that kept her from being crushed. Vera's eyes were closed, but her breathing seemed normal, as if she were simply asleep. But when I went to take her into my arms...

I blinked, trying to understand what I was seeing.

How was this possible?

"Am I dead?" she croaked, her eyes still closed, her voice rough and tired. My heart soared at the sound of her voice.

"No." I shook my head slowly, still not processing what I was seeing. "You're very much alive."

Her eyes fluttered before half opening. "Doesn't feel like it. Everything hurts."

I reached for her, but she held up a shaking hand to stop me as she tried to move on her own. I sat back on my heels, unsure what to say. The two fae behind me were just as quiet.

"Why are you all looking at me like that?" Vera groaned, giving up and slumping back against the wall. "Did that big rock hit me? Did it break me? Am I broken? My back is killing me."

Maybe it was the intense feeling of relief that she was alive, or maybe it was the knowledge that she felt well enough to be her normal stubborn self. Whatever it was, I cackled. A genuine loud-as-hell cackle.

Her eyes opened just a little more, and one corner of her mouth quirked up in an exhausted smile.

"Are you laughing at my pain?"

"No, Vera. It's that..." What was I supposed to say? "Can you reach behind you?"

"Of course I can." She shifted slightly and squeezed her eyes shut, groaning again from the pain. I wanted to scoop her into my arms and whisk her far away, but that couldn't happen. Not yet.

I could see the hint of a snappy reply start to form on her lips, but then she slowly reached behind her.

And her eyes snapped open. Two brown eyes, now big and wide and awake, looking up at me at me with a mix of confusion and excitement, no doubt wondering, like me, what the hell had just happened. Two big eyes looking to me as if I had to have the answer.

I didn't.

"What... What is this?" she asked.

What was there to say? All I could think to say was the obvious.

"They're wings, Vera. You have wings."

13

VERA

Had it all been a dream?

When I opened my eyes, the first thing I realized was that I wasn't wearing my own clothes. I didn't recognize the oversized shirt I had on, and I didn't remember changing clothes either, but when I tried to think back on what happened, everything seemed shrouded in a blanket of fog.

Caves.

Water.

Wings.

Protect them.

I sat up in my bed too quickly, blood rushing to my head and making my vision go white for a second. No time for fainting, I told myself and shook my head to get rid of the fog before swinging my legs over to the side of the bed.

That hadn't been my voice. It was someone else's. A woman's.

A shiver ran down my spine at the memory, and the noise I heard behind me reminded me.

It hadn't been a dream at all.

I had *wings*.

When I strained my head around to get a good look at them, I saw two shimmering, multicolored wings. Crimson and tangerine, citrus and emerald, scarlet and apricot, they were a swirl of many different colors, all bright and beautiful. And mine.

It was about damn time.

Protect them, the voice had said. Was that part of getting wings? I wasn't sure, but I could figure it out later because *I had wings*. Heart racing, I clenched my back experimentally, just to see what would happen. As expected, my wings moved. Slowly, awkwardly, in weird little jutting motions, but they moved all the same.

Could I fly now? What else could I do? How had my magic changed?

Now it made sense. Someone had changed my clothes and put me in a shirt that accommodated the wings. I felt like squealing right then and there at the idea that I was, for once, *normal*.

Well, sort of. These wings didn't seem normal at all. I'd seen wings that seemed to change color in the light or sparkled in different shades, but I'd never seen wings like my own, wings with too many colors to count, their hues intertwining and mixing with each other in a rainbow of vibrant tones.

My body ached, but I wanted—no, *needed*—to try them out. Could I fly around the room or maybe out of the window and do a lap around the palace? After a moment's hesitation, I flexed my wings, not expanding them totally, but enough to see if I could, in fact, move them as if I was flying.

And I could.

I fluttered them, just a little, and was surprised by how easy it was. I tried again, this time attempting to expand them completely at my sides and found the movement just as simple. Light despite their size, moving with ease merely because I willed it so. Out and in, back and forth, my wings—my *wings*—moved as naturally as an arm or leg.

This was how it was supposed to be. It felt like I now had all the pieces of me in place, as if it was the most natural thing in the world to have two wings sprouting from my back. I twisted my head around to get a clear picture of them, two big wings that dazzled with more colors than I could count, seeming to change each time the light touched them.

But then I saw something else over my shoulder.

Leo.

My heart clenched at the sight of him, a smile breaking out across my face. My face felt hot remembering Leo and steam and water, and I must have remembered too much because my wings started fluttering behind me. Leo sat in a chair, but his upper body was draped over the side of my bed, his head resting on his arms. His eyes were closed, and I wondered if he was dreaming.

He didn't stir as I moved on the bed and crawled toward him, and it was only when my fingers began to trace through his hair that his eyes opened.

The side of his head still resting against his arms, Leo's silver eyes opened and he blinked up at me. Then he jolted up and leaped out of the chair, his big body suddenly on top of mine before I had time to even let out a squeak of surprise.

"Oh shit." Leo's eyes trailed to my side where I knew he was looking at my new wings underneath me. "Is this okay? I forgot about…"

"I don't think you can hurt them."

His silver eyes flicked away from my wings back to me. "I'm not used to seeing you with them."

"You and me both."

With a loud exhale, Leo pulled me up off my back and into his lap, his arms going around me, careful of my new wings, to hold me in place.

Snuggling my head into his shoulder, I knew. This was right, this was how it was supposed to be. Him and me, together. I could barely breathe, but it felt like a fair trade for the feeling of his body against my own, for the chance to be so close that I could smell his distinctive scent of campfire and mint. I inhaled against his neck, savoring it.

"Are you sniffing me?" he asked after a second.

"Deal with it. Let me have this."

Chuckling, Leo held me there a second longer, then moved away, and I stifled a whine at the loss of his closeness.

"Help me out." I twisted around on the bed so that I faced away from him.

"What do you want me to do?"

"I'm sore. Could you rub my back?"

I heard his deep chuckle behind me, and then I felt the mattress dip as he scooted closer. I waited for his touch. Nothing happened, but then I felt a tug on the hem of my shirt.

"I can't get to your skin with this in the way."

Not needing any more instruction, I pulled the big shirt up and over my head, carefully threading my wings through the openings in the fabric. I knew that he was staring at my naked back, at my new wings. Shivering in the cold of the room, I waited.

And waited.

Come on, Leo. *Touch me.*

It felt like an eternity before I felt that initial shock from his fingertips on my skin as he gently traced down my spine.

Everything in me tingled from his soft touches.

It wasn't enough.

"Leo," I said, sounding a lot whinier than I intended.

"I know, I know, little one. They're just so beautiful."

Leo moved as close as he could get, my wings forcing some space between us, with one of his legs on either side of my body. I relaxed my wings, folding them down against my back so he could move closer. Then he started in earnest, his big, firm hands on my shoulders, rubbing before digging in, his thumbs making small circles on my upper back.

It felt so good. So damn good.

Who needed a heating pad when you had a hot demon with his hot hands to take the pain away?

The pain was going away...

With a gasp, I realized what he was doing. He was linking with me. The soreness was vanishing by the second and was instead being replaced by something else. I closed my eyes, relishing in the heat from his fingers.

"What do you remember?" he asked me as he continued pressing his hands into my back.

"You expect me to think while you're doing that?"

"Try."

"Hm... I remember heat and rocks and pain. And you. It's all a blur, honestly. Everything feels like a big fog that I can't seem to shake."

"I bet that will go away soon. You've been asleep."

"Not surprised. It's been an exhausting couple of hours."

"No, Vera. You've been asleep for two days."

"What?" I jerked my head around to look him straight in the eyes and make sure he was serious. "Two days? There's no way. How is that possible? Why didn't someone wake me up?"

"I tried."

Had it really been that long? It felt like only seconds ago that I'd been in the cave with Leo, but two full days had passed?

"I didn't know what was going on," Leo continued. "You touched that damn stone and then... Do you remember anything after that?"

"No. I don't even remember doing that much. I went to grab our clothes and then you were there and then these things were there. I pointed to my back. "And then I guess I slept for two days."

"You don't seem injured, so I assume that it was from using so much energy to create your wings. I was so... Vera, I... If we had just left, if we hadn't stayed down there..."

"You're not allowed to feel bad about this. I have wings now, Leo. You know how long I've waited for this. I don't care what happened or why, because now I have wings. I'll get to fly and use magic and... and..." I had another realization, perhaps another consequence of getting wings and sleeping for two days. "And I am *starving*."

Surveying my room, I saw plates and a pitcher of water on the table. A few hand towels and various silverware. Leo's phone.

"The food here is the worst," Leo said as he watched me look around. "It's all tiny portions and strange shit I can't identify. I wanted soup, and it came back with all these weird things on top, and then supposedly their precious chef was irritated that I was irritated. You would think the royal family would hire better help, but you would be wrong."

I grabbed the shirt from beside me and pulled it over my head again, rolling my eyes. "I've been asleep for two days, and you're complaining about the food."

"Yes, because it's awful. Can't even get a decent muffin."

"And you were just in here by yourself? Doing what? Eating and watching me?"

"What else is there to do in this place? They don't trust me, and I don't trust them either. I was a fugitive in their eyes until yesterday. I certainly wasn't going to let anyone get near you, especially not that damn—" Leo clamped his mouth shut, stopping himself from saying anything else.

"That what?"

"Nothing. None of that matters now."

"I can't believe it's been two days," I said, getting off the bed. "That's two whole days I could have been learning about these new wings. I've waited for this moment for years, and when it finally happens I decide to take a nap? I can't believe I wasted all this time."

Leo sighed and took my hand, locking his fingers with my own. "You have all the time in the world."

For the first time since I had woken up, I noticed the way his cheeks seemed slightly hollow, and the skin around his eyes was dark like when he'd stay up too late in his lab back home.

"You've been here this whole time," I said.

"I would have carried you out of here, but the situation has changed."

"Damn right it has. Have you seen these things?" I pointed to my back. "No need to carry me anywhere anymore. At least I don't think so. I guess haven't actually tried using them. The situation has changed for the better in my opinion."

"That's not what I mean. Everything here has changed, Vera."

"What do you mean? Changed how? What's going on?"

Leo's features were tight, his lips pursed together in the way he did when he was thinking. Then he exhaled.

"Do you remember a glowing stone?"

14

LEO

"*. . .* **B**ecause of me? The veil around Rowan is gone... because of me?"

"No, not because of you," I told Vera, holding her hand as I sat beside her on her bed. "Because of *her*. If the Keeper had never brought you down there, this wouldn't have happened."

"You say that, but it's not like she made me do something I didn't want to do. Leo, it's because of me." Vera's voice quavered as she stared up at me. "The veil is down because of me."

It felt so unfair for Vera to finally get what she wanted, only to be told it had come at such a heavy price. I first guessed what had happened when the stone stopped glowing, then confirmed it when my phone started working above ground as I carried Vera back to the palace. That blue-winged bastard himself went to the Gate to test my theory and came back with a face paler than his hair.

It was true. The veil that kept the city invisible, the Gate that only allowed fae into the city and kept everyone else out, was gone.

The city of Rowan was completely unprotected.

Everything had happened in a rush after that. I'd been allowed in with Vera on the condition that I stay there. The princess had given me basic information about what was happening outside the walls of

Vera's room, but I hardly listened. I only cared about Vera and when she would wake up.

She stood up and started pacing back and forth. "The Keeper said the stone would help me with my magic. That's why she flew me up to it. That's why I touched it in the first place. I never would have... Leo, if I had known..."

She stopped pacing and stared at me.

"Did you know?" she finally said. "Did you know that something like this could happen?"

"Vera, no. I had no idea she would use you like this. I would have protected you better if I had known."

She frowned, and for the first time I saw her wings droop behind her.

"Protected me. I thought... I felt... Leo, I really thought you could finally see me as an equal, as someone strong, not as someone you had to protect. But then I end up being used by that witch. I feel... sick."

"Me being here has nothing to do with that. I'm here because I love you. You had no way of knowing that it would turn out like this. It's not your fault."

"That's no excuse!" She slammed a fist down on her little table, and instantly it cracked down the middle. Her eyes flashed up to me, wide and scared.

I ran over and pulled her against me, holding her as tightly as I could.

"The table," she mumbled into my chest.

"Fuck the table."

"Maybe I am strong after all."

I had to chuckle as I hugged her against me. "Too strong, apparently."

We all had our regrets here. If I hadn't followed the Keeper to the cave, Vera never would have come to find me. If I had left days earlier, could we have avoided all this? Instead of the time Vera and I spent in the cave, what if we had left immediately?

"What are they going to do, Leo?" She twisted my shirt in her fingers. "If anyone can see their city, if anyone can get into their city…"

"For better or worse, this isn't your problem to fix."

"Maybe I could help!" She pulled away from me and ran over to her closet, rummaging through her clothes.

"I understand wanting to help them, but now that you're awake, our priority needs to be leaving this place."

"I can't sit here and do nothing, Leo. Not if they need me. She said to protect them," Vera murmured.

"What?"

"I remember now." Vera froze, staring at me. "When I touched the stone, I saw someone. A fae woman. Her wings, they were like mine."

That got my attention. "You had a vision? Tell me."

She shook her head as she finished getting dressed. "I don't know. Maybe I'm crazy. Visions? I sound crazy."

"No, it's not crazy at all. Vera, that stone—"

The door to her room flung open, and the princess flew in. "I heard voices!"

I didn't have time to speak before she flew to Vera and almost knocked her over in a hug.

"You're up! And you have wings! I'm so happy! I'm so happy, and you are… not." She stepped back, examining Vera's face, then the white-haired princess looked at me sharply. "You told her."

"Of course I told her."

"You couldn't have waited a couple of hours?"

"Mia," Vera said quietly. "I would have found out eventually. I'm so sorry. I didn't mean to—" Her voice broke, and hearing her sadness, I thought my heart might break along with it.

Mia hugged her again, gently patting her back and avoiding Vera's new wings. "I know, Vera. I know. That damn Keeper was always shady as hell, in my opinion. She used you to draw out the magic in the stone. It's not your fault. They've arrested her and there will be a trial."

"These wings…" Vera hung her head. "I thought they meant that I was finally normal, but they don't mean that at all, do they?"

Mia and I exchanged a look, both of us unsure what to say.

"We don't know," I told her. "Given the timing, it does seem fair to assume that the magic from the stone is what enabled your wings to grow, particularly since their colors are so unusual."

"He meant to say beautiful," Mia added. "I've never seen anything like them. Supposedly the ancient fae had multicolored wings like yours, but I've only heard about them in the stories Victor has told me of the ancient ways. Would you like to talk to him about it? He knows a lot about this kind of stuff, and he's..." Mia paused, looking nervous. "He's right outside."

"He is?" Vera raised an eyebrow. "I guess it wouldn't hurt anything. The more we know, the better."

As it turned out, Victor wasn't the only one waiting out in the hall. I'd managed to keep that blue-winged bastard away from Vera the past two days, but it looked like that had come to an end. Surprisingly, he stayed the farthest away from her, leaning against the wall while the girls sat on her bed and Victor stood beside Mia.

As I sat at Vera's broken table, I watched the four of them discuss everything that had happened. After the Keeper offered to bring her to me, Vera had told Mia to follow her, just in case. She was held up by several Black Guard fae who were watching the passageways, so they'd traveled above ground to remain unnoticed. It took longer, but they were finally able to find the cave.

I couldn't tear my eyes away from Vera. The serious expression on her face as she nodded along to the conversation, the rush of pride I felt when they looked to her when she spoke.

Vera was captivating on a normal day, but now... Now with her bright wings fluttering behind her, her long, brown hair draping down her back, she was something else entirely. Vera was an angel, a goddess, a woman ethereal and perfect and somehow, I hoped, still *mine.*

My fingernails dug into my palms as I watched her smile at something the fae bastard said to her. I knew that logically I shouldn't storm over to her right that instant and make sure that smile was directed at me and me only, but damn, it was hard to resist the temptation.

I'd never been very good at resisting Vera anyway.

When I stood directly behind Vera, the eyes of the other three fae flicked up to me. Noticing that their attention had shifted, Vera spun around and smiled at me. I was relieved to see her happy again, but I couldn't deny the pang of jealousy that they'd been the ones able to bring out that side of her.

"Laurie says his father is going to hold a strategy meeting tomorrow," Vera said. "We're both invited."

"And an official state dinner to welcome you, Leo."

"I don't need a fancy dinner," I told him.

"And since I knew you would say that"—Laurie nodded—"I told my father that too. He insisted, however, so that's what we're doing."

"It is kind of weird," Mia said. "Don't you think? He's throwing a state dinner even though everyone hates demons. Sorry, no offense."

"None taken," I said.

"I agree," her brother said. "I'm assuming this is to apologize for his earlier behavior. Given what's happened, if Leo can be an ally of Rowan, our father is going to have to put aside his own prejudices."

When I looked to Vera, she didn't seem bothered by any of this. Was she used to Rowan's customs now? Standing there talking with the other three fae, she certainly looked like she fit in with them.

Maybe that was why it was bothering me.

I would have been happy leaving Rowan forever and letting them figure it out for themselves. As much as I wanted to bring Vera back to my home where it could be just the two of us and pretend like the outside world didn't exist, I couldn't deny that this was the fae city and the home of her ancestors.

"Leo, were you listening?" Vera asked.

I wasn't.

"According to Victor, the legend is that the veil was created with the original fae queen's magic."

"We can discuss this with my father's advisors tomorrow at the meeting," Mia said.

"She won't be there, right?" Vera asked. "The Keeper."

"The Keeper is in jail and heavily guarded," Laurie said. "We've tried tracking down most of her followers, but they either left as soon as the veil dropped, or they're very good at hiding. The whole cave is being investigated."

"That is a sacred place," Victor told them. "It should be left alone. Let me tell you about its construction. The roots of the Great Tree once..."

The girls kept listening to Victor recount more legends when Laurie came over to me, nudging me in the side. "Leo, can I speak with you for a moment? In the hall?"

I followed him out there, wondering what the hell he couldn't say in front of the rest.

"At this meeting tomorrow, there are going to be questions about you," he said. "I've done my best to explain about Syn and what you've done in the demon kingdom, but that won't be enough—for the older fae especially. They hate demons, and they're already suspicious about the veil failing to prevent you coming through."

"What are you saying?" I asked him.

"I'm saying that unless you want to answer some probing questions about your genetics, it might not be a bad idea for you leave town."

"What? No. I'm not leaving without Vera, and I can already tell from her reaction earlier that she's not leaving here either."

"I can help you get out of the palace without being seen."

"If I go, she's coming with me."

"That's not all I'm worried about," he continued. "My father wants to protect this city no matter the cost. Now that he knows who you are and what you've done for fae, an official alliance with Vestia will be a big deal, and there are a lot of fae who will be against it. I don't know what his terms will be, but—"

"He can do what he wants. Alliance or no alliance. It won't change the fact that I'm not leaving without Vera."

"You don't owe us anything, Leo. We're not helpless without you,

you know. If you come to this meeting tomorrow, there could be consequences—not just for you, but for others as well."

"Cut the act. You want me to leave so that you can have Vera to yourself."

Laurie sighed. "Leo. No. That's not it."

"Let me say this one last time. Leaving is—"

Vera poked her head out the door before I had a chance to say more. "What was that about leaving?"

Her big brown eyes met mine, and something inside me clenched at how suspicious they looked.

"No one is leaving." I couldn't tell if she believed me or not.

"Come back in here," she said. "Victor is telling us about the first fae queen."

Throwing a sideways glance at Laurie, I followed her back in. The fae prince's warning running through my head, I couldn't get the three of them out of her room fast enough. With agreements to talk more later, I did my best to shuffle them out, and I was almost successful when that blue-winged bastard stopped by the door on his way out.

"Oh, and Leo?"

"Yeah?"

"Since you are being officially welcomed at tomorrow's meeting, there's one thing I need from you."

"What's that?"

With that annoying smile of his back, I didn't like at all the way he narrowed his eyes, as if he was examining me. "You'll see."

15

VERA

"Is this truly necessary?"

Leo stood in the middle of Laurie's studio, his arms out while a tailor held a tape measure against one and then the other. Since we'd already found a shirt that would fit him, Leo's chest was bare, and he wore black pants that matched the jacket.

I had to stifle a laugh as I watched Leo glare at the poor fae who was just doing his best to avoid stepping on Leo's tail. The tailor tried to avoid Leo's gaze as well as he fussed with the jacket, taking notes on the black fabric where it needed to be altered for Leo's wings.

Whatever the royal family was paying this tailor, he needed a raise.

I wasn't the only one holding back a laugh. Beside where I sat on the little couch in his studio, Laurie grinned and stretched his arms out along the back. A steady glare from Leo had him removing his arm from the couch behind me.

"It's a good thing we had something that could fit you," Laurie said.

"This doesn't fit me," Leo grumbled.

"It will. Gerald here learned everything he knows from me,

personally, and I am confident that he'll have your suit ready before this afternoon's meeting."

"The problem isn't *Gerald*." Leo's silver eyes shot daggers at Laurie. "Or the suit. The problem is that we're worried about stupid shit like what I'm wearing when we should be spending this time worrying about your city."

"I could take your measurements myself, if you would prefer," Laurie told him.

"I would not."

"As you wish. I took Vera's."

With a loud thwack, Leo's black wings extended, knocking the poor tailor back a step and I'm fairly certain ripping the fabric of the jacket as well. "You did what?"

I sprang up from the couch and moved to stand between the two. "My measurements. He had to take my measurements, Leo. Back when I was working at Elise's club. For my uniform."

Leo's wings relaxed. Slightly. "Oh. Is that what you meant?"

Laurie smirked at Leo. "Sure."

"Those dresses were too short," Leo muttered. "But she did look hot in them."

"Is that your way of saying thank you?"

"They fit well." I poked Leo in the chest. "And now it's your turn."

I ran my hands down the sleeves of the jacket, feeling his muscles underneath the fabric. When I reached his bare chest, I let my fingertips graze his skin and felt those familiar little shocks, little bolts of lightning that sparked where we touched.

"This suit looks good on you," I told him.

Leo tilted his head down to me. "You think so?" he asked in that husky voice that made my insides melt.

"Vera's right," Laurie chirped, bringing us back to reality. "You have to think of the optics here. We have the strategy meeting this afternoon and then the dinner. I've done my best to explain the situation, but most of the fae at court still see you as a trespasser at best, a slaver at worst."

The general fae population might not understand Leo's role in helping fae everywhere, but Leo's father seemed to once they'd had a chance to speak face-to-face. The dinner was to celebrate the alliance of Vestia, through Leo's proxy, and Rowan.

"You can't show up at court wearing"—Laurie gestured at Leo—"whatever you normally wear and expect fae to listen to you."

Leo scowled. "They should listen to me because their lives depend on it. A fancy suit isn't going to change that."

"And you think the tattered clothes you wore here will?"

"They wouldn't have been tattered if I hadn't been thrown in your jail."

"Enough," I said.

"Fine," Leo huffed. "Whatever. Just make it fast and remind me why the prince of Rowan has time to sit here watching me. I don't need an audience."

"Great point. In that case, come on, Vera. I can get your fitting for the dinner started in the dressing room next door. I think I have your sizing down, so it's really about which dress you like best. I have things I want you to try on so we can see how they go with those pretty new wings."

Leo was already walking with us, the poor tailor long forgotten. Leo shrugged off the jacket, leaving it behind on the floor. "Not without me, you aren't."

Laurie rolled his eyes as he led the way. "The more the merrier."

Leaving me alone in the dressing room with Leo and a handful of dresses, Laurie muttered several excuses for where else he needed to be and told me to pick whichever I liked best.

I was grateful for Leo's assistance because, as expected of Laurie's creations, each dress was beautiful, so it was going to be hard to choose. It was an immediate no on the blue dresses though as well as the black ones. Even though Leo was wearing black, that was too plain for me tonight. Everyone was going to be looking at my wings no matter what, so despite how I got them, I knew I had to embrace it and do my best.

There weren't any silver dresses, but there was a white floor-length gown whose lack of color would allow the vibrant hues of my wings to be the focus. There was also a very fitted short red dress that could bring out the red tones in my wings.

"We're finally alone," Leo murmured, close behind me as I shuffled through the gowns on the rack.

I spun around and ran my fingers down his chest. "That we are."

"Gods, I'm so tired of seeing how that fae bastard looks at you." Leo's hand was on my back, pressing me against him.

"Now it's your turn to look. You. Over there." I pointed to the chair in the corner of the dressing room. Other than the rack where the dresses were hanging, the chair and a tall mirror that rested against one of the walls were the only furniture in the room.

Leo grunted but obeyed, flopping down in the chair with a huff. He leaned back, watching my every move. "Feeling bossy today?"

"A little." I thumbed through the rack of clothes, finding the red dress. "Someone has to take charge, especially since you were the one acting bratty earlier, not me."

Leo scoffed, but the corner of his mouth quirked up in a devious smile. "Are you going to put me in my place?"

"Maybe," I purred, turning away. I glanced over my shoulder at him. Leo had leaned forward, elbows on his knees, waiting with anticipation to see what I was going to do. "If I'm going to try on these dresses, I guess I have to take off these pesky clothes."

Leo hummed in agreement as I pulled my shirt over my head and tossed it behind me.

Still not turning around, I bent over at the waist and slowly rolled my pants down to my ankles before taking them completely off. Out the corner of my eye, I glimpsed Leo standing up to come toward me with a wolfish grin. I held up my hand to signal him to stop, and without realizing what I was doing, my magic shoved him back into the chair forcefully.

"Whoa," I said.

Leo plopped back down in the chair, silver eyes wide. I thought that forcing him away would make him back off a little, but it seemed like my magic had other ideas. I dropped my arm and was about to apologize, but then something caught my eye. Judging by the bulge I saw growing in Leo's pants, that little display only made him more aroused.

"Using your magic on me now?" he asked, raising an eyebrow.

"Apparently."

I let him sit there as I stepped into the red dress, pulling the thin straps over my shoulders. It was tight, but it fit remarkably well, hugging my body in all the right places and barely covering my thighs. I looked good, and as I twirled in the mirror, I was pleased with the way the red of the dress highlighted the red of my wings.

Leo cleared his throat to bring my attention back to him. He had already taken his cock out of his pants, his hand lazily stroking it as he watched me.

"What?" he asked. "You won't let me get near you, so I had to take matters into my own hands."

"Literally, I see. Were you feeling neglected?" I stalked over to him to stand in front of his chair.

"Not really. I'm just enjoying the show right now."

"Oh yeah? You want a closer look?"

"Always."

Wrapping my arms around his neck, I climbed onto the chair on top of him, the short dress riding up my thighs as I straddled him. I could feel how hard he was below me, and I let myself grind down against him, rubbing my clothed pussy over his hard dick.

With one firm yank, Leo pulled the top of my dress down, and I heard it rip, but at that moment, I didn't care. All I could think about was Leo's hot mouth on one breast, his hand groping at the other.

"Fuck," I moaned as his tongue swirled around my nipple.

"That's what we're going to do, baby."

"Now who's bossy?"

"I'm always the boss."

"Not right now you're not," I said, rocking my hips over his dick. Due to how tight this dress was around my thighs, I couldn't sit all the way down on him, but that was okay. I was fine teasing both of us with only the hint of friction.

"That's where you're wrong," Leo said.

I felt something against my leg, and when I looked down between us, Leo's tail was sneaking up, writhing between our bodies. I gasped as the tip of his tail wiggled against my underwear, pushing up into me through the fabric.

"Now you're playing dirty," I breathed as it jutted up, pressing against me.

"Tell me you don't like it."

I couldn't say anything as his tail squirmed over slightly, and then the hard tip pushed my panties to the side.

"*Fuck*," I moaned, feeling the tip prod at my entrance.

"You're fucking dripping, little one. I need you closer."

His tail wiggled away, and Leo's hands grabbed the hem of my dress on one side of me, ripping the fabric in two so that I could rest on top of him.

If this continued, the little self-control I had would be gone. I wasn't ready to give in to him completely though. Regaining enough control to slide off his lap, I stepped back and out of the now-torn dress before dropping to my knees at his feet. I ran my hands up his legs and onto his thighs, feeling the way his muscles tensed under my touch. My fingers had only just barely grazed his twitching cock when I sat back on my heels, taking my hands off him completely.

Leo threw his head back and groaned in frustration. "Now who is playing dirty?"

"I was just thinking." I looked up at him with the most innocent expression I could come up with. Eyelashes batting, lips pouting, the whole thing. "Maybe you were right. Maybe we don't have time for— What did you call it earlier? Stupid shit? When the safety of the city is at risk."

"Play games with me right now, and you'll see how that works out for you."

"Is that a threat or a promise?"

"Whichever one you want it to be. Now get back over here. I want your lips around my cock."

My fingers danced on his legs, his thighs twitching under his pants. "So mean. Is that how you ask for what you want?"

"Vera."

I slid my hands up, spreading my fingers wide. "Hm?"

"Suck on my dick. Now."

"That sounded a lot like a command."

"Then you should obey it," he ordered.

I scooted forward and wrapped a hand around his cock. I was going to do what he said, but that didn't mean I had to do it quickly. Besides, I wasn't done teasing him yet.

"Like this?" I asked demurely, sticking out my tongue and giving the tip of his cock the tiniest of kitten licks as I continued to stroke him.

"Vera," he said between clenched teeth, and I could hear that deep rumble in his chest.

"Or like this?" I hovered my open mouth over the tip, barely letting my lips brush against him. My eyes flicked up to meet his, and the feral look in his silver eyes made me think that maybe I'd taken this too far.

I was right.

"No more teasing," he growled.

"Then say please."

Instead of speaking, with a loud snap, he wrapped his tail around my neck and yanked me forward, his cock going farther down my throat until my mouth pushed up against his body. I had to force myself not to gag at the sudden intrusion, but his tail kept me there, forcing me to breathe through my nose as his thick tail tightened around my throat. My instinct was to push back or grab his tail and pull the damn thing off to relieve some of the pressure, but I couldn't, not when I had to grab on to Leo's thighs just to stay upright.

He relaxed his tail so I could take a breath.

"Fuck. That's a good girl," he said, both of us panting to catch our breaths. I had barely a second to breathe though before his hand was tangled in my hair, pushing my head down his cock again. "Such a good fucking girl, taking it all the way down her throat."

As if I had much choice. His tail was still wrapped around my neck, but it didn't have that same vise grip any longer, so now that I could get air again, I focused on hollowing out my cheeks and forcing him to make more of those delicious moans that I knew were only for me.

Relaxing my jaw, I went down as far as I could, and Leo held my head there before he suddenly pushed me back, releasing his tail from around my neck.

"Damn it," he groaned, "if you keep this up, I'm going to come in your mouth."

We couldn't have that happening. Nope, not at all.

I needed him inside me. Then. Now. Immediately if not sooner.

He must have felt the same way, because Leo wasted no time standing up, grabbing the chair he'd been sitting in, and tossing it in front of the mirror.

"Bend over. There," he growled and pointed to the chair, hands on my hips, already moving my body before I had a chance to do it myself. "You're going to watch me fuck you."

Obeying in an instant, I leaned over the back of the chair, bending at the waist, and wrapped my fingers around the chair back. My eyes flicked up to meet his in the mirror, and all I saw was hunger. White-hot hunger burning in his silver eyes.

I gasped when his tail hooked around one of my ankles; it pulled my leg out to the side, spreading me for him even more. In the mirror I could see Leo looking at me, no doubt seeing how wet and open I was for him.

"What are you waiting for?" I asked, teasing him with a little wiggle. He responded with a sharp slap against my ass.

"Absolutely nothing."

"Good— *Fuck*." I was cut off by the feeling of the tip of his cock pressing against my entrance and then sliding forward, slowly, one inch at a time.

At first his thrusts were slow and deep, but that wasn't enough for either of us. Leo answered my pleas for more by fucking me harder, with rough, staccato thrusts, each one making me clench my hands on the back of the chair to brace myself against him.

"There," I murmured when he managed to hit that one spot that had me seeing stars. "Right there."

"You think I can't tell?" he snarled, giving me a particularly brutal thrust. "You think I can't feel you clenching around me?"

"I don't know what you're feeling," I managed to breathe out, my brain turning to mush the longer he kept it up.

"Then I'll tell you," he said, punctuating his words with quick snaps of his hips, each one jolting my body forward. "I feel your wet cunt sucking me in." Another thrust. "And it feels fucking awesome."

Twisting my hair in his grasp, Leo used that hold to yank my body up from the chair, my back arching hard, my new wings brushing against his bare chest. In this position, his mouth was closer to my ear, and he took full advantage, whispering a string of absolute filth as he continued to pound into me.

With a grunt, he let go of my hair. I thought I was going to fall forward, but he caught me, one hand around my waist, the other on my face.

"You gonna come for me?" he murmured into my open mouth. His hand snaked down my belly until his fingers found my clit, rubbing in furious circles that only made me arch my back more. I was his instrument, and he knew exactly how to play me. Everything he was doing, every touch from him, made my body tighten and writhe in his arms, all of it building and leaving me begging for release.

"Yes— *Fuck*." I gasped when it felt like his cock banged against my cervix and his thumb pressed down harder on my clit. "Yes, Leo. *Yes*. I want to come. Please."

"Then fucking do it."

As if on command, my entire body quivered, shaking in his hold while my heart thumped loudly in my ear. There were no other sensations other than him and the stretch of his cock inside me and the way he rolled my clit between his fingers.

"Fuck!" I squeezed my eyes shut as my body stiffened with anticipation of what was about to happen, fully aware of how close I was and how little control I had over how good he was making me feel.

Finally something snapped inside me, and I could feel myself clamping down on him, arching and howling and thrashing in his hold.

"That's it," he purred, continuing to fuck me as my orgasm washed over me. "There you go," he said, his thrusts slowing slightly as I gasped for air.

His cock still deep inside, I slumped forward, grabbing the back of the chair with both hands. I sucked in deep breaths to try to slow my heart as Leo leaned over to plant sweaty kisses down my back between my wings.

"You're so beautiful, Vera."

Even a smile for Leo felt like a lot of work, but damn, he deserved it after all that. Still struggling to breathe, I picked my head up to meet his eyes in the mirror.

"You did so good," Leo cooed, his hands rubbing soothing circles on my hips as he slowly fucked me. Still holding his stare, I watched as his eyes seemed to darken, and those circles became a fierce grip. "But now it's my turn."

All I could do was hold on. There was something selfish and mean but so fucking hot in the way he used my body to chase his own end. With the mirror in front of me, I could see it all. I couldn't have taken my eyes off him even if I had wanted to. It was all too beautiful, too mesmerizing, to not watch as this powerful demon came undone. The way he panted and moaned, the way his muscles flexed as he fucked me, the way his wings quivered when I knew he was close.

Fingers digging in deep into my flesh, Leo kept increasing his pace until with a final groan he buried himself deep inside me. I stayed still as he twitched inside me, and when our eyes met in the mirror, Leo surprised me with a big, dopey smile. My heart fluttered because I knew that this was the smile that only I saw, one of those rare moments where Leo allowed himself the tiniest amount of joy. I wanted to lock this image of him smiling forever in my heart because I knew how rare it was.

Once we had our clothes back on, Leo and I stared down at the ripped pieces of what used to be the red dress that now littered the floor. I quickly realized that both of us were thinking the same thing, even though he was the one to say it.

"Looks like the white dress it is."

16

VERA

Fae were arriving for the meeting, and now that I wasn't staying in my room any longer, I decided to get some fresh air and practice with my wings.

I pushed open the big wooden doors that led to the palace's front yard, and a group of women flew past me on their way inside, their arms filled with bouquets of flowers, their voices hushed as they went by. They seemed to float effortlessly, their dresses ruffling elegantly as their pretty wings fluttered behind him.

Leo must have had the same idea, because I saw him up ahead, not far from me. He'd already gone down the stone staircase that led to the front path and was stomping toward the palace gates.

"Hey, wait up!" I shouted as I jogged toward the stairs. Then I remembered that I didn't need to run after him at all. Picturing the pretty girls flying elegantly, I leaped into the air. I could be elegant. I could be graceful. I could be—

I crashed onto the last stone step with a thud.

Shit. Maybe I should have just jogged.

When I looked up, Leo looming over me. "Are you hurt?"

Part of me wished I had been knocked unconscious to spare

myself the embarrassment. "Just my pride. Seems like I need to practice using these things more."

"You'll get used to them."

Leo reached out his hand, and I went to grab it to get up, but
instead he was holding a single red rose.

I sat back down and eyed the flower suspiciously. "Did one of
those women give you that? They're getting bold, aren't they?"

"Vera." The corner of his mouth quirked up in a small smile.
"This is for you. I asked them for one."

I closed my eyes. Yep, dying of embarrassment would have been
great right about then.

"If you don't want it, I'm sure one of those girls—"

I snatched it from his hand and stood up. "Don't you dare."
Staring down at my hands, I fiddled with the leaves on the stem,
unsure how to ask what I wanted to know, unsure if I really wanted
the answer. I had to ask though.

"Were you going somewhere?"

Before I could blink, Leo was right in front of me, his big hands
on my shoulders. Startled by the sensation of his touch, I looked up
at him, and I fully expected to see anger in his eyes, but instead his
eyebrows were drawn together in concern. "I'm not leaving."

"Okay," I said quietly, suddenly feeling embarrassed for asking. "I
was just curious in case... I don't know. I heard you and Laurie talking
about leaving, and then I saw you walking toward the Gate."

"I'm not going anywhere unless it's with you."

"But then why were you walking toward the Gate?"

Leo sighed and dropped his hands from my shoulders. "I'll show
you."

He took a step back and took the rose from me. He broke off the
thorns and slid it into my hair, tucking the stem behind my ear. Then
he held out his hand, this time for me to take.

"Focus on me," he said. "Okay?"

After his fingers locked with mine, holding tight, we were in
the air. Leo allowed just enough space between us so that our
wings wouldn't hit each other, but I kept my eyes on him. Black

wings beating slowly behind him, Leo hovered in the air in front of me, flying backward slowly as he coaxed me toward him.

At first it felt silly, like he was treating me like a child, but then again, when it came to flying, I was like a child. I had to admit that focusing on him, on this handsome demon whose dark hair moved in the breeze created by his wings, really did help take my mind off over-analyzing what I was doing.

As we flew toward the palace gates, I heard a voice. A voice I hadn't heard in weeks. A voice I had sincerely missed.

I didn't need to follow Leo's lead any longer. I let go of his hands and flew up and over him, darting straight toward the Gate where a demon was talking to a guard.

"...I know. I just called him, and he didn't answer. We were told that the appropriate officials would be notified, so we sincerely apologize for arriving without an official royal invitation, but I believe there is someone here we need to speak with—"

"Rand!" I shouted before crashing into him.

Rand grunted as the force of my hug knocked him back a step, but he hugged me back all the same. Then he let go, setting me down in front of him. He looked the same as ever, brown hair perfectly messy, fitted black shirt unbuttoned at the top and tucked into slim black pants, a leather bag slung over his shoulder. He looked over my shoulder at my wings and then gave me a pointed look. "You look a little different, friend."

"Surprised?"

"Nah, I knew it was only a matter of time." He swirled a finger in the air, indicating for me to spin. I dutifully turned around, and he laughed. "A little wild, a little bright. Pretty. They suit you. It's good to see you too, Leo."

"Rand."

"How's life in the homeland?"

"Fucking awful."

"I thought for sure that when I saw you again, you'd be different. The fae are all so colorful, especially this one now," Rand said, nodding to me, "but you're still just as gloomy as ever. It's sort of comforting to know some things never change."

"Thanks?"

Both of us turned our heads at the sound of a dog barking. There in the grass a tiny white dog bounded over. I knew that dog, but I didn't understand why Elise's pet was here in Rowan. I reached down to pet him, but the little jerk leaped forward, teeth bared.

"What the hell?" I yelped and jumped away.

"Did he bite you?" Leo asked.

"No, but he almost did."

Rand sighed. "Apologies, but she made him take Zeus."

"Him?"

Rand crooked a thumb behind him. I had been so happy to see Rand that I hadn't even noticed the tall redheaded demon behind him. How could I have missed Zell?

With a big backpack over his shoulder, Zell had on dark ripped jeans and a loose white T-shirt, the short sleeves showing off all his tattoos. In one rough movement, Zell's tattooed arm yanked the still-barking dog off the ground and up into his arms. Then Zell smiled at me, his stupid tongue piercing rolling across his lips.

"Hey, princess. Long time no see."

"Could have been longer," I said back. "Get control of your pet."

"Aw, is the princess mad that the little dog likes her?"

"He tried to bite me."

Zell shrugged. "Like I said, he likes you."

"We don't have time for pets right now. Zell, I need you and Marcus on a project immediately. Rand," Leo said, "you weren't supposed to come here."

"Someone had to bring Marcus." Rand looked around. "Speaking of, where did that nerd run off to? He was too caught up taking pictures and scribbling in that damn notebook of his. I told him if he tried to explain one more thing to me on the way here that I was going to drop him off my back and he was going to have to walk the rest of the way."

"You flew Marcus here on your back?" I asked.

"Didn't you wonder why my clothes are all wrinkled and my hair looks like this?" Rand pointed to his shaggy brown hair, perfectly unkempt as always. "This idiot over here was too busy dog sitting, so I let Marcus hitch a ride with me."

Zell scoffed as he tried to wrestle the snarling little ball of fur into the bag he'd brought. Eventually he settled on just holding him under his arm. "I'll take Zeus over a human any day. Unlike you, I'm not used to letting dudes ride me."

Rand smirked. "Don't knock it until you try it."

I had to hold back a laugh as the little dog continued to thrash and bark under Zell's arm. Even though Leo had said Rand wasn't supposed to come, I was just so, so happy to see him again. I could go my whole life without seeing Zell again, but I'd missed Rand more than I'd realized. Just seeing his playful smirk again made me feel like I was back home.

Home.

What did I even mean by that anymore?

"How about you, princess?" Zell nodded to my wings. "I see you finally grew up. Nice pair you got there."

"Stay with your dog and away from me and we're fine."

"Oh, he's not letting that dog go anywhere." Rand laughed and clapped Zell on the back. "He would never let anything happen to Elise's favorite little treasure. She figured he couldn't get into too much trouble if he had Zeus tagging along."

Zell chuckled. "That was her mistake because girls love dogs."

The words had hardly left his mouth when Zeus growled and bit down on his arm. Hard.

"In other words, the dog is actually babysitting you and not the other way around," Leo said.

"I could fly home, you know," said Zell. "I'm only here because you all would be hopeless without my knowledge and expertise."

"To some extent, you're right," Leo admitted, although I could tell by his expression that was the last thing he wanted to say.

Those seemed to be the magic words for the redheaded demon, a crooked smile breaking out across his face. "Then can I hear you ask for my help one more time? Maybe I could even record it now that these fae finally have moved out of the stone age."

"Barely," Leo added. He looked around and no doubt noticed the fae guards watching the trio of demons. "Let's go somewhere more private where we can talk. I asked to have rooms prepared for each of you. Where's Marcus?"

Zeus started barking again, and all of us looked in the direction the dog was facing. As if on cue, a fae guard was coming closer, a firm grip on Marcus's shoulder as he walked him toward us. With a shove, the guard threw Marcus on the ground at our feet.

"That was not necessary," I said to the guard, rushing over to Marcus's side.

"Is this human yours?" the guard asked me.

"I will vouch for him," Leo said, standing close to the guard and looming over him.

"Fine. Whatever. Just know that we don't need humans, or demons, wandering around this city."

"So much for the warm welcome," Rand muttered as the guard walked away.

"Should I send Zeus after him?" Zell asked.

When I looked back to Marcus, his eyes were wide and his mouth open in surprise. He didn't say a word from where he sat on the ground and just continued staring at me. At my wings.

"I might have wings now, but I'm still the same Vera. Let me help." Reaching a hand down, I took his and pulled him to his feet. I wrapped my arms around to hug him and that's when I realized something.

"Whoa," I said when I pulled back, noticing the size of his arms. "You've been working out."

Marcus's cheeks turned as bright red as his mop of hair. "Um... Yes? I guess you could say that?" He pushed up his glasses and stood a little straighter. "No, yes. I mean, yes, yes I have." He smiled sheepishly. "With all of you gone, I've had a lot of free time."

"And Lydia is doing well?"

"Um, she's... Well, you see..." He seemed to struggle to find the right words. This was the Marcus I knew. "She's good," he finally said. "She's great."

It was bittersweet to think of those days when we all lived together, before Vestia, before the demon king, before everything that had happened here. Training with Rob and Lydia in our spare time, hanging out in our rooms doing whatever we wanted. Would we ever be able to go back to those days?

Now that everyone was accounted for, Marcus, Zell, and Leo walked ahead of us toward the palace, the little white dog running through the grass at their side. Rand linked arms with me as we followed behind them. He whistled as he looked around the palace grounds.

"I've been a lot of places," he said, "but obviously never here. Everything about this city is so... quaint."

"You hate it."

"I didn't say that. It's very pretty, I have to admit. The little cottages and gardens and cobblestone paths are all very... cute. Very retro. Very farmer-chic."

"You can actually breathe the air here without inhaling car exhaust."

"No cars here?"

"None."

"You're right, I hate it."

"It grows on you. Kind of. It's peaceful. Maybe too peaceful sometimes."

"I see. Leo filled me in on what you've been trying to do here. I wasn't surprised by anything he said though. Why would anyone want to leave this adorable utopia to go help strangers?"

"It's much easier to ignore what's happening to fae everywhere else. Laurie has been trying to get them to understand, but it hasn't been going well."

"Laurie, huh?" Rand shot me a sideways glance.

"What? Don't look at me like that."

"I wasn't looking at you in any kind of way," Rand insisted. "If you think I was, then maybe it speaks to your own guilty conscience?"

Was I feeling guilty? I thought of the other night after the bar. The kiss. Laurie. Mercifully Rand kept talking without waiting for me to explain my silence.

"Leo also filled me in on the prince and princess and their little deception. Posing as slaves, the sneaky little fae. I was glad to hear that my instincts were right. I knew something was shady about that guy."

"He's not shady."

Rand raised an eyebrow again. "Is that so?"

"Yes. Laurie hid his identity, but he's on our side. Please play nice when you see him."

"I always play nice." Rand pretended to be offended. "But your request makes me think that Leo hasn't been doing the same. I'm not surprised there. Don't worry. We'll get along fine. Fae like me."

I gave Rand a good-natured nudge as we walked. "And you like one fae in particular. A tall, green-winged guy with big muscles and adorable in that fae-next-door kind of way. Am I right?"

"We're talking about you, not me," Rand grumbled.

"Oh? Does this reaction speak to a guilty conscience, perhaps?"

Rand grunted at the use of his own words against him. "Absolutely not."

"Did something happen with Jasmine instead?" I smiled as I thought of the bubbly pink-haired demon who took care of Rand's apartment. Rand wasn't smiling though.

"That is a ship that is not going to be sailing, my dear," he said.

"Really? How come?"

"Look, I'd rather get hit with a sharp tail across the eyes than continue this conversation. Let's gossip about something else. Speaking of, did you really slap Leo?"

"Yeah."

"Damn, girl. Good for you. Did you guys have some hot make-up sex and get over it after that?"

"The first part yes, the second part sort of. There's been a lot going on," I said, gesturing to my wings. "I want to move forward, but..."

Rand stopped and turned me toward him, his hands on my arms. "Vera. Leo is an idiot, but he's an idiot who is in love with you. I'm not saying what he did was right, but I saw how sending you away tore him up. He was devastated. I've known him a long time, and I've never seen Leo like that. He stopped eating—"

"Really? Even breakfast?"

"Yes! Even breakfast. With the Ignitors dead and his father who knows where, Leo spent almost every day holed up in the royal office poring over legal nonsense to figure out the logistics of abolishing slavery. Sales of Syn were taking off, the nobles were mad at losing their slaves, the freed fae were in complete chaos, Vestia's economy was in shambles—it was a mess. He's the one who set the plan in motion to get everything back on track."

"So he really did do all that."

"Yep. With that same stubborn determination that he brings to everything in life. Leo was like a machine, grinding until the early hours of the morning. Grinding us down too. I'm not going to lie. When he left us to come here, I was excited to actually get some sleep for once, knowing he'd be gone. Of course then he ends up calling us anyway."

"You knew he was coming here? To get me?"

"Do you even have to ask? There was no other explanation, sweet girl." Rand spun me around so that I could see the three up ahead, each of them gesturing wildly as they talked. He leaned over my shoulder, pointing at the trio. "Look at those happy nerds. I know for a fact that the tall brooding one is hopelessly in love with you. If you can truly forgive him, you two are going to be just fine."

"He's miserable here. He's only staying because I'm here."

"Leo is miserable everywhere except wherever you are. Do you really think Leo would have summoned us here if he was truly unhappy? If he really wanted to leave, he would have left. Instead, he's working as hard as ever for these fools, even when it doesn't benefit him in the slightest."

Not sure what to say to that, I grabbed Rand and pulled him along to catch up to the other guys.

"Rand, why didn't Leo want you to come here?" I needed to know before we got too close to them. "Marcus isn't the best at speaking in large groups, Zell needs to stay in a lab and far away from people, and Leo is... Well, you know how he is."

"Yeah, trust me, I know."

"So why? It makes sense for you to be here. Why wouldn't he want you to come with them?"

It was Rand's turn to be silent for a change. Judging by the worried look on his face, I could tell something was bothering him. What was he trying to hide?

"I'm here now," he finally said. "I'm not sure how long I'll be able to stay, but I want to give some input on this plan. Plus I need a tour of this new home of yours."

"Sure. But first, do you have any new competitors for Syn?" I was thinking of the Dust Mia and I had found. "Or have you heard of any coming out soon?"

"Why do you ask? Fuck!" Rand suddenly yelled. He let go of my arm. "What the hell?"

That was when I saw that Zell's little dog had sunk his teeth onto the end of Rand's tail. The ball of white fluff was growling and hanging on as Rand whipped his tail back and forth to try to get him to let go.

"Get control of your animal, Zell!" Rand shouted. Leo, Zell, and Marcus turned around to see us. Instead of coming to help, Zell threw his head back and cackled, making no attempt to come get the little terror.

Leo whistled, and the dog instantly let go of Rand's tail, his head perking up to see the source of the sound. Leo snapped his fingers, and Zeus happily plodded over, ears flopping, tail wagging, to where Leo stood.

"Sit." Leo's deep voice left no room for argument.

Fuck. After the way he said that command, I almost sat down myself.

Leo ignored the dog sitting still at his feet and instead turned to our friends. "Take a few minutes to settle in to your new rooms and then wait for a message from me. We'll meet up and talk then."

"What?" Zell made a sour face. "No tour of the palace by some cute fae maid or something?" He came over to pick up Zeus, who only snarled at him.

"Good dog," I said, and Zell rolled his eyes.

"Will we meet with the royal family soon?" Rand asked. "What's the plan, Leo?"

"The plan? The plan is to figure out how to save these idiots whether they want it or not."

"Sure, sure. In coordination with the fae, I'm assuming?"

"I guess. There's an official dinner coming up, and you'll all be attending."

"Hell yeah. That's what I'm talking about." Zell grinned.

"We need to coordinate with the king and queen in private, not at a big event, Leo. It might be advantageous to schedule a meeting with their prince first. Maybe Vera could set that up for us…" A sharp look from Leo ended that train of thought. "…or not."

After plans were made, dogs were corralled, goodbyes were said, the guys left for their rooms, and it was just Leo and I again.

"Are you headed your room too?" he asked.

"I hadn't planned on it," I admitted. "You're going to be meeting with the guys, so I should probably practice with my wings a little."

"Yes, you should."

"Seriously? That's where you are supposed to say 'no, Vera, you're perfect, you don't need to practice' or something like that."

"After what I saw on the steps?"

He had to bring that up, didn't he?

"You know, when you fell."

I grimaced at the reminder. "I knew what you were talking about. Can we forget that ever happened?"

"If we forget our failures, we'll never move forward."

"Okay, okay, I get it. Fine. I'll practice." I looked around the palace yard, noticing that it was mostly empty except for a few guards walking up and down the outer fence. It might be better to go somewhere in the back gardens though, where I knew I'd be alone. Mia often trained her guards in a large open space in the eastern yard, so that was also an option.

"You don't have to come with me. It's probably better if I embarrass myself in private."

Leo took a step toward me and held out his hand. "You could hold my hands again."

"Thanks, but I can do this. Like you said, I have to acknowledge my failures and then figure it out for myself."

"That's not exactly what I said. Take my hand."

I waved him away. The last thing I needed was for him to think I was so pitiful that I needed hand-holding. "It was something like that then. Really, Leo. Go get some rest before this afternoon. I can do this."

"If you would just take my hand—"

"I can do this, Leo."

"Vera. Stop being stubborn for five seconds. I'm telling you that I would like to hold your hand." Instead of reaching for my hand though, Leo touched the flower in my hair. "That is, if you would like to hold mine."

"But if you don't want to..." He took his hand away.

I grabbed it and smiled up at him. "Let's do this."

Leo stayed right in front of me, holding both my hands as we practiced rising into the air and then coming back down. Maybe it was the way he was watching me, his silver eyes never leaving mine, but flying felt easier than it had earlier. Not needing to move my arms or legs, it was like I was weightless, yet the weight of my wings moving in the air made me feel safe. It didn't take long before we were flying higher, my confidence increasing by the minute.

Would Leo keep holding on, even once he saw that I could do this on my own?

Or would he let go?

And which did I want?

Leo chose for me, releasing my hands as we tilted and dove toward the grass.

I looked to him in surprise, and for just a second, I thought I saw a brief flicker of sadness. It was gone in an instant though, and then I was doing it on my own, easily avoiding the ground and soaring back into the sky as if it was the most natural thing in the world.

I tried out a few more moves, figuring how fast I could go, how quickly I could climb into the sky, and how to slow my wings if I wanted to decrease my speed.

"Check this out!" I called down to him when I'd made it up and over a tree. Leo was on the ground watching me, fairly far away from where I was flying. I could still see his face, however, and he didn't look sad any longer. Instead, he was a smiling, a rare, genuine smile.

Leo cupped his hands around his mouth and yelled up to me. "I love you!"

It was the sound of his pure, breathless joy that made my body stop, wings frozen, in midair. On any given day, Leo was serious and demanding, calculating and deliberate, so to hear those words spoken so easily, and with such pride, made my heart swell.

It also made me forget the number one rule of flying: use your wings.

Immediately I dropped from the air, and in less than a second Leo caught me in his arms, sweeping me along with him in one smooth scoop.

"You caught me," I said, slightly embarrassed but also enjoying being cradled in his strong arms. "You weren't even close to me."

There was that smile from him again, and I felt like I could live my entire life right there, in his arms, with that smile.

"I will always catch you, Vera. No matter how far away you are."

17

LEO

"Tell me everything you know about Hellfire rubies."

"Why do you want to know?" Zell asked me.

"Everything. I never saw them made, and you have the most experience in the Vestian lab."

"Hell yeah I do, but I never messed with that stuff. They stopped making them years ago. I know what everyone else knows, that they're made from the hearts of fae. I hear it was disgusting work, but it did make pretty gems."

Pretty? I glanced down at my ring. Could something like this be considered pretty? Was it possible to find beauty in something so horrific? No. Pretty was seeing the look of absolute elation on Vera's face when she flew without my help. Pretty was the way her wings reflected the sunlight.

The king had been gracious enough to allow us to use his study, not that it looked like he ever used it. The room was too bright and in desperate need of curtains to block the insane amount of sunlight that poured into the room. As it was, I was going to have to wear sunglasses just to read the basic reports Rand had brought.

"Marcus?" I asked. "What else do we know?"

"Leo, do you really..." Marcus grimaced. "Do you really want to know? I know that yours... It was your..." Marcus's eyes trailed to my hand where I wore the gold ring.

"Yes. I need to know."

"All right." Marcus nodded. He took out his tablet and clicked on something. "I did some research after you called us. I've never seen the process of their creation either, but from my readings, it is my understanding that fae hearts are removed, dehydrated, and then put under extreme pressure at an incredibly high temperature. They'd essentially be melted down in the lab and then built back up into the ruby itself."

Zell smacked Marcus on the back, just hard enough to send him forward slightly, the phone popping out of his hand until he caught it. "Good explanation, human. Maybe your species isn't as dumb as they seem. Now let the real expert take over. The process is called chemical vapor deposition, Leo. The guys who ran the lab before me also used chemicals to induce ionization and break down the hearts at a molecular level. I don't think a Hellfire ruby has been made in around twenty years. You should know that already, Your Highness," Zell said with a sneer. "Oh, that's right. The old demon never let you get near the crown, did he? Guess we all now know why."

"What about their abilities?"

"They're basically Dust in a condensed, crystallized form. Since you aren't ingesting them, I doubt they do much of anything other than look pretty. Elise wore one for years on her finger, and she wasn't walking around powered up all the time."

"What about their psychedelic properties? Can they cause hallucinations?" I asked.

"Dude." Zell shot me a look of disgust. "Are you planning on eating one?"

"Why do I even bother asking you?"

"Look, Leo, we're in uncharted territory here. To my knowledge, there's never been another half-fae royal who had access to one of the rubies. You tell us, because I sure as hell don't know."

"Not to sidetrack this conversation," Marcus said, "but you asked us to research the Hellfire rubies. However, it seems like we should spend our time on the Keeper Stone instead, given the recent developments with the fae city's protective veil."

The door creaked open, and we all turned to look as the rest of the group joined us. The prince and princess were accompanied by our resident mythology expert. He stayed by the princess, and even though Vera said he was a lieutenant, I had to wonder if he'd ever seen Mia fight, given how his body language seemed to be threatening all of us to stay away from her. Vera came in last, sitting down on one of the couches near the windows.

"Did you bring what I asked?" I asked the prince.

"I'm a little uncomfortable sharing anything about Vera's blood with a demon, but if this will help, here." Laurie took a piece of paper from his pocket and unfolded it, then handed it to me. I scanned it quickly before passing it to Marcus.

"When did you take my blood?" Vera asked.

"It was after you fainted," he explained. "We wanted to make sure you weren't sick."

"I wasn't, right?"

Marcus looked up from the paper. "You weren't sick at all. In fact, from this report, you're healthier than ever. There are definite changes here that weren't there before though. I've seen your blood work for many months now, including the documents from the auction, and from what I can tell, right now everything with you looks perfect."

"I'm not surprised that she's perfect," the white-haired jerk said. I cleared my throat, and when he saw my stare he held up his hands. "Fine! Sorry!"

He didn't seem sorry.

"Leo, can you explain your thinking here? I'm not sure that I'm connecting the dots."

"I suspect that the combined magic of Rowan and the Keeper Stone triggered something in Vera that developed her wings. From what the Keeper told me, in the past, fae could wield stones like that."

"Oh!" Marcus sat straight up, finally catching up to me. "So the magic of the stone transferred into Vera, and then not enough was left behind to continue creating the protective barrier."

"Exactly."

"Then this is easy." Zell scoffed. "To get their little wall back up, they just need to put more magic or whatever back into it."

"How, exactly? It was the original queen's magic that infused the stone, smart-ass," Laurie said. "It's not a 'little wall' either, it covers the whole city. That's an insane amount of magic."

"I'm a scientist, not a magician, but the answer seems obvious. Just have Vera do it."

"No."

All of us turned our heads at the sound of this new voice, the deep baritone of Victor, the purple-winged fae.

"In the legend of our original queen, it is said that she created the veil to ensure that fae live a life of peace," Victor explained. "Queen Morgana used all her strength for seven days and seven weeks, weaving a special magic into the stone."

"Could Vera do something like this?" I looked over at Vera, who grimaced.

"I wouldn't even know where to start," she said. "I can barely even fly, much less 'weave' or whatever that means. I'm happy to try though if it means helping everyone."

"It could be possible," Victor said. "However, there is a price."

"What is it?" Vera asked. "Because right now there don't seem to be a lot of other options. Surely there's no real harm in trying."

"The legend says that once the stone was created, the queen's magic had burned away, as had her life."

"This option is off the table," I said immediately.

Vera looked paler than I'd ever seen her. "She died?"

Victor nodded solemnly. "She burned out to protect her people. It was an honorable death."

"That's kind of fucked up," Zell muttered.

"I don't care about legend," I said. "This is not a viable option."

Vera chewed on her bottom lip in a way that I normally found adorable but right now wanted her to stop because it meant that she was thinking it over. "Marcus said himself that I was extremely healthy. I've seen firsthand that I do have the ability to use some kind of barrier magic. Maybe I do a smaller one that can protect everyone without burning out. Laurie, you've seen the barriers I've made. Mia too. Back me up here."

The princess sighed. "Yes, Vera, that's true, but..."

"The legend states that—"

Zell exhaled loudly, interrupting Victor as he threw his head back in irritation. "If I have to listen to more about your stupid legends, I'm going to overdose on Dust on purpose. Can we talk about reality instead? Give me Vera's blood report." Zell went over to Marcus and snatched it from his hand. The redheaded demon read it over, then tossed it behind him.

"What?" he asked when all of us gaped at him, mouths open. "It was all bullshit. Nothing worth knowing."

"B-But... But..." Marcus stumbled over his words as he rushed over to pick up the fallen papers. "When you look at the change in Vera's blood chemistry compared to her baseline, that assay shows us that—"

"It shows nothing." Zell flopped down in a chair. "This fae magic shit is too weird for us to understand with charts and graphs. Even I'm not sure about the little princess possibly dying for a hypothesis. Does someone have other ideas?"

"I do." Rand spoke up. "We coordinate with the fae to build their resources, organize an army, and develop security measures."

"Are these fae that weak? Man, they should try to live in the wild for one day and see what happens. If they can't survive without their precious wall, then they need to tell their subjects to kick the ass of whoever tries to hunt them down and let's go home." Zell reached for his drink and downed the whole thing in one gulp. "I don't see what the problem is."

"You think that wasn't already the plan?" Laurie snarled. "Leo, these demons of yours are idiots. I should have known this meeting wouldn't help."

"Hey, pretty boy," Zell called over to the white-haired fae. "How about you keep your mouth shut and let the grown-ups talk?"

"Grown-ups?" Laurie rolled his eyes. "Says the demon who can't stop showing off his tongue piercing."

"Jealous?" Zell stuck out his tongue for good measure, and Laurie flipped him off. "Leo, do all these fae have such a stick up their asses like this one?"

"That's the future king of the fae you're talking about," Mia said, moving to stand right in front of Zell's chair. "Watch your tone."

Zell leaned forward, his elbows on his knees. "Or what? What are you going to do about it, sweetheart? The last time I saw you, you were just a slave parading around in skimpy outfits in the arena. Now you're what? Some kind of warrior princess? Give me a break."

"She *is* the princess." Victor was at Mia's side. Towering over them both, his presence alone seemed to make Zell shut up, at least for the moment.

Rand came over, his black wings spread out behind him as he stared Zell down. "Is everyone trying to be obnoxious tonight? Zell, why are you being such a dick to them?"

"It's part of my charm."

"Did Elise tell you that?"

"No, because when Elise talks about my dick—"

"That's enough," I barked, my voice cutting through the chatter and silencing everyone. "We are here to work together to prevent a war, and you're all acting like children. Let's pause the discussion of the stone. For now. Rand. Give us a report from Vestia."

Rand relaxed his wings and turned to me. "It would be my pleasure. As you already know, your biggest threat is from the humans. Vestia will stay out of it. The demons will not mobilize; the general knows the basics and has agreed to this plan."

"You talked to your dad?" Vera asked him.

The scowl on Rand's face spoke volumes. I was familiar enough with my own father issues to know better than to even ask.

"Something like that. Leo, I can't speak for any rogue agents, but everyone inside Vestia will stay put. They will not hunt anyone here."

Marcus raised a hand. "If I may?"

"This isn't fucking school, nerd," Zell sneered.

"Zell, you are literally the demon in charge of the royal labs, *nerd*," Rand shot back. "Marcus, continue."

"We feel confident about demons in Vestia, but outside of Vestia... So far there's been no word from..." He adjusted his glasses and then grimaced, eyes darting to Vera as if for help.

"There's been no word from the former king?" Vera finished the sentence for him. I could feel my hands clenching at the mention of him, my fingers digging into my palms.

"Marcus is right." Rand nodded. "No word. But he no longer has access to money or a full army, so I don't see him being much of a threat here at the moment."

"The old bastard is always a threat," I said.

"Let me rephrase. He's not an immediate threat to the fae of Rowan. Even if he's aware that the veil has been lowered, which is likely, I can't see him having the means to stage anything large scale with the handful of followers that left with him."

Rand's words didn't help me relax. "Let's hope it stays that way," I said. "If you hear otherwise, tell me immediately."

"Of course. Outside the demon kingdom, from what I'm hearing from my other contacts, the wolves are staying in their dens and watching to see how this all plays out. That leaves the humans, and I'm sure they're foaming at the mouth at the opportunity to hunt down more fae. But first they will need time to prepare. Even humans aren't dumb enough to stroll into a city of thousands of fae with no plan and think they'll make it out alive. They're going to have to work on a plan first, then mobilize their hunters, all of which will take time."

Laurie nodded in agreement. "Time for us to figure out how to restore the veil."

"We need to go back to the cave," Vera said.

"No," I said. "We need to know more about what we're dealing with first."

"There's no time for that, Leo," Laurie said. "If Vera can link her magic to the stone somehow, then it might restore the veil as well."

"That is a theory. And at what cost?"

"Leo's right. That is unproven as of right now. We don't have enough information yet about the composition of the stone," Marcus added. "I'd like to do some radiometric dating on it first, and if I had a thermal mass—"

"Going to the cave is better than doing nothing." Laurie stood up and walked toward Vera, a hand extended. "Vera, let's—"

Zell was up in an instant, moving between her and Laurie. "Back up. That's not your chick, pretty boy."

"As I was saying, let's go to the cave," Laurie said to Vera, ignoring Zell completely. "I'll go with you."

"Didn't you just hear me? I said she's not yours."

"Zell." My voice made everyone stop to look at me. "Defending Vera is not your responsibility."

"I wasn't defending her. I just don't like him." Zell pointed at Laurie.

Rand sighed. "Idiots. All of you."

"There's one more thing I'd like to discuss with the group," Vera said. All eyes turned to her, and she nodded to Mia. The princess dug into her jacket pocket and pulled out a small box.

As soon as I saw the packaging, I went over and took it from her, then opened it. What the hell?

"Did you find this here?" I asked Mia.

"Yes. Even before the veil fell, someone was selling the fae real Dust."

18

VERA

The Great Hall was abuzz with the sounds of murmurs and the fluttering of wings. Laurie had told us this was only a strategy meeting, but at the moment it looked more like an elegant party than anything else. Fae milled about the room, leaving the chairs empty as everyone waited for the king to arrive.

Fae with wings of bright red or green, purple or yellow, their vivid colors dazzling in the light coming through the large windows, surrounded Laurie and Mia, trying to engage the prince and princess in conversation, but I couldn't ignore the glances everyone kept sending to one side of the room.

There was Leo, his arms crossed over his chest, leaning against the wall, tail tapping impatiently on the floor.

I wasn't surprised by the secret and not-so-secret glances being sent his way. He was a striking figure in any room, but here, in the fae's own Great Hall, he was truly quite a sight to see. This tall, dark-haired demon with black wings and tail, dressed in a tailored black suit. Handsome and threatening, striking but alluring.

I made my way over to him, his tail no longer thumping against the floor once I was there. I smoothed down my dress, just a simple yet elegant linen frock of green and gold since I was saving the white gown for tonight.

"You okay?" I asked. "There's a lot of fae here."

"Only one fae I care about." Leo slipped an arm around my waist to bring me closer.

"That doesn't stop fae magic from affecting you."

His hand tightened around my waist. "I'm hanging in there."

"You know, it's kind of nice," I said, playfully nudging him in the side. "I like not being the only oddball here for once."

"These fae need more to do if seeing a demon is the most exciting thing happening around here," he said.

"Be nice. Most of them have never seen a demon before."

Leo grunted.

"And you're not just any demon," I continued. "You're the famous demon who developed fake Dust, the prince himself."

"We need to start asking questions about the counterfeit Dust. Make a note of who you think we need to speak to later." Leo sighed and rolled his eyes. "With everything going on, this whole event is such a waste of time. Don't they know they should be preparing for what's coming? Human hunters could be here within days, and they're standing around acting like this is a party instead of a strategy meeting."

"How would they know what to do? To the younger fae especially, war is part of their parents' history, not their own. Until a few days ago, they thought their city was completely protected."

"All the more reason to be taking this seriously and planning, not wining and dining. They don't need distractions tonight."

We heard a door creaking open, and both of us turned to look as a group of fae women quietly tiptoed in through the side door near us. They were young, younger than me at least, with pretty dresses and prettier wings, the whole group giggling to each other as they fluttered closer. I'd been told that only high-level officials would be in attendance tonight, and judging by their age, I had a feeling they weren't part of the strategy meeting. Were they party crashers?

To my horror, they flew directly to us.

Or rather, directly to Leo.

Before I could stop them, they immediately started peppering Leo with questions, getting so close to him that I was practically boxed out of the conversation.

"I've never met a demon before," one said, her voice full of awe. I swear there were actual stars in her eyes as she stared at him.

"Can I touch your tail? I bet it's really soft." She reached toward him, and without thinking, I pushed my way to Leo and swatted her hand away.

"Hell no you can't," I said. "That is incredibly rude."

As if realizing for the first time I was there, the girls muttered apologies and fluttered away, leaving through the same door that they came in.

I heard a soft chuckle behind me. Placing one hand on my shoulder, Leo leaned down and whispered in my ear, "What happened to 'be nice,' hm?"

"That went out the window the second that girl reached for your tail."

"I see." Even though I couldn't see his face, I knew that he was smirking. "Is the little one jealous?"

"No," I said, trying desperately to ignore the way that endearment made me feel. I was glad Leo was standing behind me and couldn't see what I was sure was a rush of blood to my cheeks. "I was just being... protective."

"You're protecting me now?"

"As you said, we don't need any distractions."

I heard Leo sigh, and then he gave my shoulder a squeeze and let go. "Indeed," he said. I was already missing the weight of his hand. "If you'll excuse me."

Without another word, Leo left me there and made his way toward the other side of the room.

I found Leo interrogating two very confused and frightened fae in one corner of the room. He loomed over the two, his hands gesturing wildly as he spoke. When I got closer, I could see they both looked anxious and confused, neither saying anything but watching

Leo with wide eyes while he rattled off a series of rapid-fire questions.

"Have you tried converting biomass into electrical power?" I heard him ask. "With the number of farms here, it might work. Wait, how are you powering your irrigation system right now? Are you using wells too? Do solar panels work here?"

I placed a hand on Leo's arm, and he stopped talking when he saw me beside him.

"Good evening, gentlemen," I said to the group. "Solving the world's problems?"

One of the fae, a red with light brown hair, used this slight interruption to pull himself together enough to answer. "His Highness wanted to discuss ways for us to... adapt... to our current circumstances. He was sharing some thoughts on the matter."

"We are very grateful," the other, also a red but with dark hair, added quickly. "It's all very new to us since the veil has blocked all technology until now; however, now that you're here, we would like—"

Leo didn't let him finish the sentence. Instead, he turned to me. "They're hundreds of years behind on basic electrical infrastructure, and if they want even a simple security system, they need to get to work now. It's possible they could set up some generators around the rivers and then use turbines to transmit the power."

"Leo, slow down."

"There's no time to slow down! We should explore solar too. We might be able to get transformers brought in from Vestia, but that's going to be expensive, and without the proper infrastructure—"

"We?" I asked.

"Them." Leo gestured to the wide-eyed fae, who both shrank back, their body language making it very clear they were not the ones in charge and had no desire to be. "Or someone. Who runs your engineering teams? Who's in charge of research and development around here?"

"Uh..." The two fae exchanged a look, both shaking their heads. "I don't believe anyone has been appointed to those roles."

"I think one of the king's brothers is in charge of the interior," one of them said.

"We can work with that." Leo nodded. "That sounds like a good starting place at least. What's his background?"

"Um, well, you see, he mostly approves paint color on houses and design choices for new buildings."

"Are you joking?"

"Leo," I murmured, squeezing his arm. I could feel his tense muscles under my hand, his tail already starting to tap against the floor.

"I know you're all happy here," Leo said, his tone far from happy, "living in your perfect little paradise, ignoring the rest of us, but are you telling me there is literally no one responsible for day-to-day engineering or operations or anything for a city of thousands?"

"The Head Weaver organizes the distribution of cloth throughout the city. Maybe she could help?" one of them said, the other nodding enthusiastically.

"I'm going to lose my shit," Leo muttered, low enough that only I could hear.

"Please don't," I whispered back.

"I need to think of a plan," he said to them. "I'll find you another time."

Without waiting another second, holding on to my elbow, Leo spun me around and we started walking in the opposite direction.

"There's no way they can get this together," he muttered beside me.

"I know."

"They're going to have to rely on their own magic when they'll be up against an army of hunters."

"Pretty much."

"I didn't work this hard on Syn for them to lose everything to a bunch of humans jacked up on Dust."

Someone cleared their throat behind us, and we turned around. There the two red-winged fae waited. "Excuse us, but—"

Leo already had us walking away, but they followed close behind.

"I told you I needed time," Leo said over his shoulder,

The fae stumbled over their words as they tried to keep up with us. "If you could give us one more moment. We just... uh... We just wanted to..."

We stopped, and I could feel Leo tense at my side as they came around in front of us.

Oh hell.

Here we go.

"What? You just wanted to what?" Leo snapped. "I already told you that I needed time to come up with a plan."

"It's not about that," the dark-haired one said.

"Then what is it about?"

"We actually wanted to talk to you," he said to me. "There's something we wanted to ask."

"She doesn't have time for that either."

"Yes, I do," I told them. "I'm happy to answer any questions you might have. As scientists"—Leo huffed at that word—"you might be interested in what I know about fae development in captivity. Or I could tell you about the testing we did there. The humans did monthly blood draws, actually, to measure our power levels, and—"

"That would be good information for another time," the light-haired one said, shifting from one foot to the other, fidgeting with his cuffs, "but that's not what we wanted to ask."

"Oh. Okay. Then what was it?"

"Well, we wanted to know if, maybe, we can, you know..."

"No, I'm sorry. I don't know."

He looked to his friend for help, and then the dark-haired fae leaned closer to me, his voice low. "Can we see them?"

My mouth dropped open at the same time that Leo took a step forward. The two men flinched back.

"What did you just say?" Leo asked, his voice dripping with venom.

"Uh, y-your... her... wings?" the light-haired one stammered. "We j-just wanted to s-see... them? Up close?"

"Who the fuck do you think you are?"

"We've never seen wings that were more than one color up close."

"I think you've seen enough. Congrats. Now leave us alone." Leo had already put an arm around me, ready to lead me away.

"Leo, it's really no big deal. All I have to do is turn around and let them look at me."

"No. You will walk backward if you have to," Leo said to me, but his eyes didn't leave the two fae. "And you two. She is not some object to examine, so get lost."

Before they could respond, Laurie was beside me, clapping his hands. "Look at how well you're getting along with everyone, Leo!" Laurie's smile was broad and exaggerated, his eyes wide. "Gentlemen," he said to the two fae men, "I see you've been picking the brain of Vestia's own celebrated genius. I'm afraid I need to consult him on matters myself, so if you'll please give us a moment alone."

Not waiting another second, the two men eagerly darted away.

"I'm glad to see you making friends," Laurie said to Leo.

"I'm not here to make friends."

"Then maybe it's time to start. You're not going to get anywhere in this city if you're over here making angry faces at anyone who looks Vera's way."

"This is my normal face."

"Right. I know. That's the problem."

"Do you have a problem?" Leo asked.

"You seem to enjoy giving me problems," Laurie said.

"Guys." I looked back and forth between the two, hoping that would be enough to get them to stop arguing. It wasn't.

Leo pointed a finger right at Laurie. "Maybe I shouldn't have solved that little problem of you dying back in Vestia then."

"Are you going to hold that over me forever? I did what you asked and got Vera out of that hellhole of a city."

"Stop it!" I yelled, standing between them. Noticing more than a few glances our way, I cleared my throat and lowered my voice. "Leo, we are here to help. Laurie, thank you for allowing us to attend this meeting tonight."

"I'm not allowing you to do anything. You will never need my permission to do anything, Vera," Laurie said, looking pointedly at Leo.

Leo took a step toward Laurie. "What is that supposed to mean?"

"Oh look, I think the meeting is about to start!" I said, hooking one arm around each man and dragging them at my sides toward the long tables.

Two long wooden tables had been set up in the center of the room on either side of the dais. The king took his place at his throne, and the rest of us sat at the tables.

The king began the meeting with formalities and then dove right in, explaining what had happened with the veil. He told the group they had been assembled to determine the best plan of action for their city. Watching the king speak and the way the heads of the assembled fae nodded along, I realized immediately where Laurie's charm and charisma came from. The longer the king continued to spin this as a positive thing for Rowan and how he was confident that a solution would be found soon, the more I could feel Leo tensing next to me with each passing second.

When one of the city leaders suggested that citizens might benefit from guided meditation to relieve the stress this was causing, Leo leaned over to me. "This is going nowhere," he whispered. "They are completely out of their league."

He was right. They were dancing around the main issue.

"Your Majesty, if I may interrupt?"

I knew if I looked down from where I stood I'd see Leo's silver eyes staring at me in shock at my boldness, so I kept my eyes focused ahead on the king's table. Mia gave me a small thumbs-up, the gesture giving me a little more confidence to speak.

"Vera," the king said, smiling warmly. "Please. Go ahead."

"If the Keeper Stone held the magic that sustained the veil, can we not just put more magic back into it?"

"She makes an excellent point, Your Majesty."

The crowd gasped.

I'd been so nervous to speak that I hadn't heard the door open. All heads turned toward the unexpected voice, and there stood the Keeper.

Her hands were cuffed behind her back, and a guard stood on either side. Instead of her normal black cloak and silk gown, she wore a simple linen dress, and her dark hair hung down her shoulders, messy and unkempt.

I gasped at the sight of her, and Leo was on his feet in seconds, standing beside me.

"Your Majesty, I object to her presence here," Leo said.

The king held up a hand. "I understand the concern. I brought our former Keeper here since no one else knows as much as she does about the magic of Rowan. We are still investigating her crimes, and we will have a thorough trial, but for better or worse, right now we do need Selena's help."

"His Majesty is wise to trust my knowledge," Selena purred, and I hated how damn smug she looked. "I had suspected that Vera's magic might allow her to control the stone, but I didn't know it would go this far. But I'm glad it did."

A murmur ran up and down the tables.

"This city is rotten to the core," Selena sneered. "Fae are meant to rule this world, not cower behind a fake sense of security. The true strength of the fae resides in those who go beyond the city, those who dare to live in the wild, not tremble in fear of it. This city deserves to be ravaged by hunters. Anyone not strong enough to fight back deserves everything that is coming."

"That is enough!" The king slammed his fist down on the arm of his throne. "You are not here to lecture us. Tell us what you know of how we might repair the veil."

"Repair it?" Her red lips turned up in a smile. "Impossible. It was created by the original queen herself. The amount of magic required to restore the veil is beyond what any of us are capable of, even myself. Instead, it is time to plan the move forward. I see the demon is here, so you must have already considered how we might bring demons to heel in our war against humans. You've chosen one who has already turned against his own attendants, against his own family."

Leo was still standing. "Your Majesty—"

The king spoke over him, his attention on Selena. "That is not what we are discussing," he said. "The demons will be our allies moving forward."

"Allies?" Selena barked a laugh. My skin crawled with the way her eyes raked over Leo. "Once the demons recognize our true power, they'll have no choice but to do what we say. The fact remains that the veil cannot be repaired. Only the original queen possessed that amount of magic."

"Father, if I may?" Laurie adjusted his suit before continuing to speak. "I propose a dual approach. Vera can work with some of the other experts on restoration of the veil while we prepare defenses for the city at the same time. It is my understanding that Vera's magic could be related to the original fae queen. She was visited by Queen Morgana in a vision."

"Vera, is this true?" the king asked.

I stood up again. "Yes, Your Majesty. Or at least I think so."

"And what happened in this vision?"

I swallowed, thinking back on what I'd experienced. Even the memory still made me shiver. It had seemed so real at the time. "When I touched the Keeper Stone, I saw a woman with large wings, larger than any I'd ever seen. They were so many different colors, sort of like my own."

"And what did she do?"

"All I remember is seeing her, and then she just said two words. She said, 'Protect them.'"

The room was eerily quiet.

Until the Keeper laughed, a loud cackle that made all eyes turn to her. Selena kept laughing, even as her two guards gripped her arms.

"A new age is coming, fast," she said loudly so the whole room could hear her. "The ancient magic flows through her. If Vera's new wings weren't proof enough, then this vision confirms it. You should be worshipping the ground she walks on."

"Silence," said the king.

"You can't silence the truth. The end of the veil marks a new age for fae, an age when the strong will survive. An age that will cull the weak from our ranks so that we can retake our place in this world."

"This is a distraction. Guards, please remove the former Keeper," the king ordered.

"Hunters are coming!" she shouted as the guards started to lead her away. "Many of them. And when they do, Rowan will be brought to its knees and only those strong enough to survive will remain."

She continued shouting, despite the king's insistence she stop, as they pulled her out of the room. The doors slammed behind her, and Leo sat back down, taking my hand in his under the table.

"What if she's right?" I whispered to him. "What if there really is nothing we can do? Nothing I can do except try..."

Leo might have had my hand in his, but he was staring straight ahead. His tail tapped against the floor with irritation.

"Leo?"

"How did she know?" he whispered.

"Know what?"

"What I did in Vestia. My father's councilors. She knew..."

19

___

VERA

Rand leaned back against the couch in Mia's office, the leather creaking against his wings. "You didn't tell me he would be here."

"You didn't ask," I told Rand.

The two of us watched as Rob spoke with the servant who had just brought us food. She had pretty green wings like Rob and a matching tattoo of intricate green leaves twisting around one of her arms. She was laughing at something Rob said, and Rob was smiling back as he continued talking to her.

We had a few hours until the official dinner, and since the table in my room had been removed after I broke it, Mia had graciously allowed us to use her suite of rooms until it was time. Leo and Marcus were doing something science-y somewhere, leaving Rand and me and, unfortunately, Zell who had jumped at the chance to have drinks before the dinner.

After Selena's outburst earlier, I needed a drink. Maybe four. Hunters were coming, she'd shouted to everyone. Were they? And if so, when? Could we figure out how to put back the veil first?

"Less thinking, more drinking. At least right now, okay?" Rand said, giving me a nudge. "That lady was crazy. We can't believe everything she says."

"I know, but..."

"But what? Now what the hell are they doing?" Rand asked, nodding toward the door.

Rand and I watched Rob disappear into the hallway with the woman.

"Just go out there," I said. "Now's the perfect time to do something."

Rand looked doubtful, his tail flicking back and forth on the floor. "Like what? Should I demand that he come back in here and talk to me?"

"Okay, maybe that's not the best idea. How about this? When they come back, you could put an arm around him. Or wing? Just do something to let that lady know that you're the one he's in a relationship with."

"Texting nudes back and forth is not the same thing as being in a relationship."

"It doesn't mean you're *not* in a relationship. Or does it? This is sort of out of my wheelhouse here."

"Exactly. I'm pretty sure you should not be giving me advice about my relationship. Or whatever this is. Besides, Rob has been living in the fae colony Leo set up. It's too far away for anything real."

"He's here now."

"That he is."

"I don't think he's going back. So are you going to do something about it?" I asked him.

"Let's see. The fae city is about to be attacked, there's a bunch of rogue demons out there somewhere, not to mention a group of crazy fae on the loose, but sure, I'll go confess my feelings to Rob, no problem."

"You sure you're really Leo's chief communicator?"

"I've questioned his judgment many times over the years."

We stopped talking when Rob came back in balancing three

drinks in his hands. I took mine from him, and he held one out for Rand.

"I got this for you," Rob said. "Hope it's okay."

"For me?" Rand eyed the red liquor suspiciously.

"Yeah. I hope you still drink those. I know it's been a while." Rob sat on the couch across the table from us. "I'll get you something else if it's gross. It took forever to explain the recipe to the server."

"I'm guessing they aren't well versed in demons' favorite drinks," I added.

"You would have thought that I'd asked for the something bizarre. Really, if you don't like it, I will go back, but no guarantees since she didn't seem like the most experienced bartender. I had to explain it to her three different times."

Rand still had the drink in his hand, staring at it blankly as if he didn't understand what he was looking at. "That's what took so long?"

"I'm sorry, guys. Really. Man, I feel terrible. I just wanted this to feel like old times. I know it's been a while since we all drank together."

"Will you stop?" Rand's voice was as tight as his grip on the glass he was holding.

"What?"

"I think what Rand is trying to say is thank you," I said.

Rob's face fell. "No, I get it. I'll be right back. I'll find a different bartender this time."

"Rob!" I called after him, but he was already gone, green wings vanishing out the door again.

"Wow." I took a sip of my own drink. "That was shockingly awkward."

Rand closed his eyes and exhaled loudly. He leaned his head back against the couch. "What do I do?"

"How about you communicate, Mr. Communicator?"

"That's too hard. Give me something else."

"I love both of you, but I've known Rob longer. He will do anything for anyone and—"

"And I won't?"

"I didn't say that. Rob likes to take care of people. He's big and bulky, but he has the softest heart, and you're not going to find anyone as loyal as him. Show him that he's important to you. He needs some kind of outward sign."

"An outward sign…"

We didn't have time to talk further because Zell plopped down on the couch beside me. He started to drape an arm over my shoulders, but I scooted away, closer to Rand.

"You shy tonight, princess?" Zell tilted his head toward me, his tongue piercing rolling across his lips.

"No, you just give me the creeps. Don't you have a dog to walk or something?"

"Would you believe that none of the servants wanted to watch him?"

"I would believe that," I said, "because that dog is a menace. So where is he?"

"There are so many hot girls here too." Zell continued as if he hadn't heard me. "I thought for sure that one of them would take him. He's running around in the back garden somewhere."

"By himself? Zell, go get your dog." I mentally made a note to say something to Elise when I got the chance.

"Nah, I'm waiting for a cute little fae to find him and then come looking for the owner."

"Don't you have a girlfriend?" Rand asked, looking over me at the redheaded demon on my other side.

"Don't you?" Zell asked back.

"No."

"Boyfriend then?"

Rand took a long look at the drink in front of him before setting it down on the low table in front us. "No time for that."

"That's the Rand, I know. This whole relationship thing is a lot of work. You know, I bet with your new job you've got a line of girls and guys just dying to fuck. I used to live that life," Zell said, wistfully staring off into the room. "Do you have an assistant to weed out the ugly ones or what?"

"You're disgusting," I said.

"That wasn't what you said when you used to serve me drinks at the club, princess. Then it was all yes, Lord Zell, anything you need, Lord Zell."

"You have a bad memory then. Didn't I punch you one time?"

"Oh yeah, maybe you did do that. Anyway, that's the past. Rand's the top dog now. Let us live vicariously through you, dude. Tell the princess and me all about your latest hookups."

"Whose hookups?" Rob appeared beside us, next to Rand. He placed the new drinks on the table and then put a hand on Rand's shoulder. His features tight, Rob stared pointedly at Zell.

Zell huffed a laugh and then stood up. "Better get your man in line, fae." He smacked Rob on the shoulder as he walked past him. "If you can. See you guys at the dinner; I have a dog to find."

"What was that about?" Rob handed Rand a second drink.

I shrugged my shoulders.

"Was that guy making you uncomfortable?" he asked me.

"Zell exists to make people uncomfortable."

"I can say something to him if you want."

"Thanks, Rob, but it's really okay," I said. "He's just being a jerk because the girls here don't think he's the hottest thing they've ever seen."

"Why do hot guys think they have a right to be assholes?" Rob asked.

Rand turned around to look at him. "You think Zell's hot?"

"Do you?"

"Objectively he's not ugly, I guess."

"And all the piercings and tattoos? You like that?" Rob asked, his brow furrowed.

"Do you?"

"I guess?"

"This is so awkward," I muttered.

Rob seemed to feel the same because he put down his drink without finishing it. "Where did that lady go? I'll see you both there tonight, right? I'm going to head out."

"Hey, Rob, wait a sec," I said, trying to stop him.

He didn't wait, and when the door closed behind him, Rand groaned.

"Great communication," I said, giving Rand a big pat on the back. "A-plus communication. This alliance is so screwed."

Just then the door swung open, and Mia came in swinging a bottle of champagne, her words flying out just as fast as she flew herself. "Did someone say alliance? Who's ready to celebrate demons and fae aligning together even though it's only because we have to because our city isn't safe and crazy humans want to come and enslave us all?"

"Is she always like this?" Rand whispered to me.

"Yep."

"I like it."

The drink I already had was enough for me, but Rand and Mia seemed more than eager to split the champagne, and soon they were bonding over their shared relationship drama. After more than a few glasses, it even seemed like they were talking about the same person.

"I'm so tired of being in charge, you know?" Mia whined while Rand nodded in agreement.

"Right? Being in charge is the worst. Yes please. Thank you," Rand said as Mia poured him another glass. "I want someone else to take charge for once."

"Exactly!" Mia said, her own drink spilling onto the table as she leaned toward Rand. "He has all those muscles, but has he ever just thrown me up against a wall and kissed me? Of course not."

"That's what I'm saying! Why have all those muscles if you're not going to use them?"

"You are so right. Vera, we need your help. Leo is obsessed with you. Spill all your secrets of seduction. Immediately."

Two sets of eyes, one blue and one silver, stared at me expectantly like little puppy dogs.

"Well," I said slowly, slightly unnerved by the way they were looking at me as if I had all the answers. "I'm no expert, but Leo and I are working on trusting each other and communicating better."

Their eyes seemed to light up as if I'd just dropped some deep, mysterious wisdom.

"To communicating!" Mia said, raising her glass.

"To communicating!" Rand echoed, the two of them clinking glasses. Rand took a long gulp and then slammed his glass down, his tail flicking against the floor. "Princess, would you happen to know anyone who does tattoos?"

Fuck.

It was going to be a long night.

WHEN I PUSHED through the giant wooden doors into the Great Hall, I saw that it had been transformed from the strategy meeting. Several musicians played soft music, and more long tables had been added, each one covered in yards of white silk and decorated with elaborate floral arrangements. I recognized several of the flowers from the ones I'd seen the women bringing in. Lit candelabras on each table gave the room a soft glow, their light reflecting off the champagne glasses at each place setting. The other meeting had only been for a small group of less than twenty, but now a hundred, if not more, fae filled the space.

It wasn't difficult to find the demons.

Zell was leaning back in his chair, downing champagne while fae women giggled over Zeus. They kept passing the little dog around no matter how much he snarled at them. Did Elise know that the dog acted like it wanted to murder any woman who wasn't her? Had that been Elise's plan all along? I had to hand it to her. It would have been a smart plan if Zell had seemed at all bothered by the dog's antics. As it was, he seemed more interested in flirting than dealing with the little terror.

Marcus sat near him, his face red, looking like he was torn between wanting to rip out his notebook and take notes and wanting to hide from everyone there. I wondered if those scientists from the other meeting were at this dinner and if I could introduce them later.

But where was Leo?

If he had skipped out on this because he thought it was pointless, I was going to have to say something to him.

What if he had decided not to attend at all, thinking that Rand could handle it?

What if he had decided that he wasn't needed in Rowan at all any longer?

What if—

"Vera."

I spun around, and there was Leo. Relief washed over me. He wasn't alone either. I could tell from the way that Rand leaned onto Leo's shoulder, and the irritated look on Leo's face, that the second bottle of champagne had been a mistake.

"What the hell were you guys doing earlier?" Leo whispered to me. "He looks like a mess."

"Communicating, Leo," Rand slurred. He propped his elbow on Leo's shoulder, swaying against him. "You two think you're *so* cute because you're *so* in love and the rest of us are just figuring it all out. But you." Rand poked Leo. "She doesn't trust you. I don't blame her, because what have you done to—"

I smacked my hand over his mouth to keep him from saying anything else.

What the fuck? Leo silently mouthed to me.

I just shook my head with a promise to explain later. "Marcus and I have been discussing what happened earlier with the Keeper. I don't think her comments were a coincidence. The veil, the Dust—there's more going on here. I think we need to—"

"Vera!" Mia appeared beside us. "Can I steal you away for a second?" she asked, even though we were already walking, her arm looped through mine.

"We were kind of in the middle of something," I said at the same time I heard Leo say, "No."

"I'll bring her back in a few!" she called out to him over her shoulder.

"Sobered up already?" I asked as I resigned myself to walking with her, noticing that she wasn't in her normal guard uniform. Nor was she wearing the colors of the royal family.

"Yep. I linked with Laurie earlier to get some of it out of my system."

"Nice. Where is the prince tonight?"

She nodded to where her white-haired brother stood not far away. As usual, a group of fae women surrounded him on all sides, the laughs and voices carrying over the crowd toward us. Over their heads, Laurie saw us and raised his glass in our direction. Several of the fae women turned around to see what he was looking at, giving me an evil stare until they saw Mia at my side.

"It's easy to know where my brother is all the time anyway."

"Why is that?"

"Because he's never far from you."

"Mia..."

"Yeah, yeah, yeah. Hot demon guy is back, so I know there's no chance for my poor, lovestruck brother. A girl can still wish though! Argh!" She clenched a fist in the air in mock frustration. "I was really hoping that we'd end up related one day!"

"*Anyway.*" I dragged out the word to change the subject. "Your dress is beautiful."

Unlike her normal pants and jacket, tonight Mia wore a floor-length gown, gorgeous and feminine, tucked tight at the waist and then flowing down to the floor. The top was dark purple, plunging in a *V*-cut neckline to a thick purple band around the waist. From there, the color softened; the gown's deep purple skirt gradually fading to a light lavender as it touched the floor. Her white hair was pinned in braids on both sides, and I couldn't help but notice that she was wearing more makeup than normal as well.

"I've had this dress for a while." Her pale cheeks flushed, and she fussed with a strand of white hair. "I was waiting for the right moment to wear it."

"It's very pretty and very... purple. I'm sure your choice to wear this tonight had nothing to do with a certain purple-winged lieutenant, right?"

"Of course not! Okay, maybe. Come on, we're going to stroll elegantly over there." She nodded in front of us. My eyes followed, and I saw Victor standing along the wall with several other members of the guard that I recognized.

"Why are we strolling elegantly again?"

"Because! You're the one who said I needed to communicate."

"So we're going to go talk to Victor?"

"Talk? Oh no. Not that."

"But—"

"We'll stroll by him and smile demurely, and then I'll say something, and you'll act like it's funny, and we'll both do that little giggle thing I've seen girls do. Come on, let's go."

"And then we will actually talk to him?"

"No way."

"Then what are we doing?"

"We are going to make Victor see me."

"Mia. He already does. I promise."

"No. He sees soldier Mia. Captain Mia. That's fine and all, but I want him to see me as more. I want him to see me as a woman."

"I don't think you have anything to worry about there."

"Then why hasn't he kissed me? We're alone all the time. I even make sure to pin him down when we're sparring, and then I'll close my eyes and wait, but nothing happens. He never makes a move."

"Maybe because you're the princess? And technically he works for you?"

"Technicalities." She gripped my arm, walking faster. "We are strolling. Elegantly. Now."

"Is that an order from the captain?"

"Damn right. Be ready to giggle. On my command."

Wondering if I'd ever been commanded to giggle before, I glanced over my shoulder and saw Leo watching us. I shot him a weak smile that I hoped communicated that I had no idea what was going on, and he raised an eyebrow. Mia continued talking at a rapid pace as we got closer to Victor until we were finally walking by him.

This whole thing felt so silly. Why couldn't the two of them just talk? Why did they have to do this whole act just to be together?

But wasn't I doing the same thing? The sex was great, but had Leo and I truly addressed the issues that separated us in the first place? If we had, why was I so unnerved every time I walked into a room until I was sure that Leo was there?

"...because as you know, you can't have too many shoes!"

It took me a second to realize that Mia was talking to me, because since when did she care about shoes?

Which meant I had missed the moment to giggle.

"Oh! Ha!" I forced a loud laugh and earned another glare from Mia.

Sorry I mouthed, and she was about to say something when Victor stepped in front of us.

"Princess, if I may?" Victor asked, offering his arm.

·In contrast to all the elaborate gowns and stylish suits that everyone else was wearing tonight, the purple-winged fae wore a traditional suit in a simple black. As the second-in-command of the palace guard, I shouldn't have been surprised at how big Victor was, but I always forgot until he was standing right in front of me. Mia was just so small in comparison, even though her size was deceptive when it came to her strength.

"You may," I said for her, giving her a little shove forward so she could take Victor's arm.

"Your dress is very beautiful, Princess," he said in that deep voice of his.

"Oh, you know, Laurie had this in a closet somewhere..."

I hoped she didn't see me roll my eyes as the two of them walked away and I hurried to my assigned seat. It was no surprise that Leo was seated at the table with the royal family, but I was surprised to see that I was as well. We weren't next to each other, however. Leo ended up sitting on one side of the queen, next to Mia, and I ended up sitting on the other side, next to Laurie.

The king started with the normal introductions and then launched into the details of the alliance. One fae, much older than the king, with gray hair and delicate red wings came to the front of the room and stood on the other side of the dais. He wasn't speaking to the king, however. He was speaking straight to Leo.

"Why would a demon want to help the fae?" he asked. "I was alive during the war. I know what demons did to betray our trust. His Majesty claims that you want to help fae, but I do not understand your motivation. Why would we ever trust you, a demon?"

Murmurs of agreement sounded throughout the room.

Leo stood up from the table.

Crossing one arm over his chest and lowering his head, Leo spoke loud enough that his voice carried over the room.

"I understand your distrust in me. I barged into your city uninvited and unannounced. I can't make up for what demons have done in the past, but I want you to know that you have one demon on your side. I promise that you can trust that I only want to protect not only you and the fae of Rowan, but all fae in the world."

The old man scoffed. "I put my trust in fae, not demons."

Leo straightened up. He glanced over at me, and right then I knew what was about to happen. I held my breath.

"Then you can trust me as well because I am half-fae."

Several of the fae in the room gasped, but Leo kept talking.

"My mother was fae. She met my father during the war and then posed as a servant to the royal family during my childhood. I was able to get through your veil because of both my genetics and because I used this ring." He held up his hand to show the room the red stone on the golden band.

"You proudly wear a Hellfire ruby," one of the king's advisors shouted out, "and then have the audacity to ask us to trust you?"

Leo held his hand to his chest, the red stone shining in the candlelight. "I share your disgust for these rubies, but this one is an exception. This stone was made from my own mother's heart." Leo's hand balled into a fist. "It is the last Hellfire ruby that was made, and no more have been made since or will be made."

The king nodded in approval. "I appreciate and understand the concern," the king said to everyone. "But we need to secure this alliance so we can all trust that we're working toward mutually beneficial solutions."

While the king explained what Leo had accomplished by developing Syn and freeing the slaves of Vestia, there were several hums of approval, and I watched the expressions of everyone at the meeting to get a feel for what they were thinking. These were the most important fae in Rowan, and we needed them to understand the reality they were facing. As the king spoke, most seemed confused, some of the younger fae looked curious, but several still looked outright hostile.

Their general reluctance wasn't surprising, but it was still disappointing. I could see it in Leo's face, the way the muscles of his cheeks clenched, the way his hands curled into fists at his sides. The king had to notice it too. The two sides had to trust each other, but it seemed like we were a long way from that ever happening.

Everyone moved out onto the back terrace after dinner. Fae with wings of all colors and sizes milled around the gardens with their champagne in the fading twilight.

I saw the king and queen walk into the room with Leo close behind. Laurie wasn't with them, but Mia was. I grabbed another glass of champagne so I wouldn't look suspicious if caught and followed behind them at a distance, wondering what they were doing. They weren't being trailed by the usual assortment of guards. Was this a secret meeting? Had Leo known about it and not said anything?

They entered the king's study, and I stayed outside the door, listening. At first it all sounded muffled, but then I heard the loud and proud voice of the king.

"Prince Leo, to signal the alliance between our two kingdoms, tonight I give you my daughter, the Princess Mia."

20

VERA

What?

Surely I'd heard that wrong.

Really wrong.

"Your Majesty, I... I think—" Even Leo was stumbling over his words.

It was like my brain had completely turned off, which was probably why I dropped my glass.

The glass shattered on the stone floor. I stared down at the broken pieces and champagne that had spilled.

Shit.

They'd probably heard the crash.

I spun around to fly away, but there was Laurie, right in front of me. He put a hand on both my shoulders. "Vera. What's wrong? Talk to me."

"Did you know about this?"

"About what?"

"Your father..."

Laurie sighed. "What'd he do this time?"

"I just overheard him talking to Leo. About the alliance. Laurie, he said he was giving Mia to him, that they were going to be married."

Laurie's blue eyes blinked rapidly. "I didn't think he was serious."

"Hold on. You knew he was planning this?"

"Okay. Full transparency here. I thought something like this might happen, but I didn't know for sure."

"And you conveniently didn't tell me? Or Mia?"

"I didn't want either of you to worry about something that might never happen. I thought my father was just throwing around ideas. The way they interrogated Leo tonight must have made him nervous that Leo might back out. Not to mention that it's obvious some fae still don't trust him. From my father's point of view, what better way to gain their trust than to show that he's invested in the city by marrying the princess?"

"Leo's not like that. He doesn't think like that."

"As much as I hate to admit it, you and I know that to be true."

"There's no way he'll agree to marrying your sister. There's no way Mia would ever—"

"You don't have to convince me. If I know my sister at all, she's probably in there ready to smack my father over the head with whatever blunt instrument is nearby." Laurie took a step toward me. "But let's say Leo considered it..."

"He won't."

"Let's say he did. He was engaged to Elise because his own father arranged it, right?"

Laurie must have sensed my hesitation as he took another step toward me. I took a step back, my wings brushing up against the wall. He didn't come closer though. Instead, Laurie went down on one knee in front of me and reached forward, taking my hand in his. I tried to pull my hand back, but he held firm.

"Laurie, we've been over this. I care about you, but I love someone else."

"What has he done to deserve that love? Vera. Look at me. Really look at me. The prince of Rowan is on his knees at your feet. If you let me, I will never leave you."

"What the hell is going on?"

At the sound of Leo's voice, I pushed Laurie's hand away and looked behind me to see Leo standing outside the room, his silver eyes gleaming and black wings already starting to expand at the sight of Laurie kneeling in front of me.

Feeling heat rushing to my face, I pursed my lips. "That's a great question. You tell me."

Leo looked past me and pointed at Laurie. "You. Outside. Now."

"I am the one talking to you right now," I snapped.

"Leo, listen—" Laurie stood and held up his hands as if surrendering.

"I've listened quite enough. We're settling this right now. Prince to prince."

"Leo. This is silly. I don't want to fight you."

"Because you know you'll lose?"

"You know what? I think I just changed my mind."

"Leo. Laurie. Both of you. Stop this!" I yelled after them, but they weren't listening. They were already zooming down the hall like a couple of idiotic hormonal teenagers. I felt like following them and kicking both their asses for this stupid rivalry that they couldn't seem to let go. Laurie had no right to continue to push me when I'd made my feelings clear, and Leo had no right to act like he had a right to handle my problems for me.

By the time I managed to catch up, fae were already lined up to watch where Leo and Laurie circled each other in the grass below. Their champagne glasses raised high, fae cheered on their prince and booed when Leo got too close. As I tried to get nearer to them, I could hear the bystanders' comments, each one making me madder by the second.

"I hope he kicks that demon's ass."

"As long as he doesn't touch his handsome face."

"I wonder how hard that tail can hit."

"I'd let it hit me anytime."

When I made it to the edge of the terrace and leaned over the railing, the shouts of the crowd drowned out all other noise. The sun was setting, but the back garden was illuminated by the last bit of sunlight, and in that light I could see the two of them, their bodies a swirl of black and blue flying all over to the sound of cheers from the crowd.

It would have been an amazing sight to see if in any other context that didn't make me this angry. By most measurements, the two seemed evenly matched, so I had no idea how this was going to turn out. Laurie was similar in height to Leo, with wings just as large, but he moved quicker, using those big blue wings to dart this way and that, easily outmaneuvering Leo.

Not to be outdone, Leo was able to counter Laurie's speed with strength and skill. His large frame hovering in the air in front of Laurie, no one could deny that the demon was a force to be reckoned with. The muscles of his broad shoulders flexed as his black wings beat behind him, their cadence slow and menacing as Leo deliberated each move.

Laurie didn't give him much time to think. As I watched, he dove through the air right at Leo, his shoulder colliding with Leo's chest. The force knocked both of them out of the air, and together they tumbled to the ground. The crowd erupted in cheers at the sight of their prince taking down a demon, but those shouts of joy immediately fell silent when Leo sprang back up onto his feet, his big black wings spread wide.

Laurie was back on his feet as well. Leo took one slow step toward Laurie, and then another. I didn't even have to see his face to know that he was pissed; I could tell from his measured movements he was serious. Not waiting for Leo to come to him, Laurie rushed forward, and for the briefest of seconds, it looked like Leo wasn't going to move or even defend himself, but then Laurie fell forward, hitting the ground with a thud.

I realized then that Leo's tail had wrapped around the fae's ankle and tripped him. Leo's tail jerked to the side, whipping Laurie with it, and then it released, flinging Laurie a few feet away as the crowd booed and hissed.

"Stop this!" I screamed as I saw Laurie get up again.

Not hearing me or not caring, the two men hovered in the air a few feet away from each other. I had to do something. I had an idea, but I didn't know if it would work. I was just mad enough to try though, and there was no better time than right then, when they were still separated.

They were flying straight at each other, so I only had the smallest fraction of a moment to get between them. Zooming faster than I knew my wings could go, I barely made it, coming down hard between the two before they ran into each other. I held out both hands as if to stop them, hoping I could use my barrier magic quickly enough. I only saw Leo's look of shock for a split second before both men were flung back into the grass, landing with a hard thud that I hoped didn't break any bones.

But if it had, it was their own damn fault.

Fae were already flying over to Laurie as I walked to Leo. When I got there, I loomed over him, glaring down. "Did you get that out of your system?"

Leo closed his eyes and exhaled loudly. "Vera."

"Do you feel like you accomplished something?"

"Is that bastard still standing?"

"No, but neither are you, and it wasn't because of him either. Since you couldn't wait for me to handle it myself, you had to jump in and act like an idiot."

Leo's silver eyes snapped open. "An idiot? I did this for you."

"I didn't ask you to do anything for me. You didn't see me challenging Mia to a stupid duel or whatever this was. And now look," I said, pointing over to Laurie, who was also still on his back in the grass, but with a team of fae no doubt linking with him to heal any injuries. "You're both hurt because you two had to act like immature teenagers. I shouldn't link with you just to teach you a lesson."

"I'm fine." Leo groaned as he tried to sit up. Then he flopped back in the grass.

"It is so like you to not admit that you're hurt." I glanced behind me to Laurie and the fae around him. "You knew how fae here felt about demons, and you just made it ten times worse. Why would this city want to form an alliance with someone who attacked their prince?"

"Because without me they have nothing!"

"That's not true."

"Yes, it is. They're willing to sell off their princess to make sure I don't leave them stranded. They have no organization, and they're blind to reality. Without me, they don't stand a chance."

"And they should trust that you're going to help them? How can any of them trust you now? How can they be certain that you're not going to just abandon them because they aren't good enough?"

Leo finally sat up. "Wait, what did you just say?"

Shit.

What was I even saying?

If I stood there for another second, I was worried I wasn't going to be able to hold back the tears starting to sting the corners of my eyes. Instead, I turned away and started to fly back to my room when I saw Laurie. He was on his feet already since he'd been healed but still draped over a fae who was holding him up.

When he saw me, he cocked his head and grinned. "Did I win?"

"Don't give me that smirk."

"And don't you look at me like that. I didn't start this."

"But you participated. You're the prince of Rowan, Laurie."

He sighed. "I know. What do they say, that love makes idiots of us all?"

Unlike him, I wasn't smiling. Without another word, I turned and started to walk away, but then I felt Laurie's hand on my arm.

"Hey," he said when I turned around. Laurie had stumbled closer to me, and he wasn't grinning anymore. "Are you completely sure this isn't what you want? Are you sure I'm not..."

No matter what we did, it felt like the universe was continuing to torture us both.

"I'm so sorry. You already know the answer to that."

"Yeah." He swallowed. "I figured you'd say that. I'm... sorry. I'll talk to my dad."

"Do it tonight."

21

VERA

As I waited for Mia outside the palace, I watched the early-morning stars above me, thousands of tiny lights flickering in the black sky. Were these the same stars I'd stared at when I lived on Alliance Island? Were there still enslaved fae there staring at them right now, just like I was doing here in Rowan?

Ever since the veil came down, I'd kept my focus on protecting the fae here, but I couldn't forget the fae that were slaves across the ocean. I'd fix things here first, I promised the stars, then I'd help the rest. No matter what.

"Vera?" When I turned around, Mia was waiting for me. We were both dressed in comfortable clothes, and judging by the way she rubbed her eyes, it seemed like she could use a few more hours of sleep just like me. But for what I'd planned, we might need all day, and I was grateful she'd shown up at all. Mia had taken a while to be convinced to meet me, and after what happened between Leo and Laurie last night, I didn't want their help. At least not yet.

"You ready?" I asked her.

"Yeah. Are you sure you want to do this?"

I nodded.

Mia's blue wings fluttered behind her. "And just to double-check, you're not, you know, mad at me? My father is an idiot. You know I had no part in—"

I held up a hand to stop her. "Of course not. I was never mad at you, Mia. I was frustrated with those two idiots who thought that a public brawl last night was a good way to settle things."

"It's my dumb father's fault. I have no idea what the old man was even thinking by making an announcement like that. He must be out of his damn mind. You better believe he got an earful from me last night. And Victor, well, when he heard—"

I raised an eyebrow.

"Let's just say maybe the only good thing to come from last night was it seemed to give him a little push. I think we're, like, dating now? But that's not what matters right now. You really want to go down there? There's no guarantee that Selena's going to tell us anything."

"I know. Were you able to get what I asked?"

"Of course I was. Took me all night, so you owe me." Mia handed me a small bag. I glanced inside, and it looked like everything I might need was there.

"Then let's go."

After the flight down to the palace dungeon, it didn't take long for Mia to convince the guards to give us a moment alone with the prisoner. The cells lined a hallway lit by torches. Selena's cell looked like all the others, a small space with metal bars along the front. Even though it was early in the morning, she was awake, but she didn't bother standing or bowing to Mia. She sat on the floor of her cell as if waiting for us to speak first. Her wavy brown hair wasn't as polished or brushed as yesterday, but the way she stared at us made her seem just as proud and defiant as she had seemed in front of everyone yesterday.

I wasn't going to wait around for formalities.

"You said hunters were coming. Humans. Is that right?" I asked her.

"It is."

"When?" I asked.

"If they know the veil is down, it could be any moment."

"Why would you do this, Selena? Why would you bring humans here?" Mia asked. "What the hell were you thinking?"

Selena seemed unbothered, her face unflinching. "We are the gods of this world." As if it was the most normal thing in the world to say out loud. "Any fae who cannot survive against mere humans does not deserve to live in the world to come."

Mia knocked me to the side to get right up against the bars, her finger pointed right at Selena. "How dare you—"

"Mia." I placed a hand on her shoulder. I was mad too, but we hadn't accomplished what we were down here so early in the morning to do. "Let me ask you this, Selena. Why do you hate the fae so much?"

Selena scoffed. "I only hate cowards."

"And you think it's cowardly to stay behind the veil?"

"Yes."

"Then we actually agree on something. The prince and princess too. All of us want to go beyond the veil and help fae everywhere."

"I don't want to *help*, as you put it. I want to *crush* our enemies."

I understood that feeling. I'd felt it too back when I lived on Alliance. Back when I hated all humans except Henry. I remembered seeing them that night he took me out to an auction party, feeling disgusted at how they could live their lives as if fae weren't being bought and sold the next morning.

"Did you know that I'm an orphan like you?" I asked her.

Her eyes darted up to meet mine. "What?"

"I never knew my parents. I was taken to the fae dorms on Alliance Island when I was very young, and I lived there my whole life, waiting to be bought. Unlike you, I didn't have any special magical talent. Hell, I didn't even have wings until that stone forced them on me."

"Humans stole your childhood from you," she said.

"They did. And trust me, there was a time I wanted to make them pay. I won't lie and say I don't still think about it. But more than making them pay, I want to make sure that no other fae lives the way I did. That no other fae child stays up at night wondering if they'll have a cruel master. If they'll be raped. If they'll be killed. I hate the humans who enslaved me, but I also won't sit back and let fae be harmed, no matter who is doing it. Even if it's you."

I opened up the bag Mia had given me, taking out the file. I flipped through a couple of pages, reading over the details. "You grew up in an orphanage not far from the palace here, it looks like."

Selena sat up in her cell, scooting forward. "You researched me?"

"You're the official Keeper. Or were. It's not like these were hidden records." I thumbed through a few more pages. "From what I can tell, you were an exceptional talent, your magic manifesting at a very young age. No wonder you were recognized by the royal family. The king and queen took an interest in you quickly, and you moved through the ranks to become the youngest Keeper ever in Rowan. That's why I couldn't understand your anger, because by all accounts, it seemed like you have lived a very privileged life, at least compared to mine. That's why I had the princess dig a little deeper into your family. Your parents."

"They're dead."

"Are you sure?"

"What are you talking about? Of course I'm sure. They died when I was an infant. They were guarding the Willow Gate—"

"That's not true," Mia piped in.

"What?" Selena stood up, coming close to the bars. "What do you mean it's not true?"

"I have access to all the guard files, including their schedules and assignments. I'd never gone back this far in time, but someone over here asked me to, so I did." She gave me a wry smile. "I searched for their names, but I couldn't find them. You don't deserve it, but I stayed up for hours looking for their guard assignments. They don't exist."

"Of course they exist."

"No, really." I flipped to another page in the file. "From what we can tell, they were on an undercover mission in Vestia when they went missing. The official report said they were guarding the Gate to keep the story under wraps."

"An undercover mission? My parents..."

"Yes," said Mia. "I found the records myself. I could only access them because I'm the princess. It seems they were just as talented as you with magic and were some of the elite selected for information-gathering missions outside Rowan. Since they didn't come back, they are officially marked as missing, and while you're right that it's possible that they're dead, it's not guaranteed."

"What are you saying?"

"I'm saying," I told Selena, "that if you give us more details about whatever plan you've concocted, about what the humans know and what they're planning, then I'll do everything in my power to find out what happened to your parents. I can get records from Vestia. If they were ever slaves, it will be easy to track since only nobles in Vestia can have slaves. If they were sold at some point, I'll get auction house records. I'm friends with important people there. I can't promise that you'll like what I find, but I can promise that I'll get you answers."

Selena was silent, and I could see the conflict in her eyes as she stared at the two of us.

"Why should I believe you?" she asked.

I was ready for that part.

"I have these wings, don't I? Don't they count for something? Didn't you tell everyone that they should be worshipping the ground I walk on because I've been blessed by some goddess queen? I'm not asking you to try to put the veil back up, but I'm asking you to help me give the fae of Rowan a fighting chance."

She still didn't say anything, and for a second I wondered if this gamble wasn't going to pay off. I had one more card to play, and it seemed like now was the time.

"If you won't tell us, then give us the name of someone who will. I know you're not working alone. I couldn't figure out how you knew what was happening in Vestia or why you'd have demon tech," I said, taking Selena's holo-watch out of the small bag. "But the only explanation is that you have a demon informant. I know someone is sneaking in counterfeit Syn too. Many have left Vestia recently, so all I need is a name and I can take it from there. Tell me who you're working with."

"It won't matter. Not now."

"It might," I insisted.

"It won't."

"If it doesn't matter, then it won't hurt to tell us."

Selena stared at us for a long time, but then she finally mumbled a name. Suddenly my chest felt ten times heavier. It was like there was a weight pressing on my body, my heart wildly thrashing against it. I grabbed one of the bars of her cell, the metal crunching beneath my hand. I couldn't have heard her right. There was no way, right? Surely not...

"Are you fucking kidding me?" Mia yelled, her voice bringing me back to reality.

"Why?"

That was the only word I could think to say.

"Before the prince arrived, I didn't think there was another way to get rid of the veil other than by using demon tech," Selena said. "When the former demon king offered his assistance, it seemed a logical choice."

"Knowing that he hates fae?" Mia demanded, her blue wings rapidly fluttering behind her. "Knowing that he wants us all dead?"

"A fae who cannot defeat a demon doesn't deserve to survive."

"Oh, shut up!" Mia shouted back at her. "You are even more of a traitor than I thought."

"And you've been communicating with him, all this time?" I asked her.

"Yes."

"So he knows Leo is here. He knows I am here. He knows..." My head was spinning. "We have to go," I said to Mia. "Now."

Without another word, both of us were flying down the hallway as quickly as we could.

"Vera!" Selena called out my name.

I landed, looking over my shoulder toward her cell.

All I could see was Selena's hand wrapped around the metal bar that I'd crushed. "Go to the eastern edge of Rowan. I suspect that's where he's sent the first group."

22

______

LEO

"Are we all going to pretend like last night didn't happen or...?"

Even if we didn't talk about it, my still-sore wings from when I'd bounced off Vera's barrier were a constant reminder. I didn't need Rand to bring it up though.

"I am barely over my hangover," Rand added, picking up the cup of coffee in front of him. "So I'm fine if we avoid the topic of last night altogether."

I grunted in agreement. "Then it's settled."

The top buttons of Rand's shirt were undone, and as he leaned over the table, I could see some kind of new mark on his collarbone. Black ink. Was that writing?

"Is that a tattoo?" I asked him.

"I thought we were pretending like last night didn't happen."

I rubbed my eyes in frustration. I'd hardly slept last night, and then when I woke up, Vera was nowhere to be found. "This is such a disaster. I insulted the fae king by turning down his daughter, fought the fae prince in front of everyone, pissed off Vera, and you inexplicably got a tattoo."

"I've had worse nights."

"I haven't."

"What about that time when we were ten and accidentally locked ourselves in the bio-storage unit in the palace lab overnight?" Rand shivered at the memory.

"Thank you for that pleasant reminder. I wasn't sure I'd ever forget that smell. But this is different."

"Well, pull it together, because it's time to be a leader. With everything going on, you need to convince Vera not to do something stupid. That's why you're here sulking, isn't it? You guys didn't kiss and make up last night?"

"We did, but then she wasn't there this morning. I'm sure I'll see her later, but it was too depressing to stay in bed."

"So what you're trying to say is that waiting for someone to come back sucks, right?" Rand asked as he sipped his coffee.

"Shut up."

"You two really are a perfect match, you know. She's just like you, willing to do something totally dumb because she thinks it's right."

"You got drunk and got a tattoo, so I don't think you get to lecture me on this."

"Yes, I do. That's sort of my job."

"Vera and I were on the right path, but now she doesn't trust me at all."

"Can you blame her? You were literally rolling around in the dirt in a fist fight with another guy. Not your finest moment, I have to say."

"Shouldn't that show her how serious I am about her?"

"Or it shows her that you're unreliable."

I hung my head, the truth of it sinking in. "I need to do something to get her to trust me again."

"Good luck with that because I don't even trust you right now."

"I don't trust myself either."

Rand groaned and stood up before coming over to stand in front of me. "Okay, time for tough love."

"Maybe I don't deserve her love."

"Holy shit." Rand exhaled loudly and ran both his hands through his hair. "This is too much. You are the prince of the entire fucking demon kingdom. Quit acting like a little bitch and get your shit together."

I stared up at him sharply. "The fuck?"

"I didn't fly all this way to hear you complain about not being good enough. If you're not good enough for something, the rest of us definitely aren't either, so get it together. Be the prince Vera needs and deserves, and then, for the love of the gods, shut the fuck up about it."

I stared at him in silence for a moment, then nodded. "You're right."

"Of course I'm right."

"I have to do better."

"Yes, exactly."

"I need to communicate with her better."

"That's what I've been saying."

"So that when we go home I can protect her."

"Wait, no. Full stop. That's not what I meant. See, this is part of the problem. Quit looking at her like a delicate flower to protect. Vera is a whole damn forest, Leo, not one frail little flower."

"You think she's a forest?"

"Uh, yeah. Have you paid attention to her recently?"

"Yes, I have." I squinted up at him. "Have you?"

"Whoa, don't give me that look. I didn't mean it like that."

He was right though, and Rand's words gave me a sickening feeling at the realization that I had been trying to protect her like she could hurt herself at any step. I had thought that we'd made progress, but for every step forward, it felt like we were taking several steps back, mostly of my own doing. It wasn't that I needed her to trust me; I was the one who needed to trust *her*.

Every time we were together, I could see it in her face: the disappointment, the suspicion. She was doubting herself in part because I was doubting her.

How could I win back that trust?

How could I get her to understand that I knew how amazing she was?

"Prince or not, I'm literally going to murder you if you whine one more time about your love life. You need to focus on being a leader and not on all this petty bullshit."

"A leader? For who? I'm not leading Vestia, and with the way things are going since I arrived, I'm certainly not leading here."

"You're right, for once. That's why I have something for you."

Rand grabbed his bag, rustled in it for a second, and then pulled out something I hadn't seen in months. I was glad I hadn't seen it in months. I didn't want to see it ever again.

He held out the crown to me, waiting for me to take it.

"I don't want that," I told him, shaking my head.

"Leo. Take the damn crown. It's time to lead."

"I said that I don't want it. I never have. Those rubies…"

I stared at the red gems, the Hellfire rubies that lined the crown. They were larger versions of the stone on my ring. My thumb rubbing against the gold band on my finger, I remembered the vision of my mother. What would she think about everything that had happened? She'd told me that I didn't always need to be focused on protecting Vera, but I'd basically done the opposite.

Rand placed the crown on the table in front of me, his head tilting as he examined it. "I never really liked the crown myself either. The design is too over the top. Not to mention the whole fae-heart thing. So macabre."

"I can't believe you even brought that thing here. The fae hate my ring enough as is, but that crown?" I leaned forward to look at it closer. Each one of these rubies had been created from the hearts of how many fae? How much pain and sadness was represented in these gems? I ran my fingers over a few of the stones, careful not to let them linger for longer than a second, and shivered. "This crown is unforgivable."

"It represents demon power."

"Demon oppression. So many lives ended early, and for what? So many lives I couldn't save."

Rand sat down next to me. His voice was quieter. "You weren't alive to save them, Leo."

"And now? How can I save them now?"

We heard a knock on the door before Rand could answer. It was a messenger with an envelope for me. Zell had completed the analysis of the Dust Vera and Mia saw the men using at the club. According to Zell's letter, it was real Dust—that was true—hidden under the guise of Syn's packaging, but there was something else.

I was familiar enough with Dust to know that components had been added to this sample. Components I'd only seen come up when analyzing my own blood after my father injected me with the serum designed to eliminate my fae genes. I read over Zell's report quickly, my stomach turning into knots when I thought what this might imply.

"Not the news you wanted?" Rand asked.

"Not at all. I need time to think."

I wasn't given much time, because Rand's door opened and Rob came flying in.

Aside from the first day Rob came to my mansion as a slave, I'd never seen his face this pale.

"Thank the gods you're here, Rand. Leo? I didn't expect you to be here," Rob said. "Come quickly. The princess just returned with her team from a scouting mission. They're in the courtyard. It's not good."

Rand was already up and stalking toward the door. "If anyone fucked with that cute little princess, they're going to learn a new definition of pain."

I moved to join Rand, and as I passed Rob, he caught my arm. Something on his wrist caught my eye. "Is that a tattoo?" But Rob's face was blank, as if I hadn't said anything at all. "Rob. It's nothing to be embarrassed about. I have plenty of them."

"No, it's not that. Leo, I tried to find you first. I only happened to see the scouts coming back because I was on my way here, but..."

"Rob. What is it? Just say it."

"They ran into hunters. Humans, already on their way to Rowan."

"Already?"

"Yes. Leo, Vera was with the fae."

• • •

WHEN I GOT THERE, she was sitting beside one of the fae soldiers, her eyes closed, one hand on his head. Vera was okay. My relief quickly dissolved into irritation. I knew from the way Vera's skin sparkled that she was linking with him. As if whoever the hell that was deserved her touch. Heart thumping in frustration, I flew over, landing with a thud beside her.

"What were you thinking?"

"We can talk in a second," she said.

"We can talk right now."

With a sigh, she stood up. I knew from the way her eyes looked that she was tired, probably from linking with these stupid, undeserving fae. She crossed her arms over her chest and stood there, waiting for me to say something.

"Are you okay?" I asked her.

"I'm fine. Didn't you get my message?"

"Message? No. You didn't leave me a message."

"Yes, I did. I sent one after I talked to Selena."

"You talked to Selena? Vera, what's going on? I was with Rand, so I didn't get any message. Your wings," I said, looking over her shoulder. "Are you sure you're okay?"

"I'm fine," she repeated. "There's a bigger problem."

"Why did you go out with them?"

"Can you just listen to me for a moment? It was a good thing I did. I was one of the few who was still able to use magic."

I wrapped a hand around her arm, pulling her closer to me so I could see it better. "Where did this come from?"

"It's just a bruise, probably from carrying one of them," she said, gesturing to the other fae. Then she looked off in the distance, thinking. "Are you familiar with magic-dampening devices? They must have used something we couldn't see. That's the only explanation I can think of for why—"

I didn't care about any of that.

"Are you trying to kill yourself to prove something to me?"

"Leo, what? Prove something? I'm trying to talk to you, and you're acting crazy."

We heard Rand call for us, both of us turning our heads to look in his direction.

"Good. He's here too," she said. "Since you didn't get my message, we can talk about this together."

"Are you listening to me?"

Vera stopped walking, facing me head on. "I am listening, Leo. I'm listening to you and everyone else, and then I'm making my own decisions."

"Even if those decisions end with you being injured? Or worse?"

"That's why I trained with Mia. It's why I trained with you too. Or were all those lessons just for fun?"

"You know that's not the case."

"Leo. I have been given this huge responsibility. I owe it to Rowan to learn how to use this magic if I'm going to help anyone. Mia told me they were going scouting, and I thought I could help. I can't just sit around here and do nothing. I thought you of all people would understand that."

"You don't owe them shit."

"I do though. Whether I like it or not, I'm the one responsible for the veil coming down. I won't be able to live with myself if I don't do everything I can to help with the consequences. That's who I am. It's who I've always been."

Damn it.

I knew when she looked at me like that I wasn't going to be able to convince her to see my side.

Rand put a hand on my shoulder. "Leo, come listen to the princess. You need to hear this."

"Human hunters," Mia told us, once we were alone. "Spotted pretty far from the border. Took us all morning to fly there, but then as soon as we saw them, something went wrong. For almost everyone, flying was difficult. I thought they were just tired, but then they started dropping and could hardly stand. When I ordered them to use their magic, I was one of the few who could do anything at all. Everyone else was almost powerless and only able to use the smallest amount. They must have had some kind of weapon that could suppress our abilities at a distance."

My mind started racing with the possibilities. Did a weapon like that exist? I knew about the suppression cuffs and collars, but they didn't work from far away; the fae had to be wearing them. Somehow the humans had managed to immobilize most of this group without coming in contact with them. How?

"After that, my priority was to get everyone out of there. Once I knew that we wouldn't be able to overpower them in combat, I called for the retreat. Those of us able to still use magic carried the rest back." Mia cursed as she stretched her back. If she was sore from carrying other fae, Vera must be too.

"Thankfully, the humans are moving on foot," she said. "This gives us a little time before they'll get here, but not much. Vera... Have you told him?"

Vera let out a breath and looked up at me. "Since you didn't get my message, I'll tell you now. Selena was working with your father. He's coordinating all of this."

What?

Rand started to speak, but Vera held up her hand. "That's really all the info I have," she said. "Selena admitted that she thought his demon tech could take down the veil, that was why they were working together. But now he's running the show. I don't know where he is, but... Leo, are you okay?"

No.

I wasn't.

He had even followed me here?

In some ways, it felt like the puzzle pieces were clicking together. Her holo-watch, the way she knew who I was, all of it.

I hadn't really believed that the old bastard would fly off into the sunset and never be heard from again, had I?

Vera was watching me. Everyone was watching me, waiting for my reaction.

"It doesn't change anything," I finally said. "Whatever he throws at us, we'll throw right back."

Vera's face wrinkled in that way she did when she was thinking. "Those two." She pointed at two of the guys, one with green and one with bright yellow wings. "They were at the club the other night."

"And? Vera, why does that matter?"

"I'm not sure if it does, but it's weird." Vera rushed over to them. "Hey. You. When's the last time you took Syn?"

These fae were the ones taking the tainted Dust, the sample I'd just read the report about.

"This is important," I said to him. "When was it?"

"I... I don't know?" the guy stammered.

A stern look from me had him changing his mind.

"Okay. Um... I guess this morning? Before we left. I thought it would help."

Vera ran over to the other guy. "And you?"

"This morning too."

"When I'm fully healed, I am kicking everyone's ass and you're all running laps until your legs fall off!" Mia shouted from where she sat on the ground.

"Do you still have any of it left?" Vera asked him.

"Maybe a little."

"Let me see it. Who else took it?"

"I shared it with most of the guys here," he said, sheepishly gesturing to the rest of the injured fae. "We've never seen real combat, Captain. We... we... were cowards."

Instead of yelling at him, Mia sighed. "Give him what you have," she ordered.

He dug into the pocket of his jacket and pulled out a vial, then handed it to me.

Once I took off the lid and saw the powder inside, I knew immediately from the color that this wasn't Syn. It looked like regular Dust, but it was inside my packaging. Just like the other sample.

"Get this to Zell and Marcus immediately. Have them compare it to what we saw before."

"Some sneaky bastard is selling counterfeit product," Rand said.

"Making them think they're taking a synthetic product when it's actually fae blood. Disgusting."

"I agree, but... There's something else here. It's not normal Dust either."

The demon tech. The fake Syn. Fae with reduced magic. There was only one explanation, really, one I'd been trying to avoid. Now that I knew my father was involved, it all made sense. This was his doing.

"Captain! There's been another report of a sighting to the north. More humans. They're not at the border yet, but they will be soon."

"If they're able to use a magic dampener on the city as a whole, and they're coming from multiple directions, we're going to need a new plan," Mia said. "Everyone is at risk."

"Do we evacuate, Princess?" one guard asked.

"I need to speak with my father."

"If only the veil was still there to protect us," another mumbled.

What a fucking moron. I was about to call him that to his face when I saw Vera. She stood still, very still, and it was as if I could see the wheels in her head turning. She made some excuse about going to her room to rest and then was gone.

She was about to do something stupid.

And I was too.

"Rand. I need that crown."

Back in his room, Rand took the crown from his bag and held it out to me. "I'm glad you've finally understood. It makes sense that seeing the consequences for the fae like that would lead you to reconsider."

I started unbuckling my belt.

"What the hell are you doing?" Rand took a few steps back, holding the crown up to cover his eyes.

"Give me that." I took the crown and looped my belt through it, attaching it quickly without having to touch it for more than a second. After I secured my belt again, the crown hung against my hip; it was closer than I preferred, but at least I wouldn't have to wear it. Not yet.

Rand was still staring at me with his mouth agape. "That's not exactly how I pictured you with the crown, but okay. This works. I think?"

"Weird shit happens when I touch it, so this will have to do for now." I started walking toward his door. "You've sent word to Vestia about what is happening?"

"Yes. That's the first thing I did."

"And the wolves are staying in their dens and out of this mess?"

"Yes, from recent reports, but you never know if—"

"And you will communicate all this to the fae king and queen?"

"Of course I will. Leo, stop!"

I didn't stop, taking long strides down the hallway and not waiting for him to catch up even though he did.

"I'm not surprised. I knew I could trust you to take it from here. The general knows what to do if you need advice. When all this is over, the two of you need to have a long talk."

Rand flew around to get in front of me and grabbed my shoulders. "Stop it. Why won't you listen to me for just a second? Where are you going?"

"I'm sorry you won't have this crown to help you, because I think I need it, but I'm sure you'll figure something out."

"You're talking like you won't see me again."

"I might not."

"Vestia needs its king, Leo."

"Good thing they'll have one then."

"What?"

"Congratulations, Rand. You're the new king."

"What?" he asked again.

"You heard me."

"No, I don't think I did. I heard words, but they were nonsense."

"I'm abdicating. All of it. That was always the plan anyway, right? Before all this mess? You'll be better at being king than me anyway."

"No. You can't abdicate now. Not like this. The world is this close to burning to the ground, Leo."

"The world can burn all it wants. As long as I'm with Vera, I don't care."

"What? This isn't the Leo I know. The Leo I know puts everything ahead of his own desires. The Leo I know—"

"—has changed. Now Vera needs me. Fuck everything else."

I kept walking, with Rand following close behind as I made my way out of the palace.

"Even if I didn't think you were possessed by some weird fae magic right now, it still doesn't work like this. You can't just say that I'm king and that's that."

I exhaled loudly and finally stopped long enough to tap him on the head. "By the power vested in me by something somewhere, I now pronounce you king. You may kiss the crown. Later, if I bring it back."

"Leo!"

"Sorry, Rand." I pushed open the door and leaped into the air. "I'm trusting Vera for once," I called down to him. "Wasn't that what you told me to do?"

Rand sighed loudly. "Why couldn't you just get a tattoo of her name like a normal demon?"

I waved and kept flying. This was probably the heaviest decision I'd ever made, but for some reason I felt light as air. I had to catch up with her. I had to let her know that I supported her, even if I disagreed with her. That I was going to be there for her, always, no matter what.

Vera. I get it now.

23

———

VERA

I wasn't at all surprised to see Leo standing in my doorway. I'd just finished changing clothes when he came in, not even bothering to knock. He leaned against the frame, his wings and body taking up almost all the space.

"If you're here to stop me, don't bother," I told him.

"I'm not here to stop you."

"Good, because I've made up my mind. I'm going back to the cave."

"I know."

"I'm the only one who can put the power back into the stone. I have to try."

"Okay."

"Stop being so agreeable!"

Leo crossed his arms over his chest and stared down at me with those intense silver eyes. "Do you want me to argue with you? Slam this door shut and force you to stay here? Or better yet, throw you over my shoulder and take you home with me?"

"No, not exactly..."

"I didn't think so. Here's the thing. If you're going to do something crazy, I want to do it too. I'm not stopping you; I'm joining you. Is that okay with you?"

He was actually asking. The way he was acting was weird enough, but him asking for permission to go with me was even weirder. When was the last time Leo had asked for permission for anything? Against my own pride, I had to admit that I was scared of doing this alone, and having him nearby did make me feel safer.

"Fine. But don't slow me down. And why is your crown hanging from your belt?"

Leo shrugged. "Why not?"

"We need to be careful," I told him when we made it to the dungeon under the palace. "Any hunters we see may have technology that can suppress magic. If they use it, we might not be able to fly."

"You don't have to worry about that," Leo whispered back.

"Why not?"

"It was the Dust. That Dust was tainted. I had Marcus and Zell take a look at it. I suspect it's a lesser version of the serum my father used on me. Since the effects didn't happen immediately after taking it, I'm assuming it has a delayed reaction, possibly triggered by extreme magic use."

"So if Mia's guards were trying to fly fast or power up, it would lessen their abilities."

"That's my best guess," Leo said. "They're still running some tests."

"Why use your packaging?"

"To get it in the hands of more fae. So fae would take it thinking they weren't using actual fae blood."

"And then, when hunters attacked, and fae tried to fight back..."

"They wouldn't be able to. Vera, we need to get to the stone. We're going to have to move fast."

So we did. Leo remembered where to go, at least until we got to a large open area with several passages leading off it. Some of the ceiling had caved in, leaving huge boulders around the space. One passage was completely blocked, but the others looked open.

"You two thought you could save the city without me?" A voice echoed in the open room.

Laurie walked out from behind one of the big rocks.

"We don't need an escort," Leo grumbled at the sight of him.

"But it won't hurt to have a fae guide, right? Some of our scouts spotted humans near the grotto. That means they're already in these passages. You have to avoid them to get through these tunnels again, and I can help."

Leo and I exchanged a glance. It wasn't like there was much we could do, and having him there wouldn't hurt.

"Both hallways will take us to the grotto," Laurie said. "We could go either way. Sure wish I knew which one had the bad guys in it."

"I think there's one coming," Leo whispered. "No, more than one."

"How did they get here so fast?" I asked.

"They knew where to go. Hide, quick."

The three of us scrambled behind one of the rocks, listening. Leo peered around the side and then came back.

"Human hunters. High as hell on Dust from what I can see. They're carrying bows and a bunch of arrows."

"Let's kick their asses," Laurie whispered back.

"Hell yeah!" I agreed with this plan.

"And attract more of them? No."

"Then what do you propose?" I asked him.

"We do this quietly, and we don't draw attention to ourselves. I'll go this way," Leo said, pointing to the right. Then he gestured in the opposite direction. "Laurie, you go that way."

"Don't tell me what to do."

"I don't like us splitting up," I told them.

"Listen closely," Leo whispered. "Vera, the two of us will fly in opposite directions. Since they can't follow us both, you need to hide here and then go in the direction that takes you away from the hunters. If they go after him, come with me, and if they come after me, go with him."

"What if that means…" I couldn't even bring myself to say it, but Leo understood.

"Even if it means you're running away from me," he said. "If we stay here, all three of us could be shot. We need to give ourselves the best possible chance to get you to the stone."

"I hate to admit it, but Leo's right." Laurie nodded.

Logically, I knew this was a good plan. If a group of hunters was coming after us, splitting up gave us the best chance to escape, but that didn't guarantee that the one to escape would be Leo or Laurie. Emotionally this felt like the worst plan imaginable.

"No," I said.

"It's the best option."

"Bullshit!" I hissed, but Leo put a hand over my mouth.

"They're close," he whispered. "Vera, stay here until you see who he goes after. Ready?"

Laurie smirked. "Born ready."

When I peered around the corner, I saw the first one. A big guy, a human, tall with huge shoulders and a threatening walk. His entire body seemed to radiate with heat, no doubt from the Dust he'd taken. The hunter had a bow in his hand, a full quiver of suppression arrows across his back. As soon as he saw Leo and Laurie moving, he pulled out an arrow and aimed as he ran toward him.

He had picked Laurie.

I wanted to yell, scream, do *something* to tell Laurie that this asshole was coming for him, but that would have given away my location and possibly Leo's as well. But Laurie wasn't looking, and if he didn't turn around and was shot by this guy, when I could have done something…

"Behind you!" I shouted.

At the sound of my voice, Laurie spun around in the air, just in time to dodge an arrow. He shot me a surprised glance and then flew back headfirst, ramming his shoulder into the hunter's chest and knocking him over before he could nock another arrow.

"Vera, come on," Leo said behind me.

"Shouldn't we help?"

"Go on! I've got this!" Laurie shouted at us, delivering a punch to the side of the guy's face. "See?" he said, smiling back at us.

But the hunter used that momentary break to flip Laurie over and slam him onto the ground.

"Laurie!"

I kept yelling his name as the hunter delivered punch after punch, but Leo's arm was around my waist, pulling me away no matter how much I screamed. I could barely see Laurie over Leo's shoulder. All I could see was a whirl of blue and white, receding into the distance. Holding me in his arms, Leo flew, faster than I'd ever seen him fly, his wings moving us through the passageway at an insane speed.

"We should go back!"

"No time. Have some faith in the guy. He is the prince of Rowan, right? If one little hunter is enough to take him down, he doesn't deserve the title. Besides, we have our own job. Are you ready for your part?"

I swallowed. It didn't matter if I was ready.

Even though we were being chased by humans who wanted to kill us, Leo smiled at me, and suddenly I thought that maybe we had a chance after all.

"You're not alone, Vera. We do this together."

Eventually he put me down, and we followed the trails of steam to the cave but stopped outside the entrance when we heard voices, flattening ourselves against the wall.

"Stay here," Leo said. "I'll go check it out."

Using his wings as cover to shroud himself in darkness, Leo stayed in the shadows as he moved down the passageway. My heart thumped in my chest and echoed all the way up to my ears as I watched him sneak closer, hoping to any god or fairy queen or anyone who would listen that no one would see him.

"More hunters," Leo whispered to me when he came back. "Maybe twenty."

"That's too many. Even for us. There are probably more in the grotto, especially if they know where we're heading."

Had we made it all this way for nothing?

Was Laurie okay?

Would we be okay?

Would I be able to do this after all?

Time was ticking.

"Vera." Leo reached for my mouth, wiping his thumb across my bottom lip. "We have options. We're not powerless here."

When he took his hand away, his eyes were wide, his mouth parted slightly, and I saw the red streak of blood staining his thumb. I must have bitten my lip while we waited.

"I don't know when I did that," I told him, touching my lips. They felt raw and cracked from where I must have been chewing on them.

I should have known that Leo wasn't listening at all.

His pupils blown wide, chest heaving as he sucked in air, Leo knocked my hand away and wrapped an arm around my waist, pulling me hard against him.

We might have been mere feet away from people who surely wanted us dead, but right then, when his lips smashed against mine, with my fingers raking through his dark hair, curly from the humid air, his kiss felt like lightning shooting straight through me.

Leo had spent so long practicing how to take in my magic, bit by bit, so that a mere touch didn't overwhelm us both, but now all restraint vanished. I knew he was using this kiss to get a boost of power, that was obvious, but that was okay. We both needed as much power as we could muster. A kiss like this didn't drain me like it used to when we first met; instead, kissing Leo gave me energy. My body felt like a struck match, burning bright.

Remembering where we were and why we were there, I put a hand on his chest to stop him. Leo was glowing, a deep, dark red that shone through the mist.

He smirked down at me. "You ready?" he whispered.

I nodded.

"Let's go save Rowan."

24

VERA

Swatting away the steam as we entered the cave, suddenly I was shoved to the side. Before I could hit the stone wall, I held my hands out to brace myself for the impact, but I didn't fall. Leo had caught me, or at least that's what I assumed happened, until I heard a snap.

My hands immediately went to my throat, trying to rip off the metal that had been circled around my neck. But I wasn't strong enough. I couldn't use my magic, which meant—

A suppression collar.

The humans had brought these with them?

As I struggled to pull off the collar, a big arm looped around my waist and I was yanked into the air. As we flew up into the rising steam with me pressed against his chest, I knew this wasn't a human, and it wasn't Leo, which meant...

Oh fuck.

"Leo!" I shouted, but a hand clamped over my mouth.

"It seems the little insect got wings after all." A dark chuckle rumbled in the demon king's chest.

If I'd seen Leo's father coming, I would have been able to create a barrier, but now all I could do was thrash in his arms and try to summon any bit of magic that might work against the suppression collar. But nothing did.

"Vera!" I heard Leo shout, and then there he was, zooming through the steam right toward us. His father held me tight in front of him as he flew backward, and Leo was forced to stop so that he wouldn't ram straight into me.

The fog from the water danced in the dense, hot air all around us, and the two demons hovered in the grotto. In front of me, Leo's black wings fanned back and forth, his thick tail swishing beneath him.

"Back up, boy."

"I'm not a boy." Leo's deep voice rumbled off the walls of the cave. "Let her go."

"That's right. You're a prince, which is why you have no business with an insect like this. Even if this insect grew wings."

Leo scoffed. "It's time for you to leave the fae alone. All fae. You already ran away from Vestia with your tail between your legs. Do I have to make you do it again?"

"You are the one who ran away, son. Ran away from your destiny because of a woman." He sneered, tightening his hand over my mouth as I struggled against him. "You still haven't had your coronation, and now I see you here with the Hellfire Crown dangling from your waist like a toy. Not that it will help you protect her. Insects aren't meant to be protected, they're meant to be squashed beneath your boot."

"Vera!"

I couldn't respond. The demon wasn't letting go of my face.

"They're not worth it, Leo. Their intelligence is no match for ours. Even that fae witch was too easy to manipulate, her followers too eager to help. Once she lowered the barrier around the city, everything else went according to plan. She was a useful tool, but even tools outlast their usefulness."

I kicked him as hard as I could, and for the briefest of seconds he relaxed his hold on my mouth.

"Shut up," I managed to croak.

Leo used the opportunity to dart toward me, but just as quickly his father flew us up higher into the cave.

"I just want to talk to you," the demon called out to Leo. "Father to son."

"I have nothing to say to you," Leo growled before coming straight for us again.

I shrieked as his father held me out in front of him, forcing Leo to dodge to the side again.

The demon king landed on the side of the pool, the steam wafting away from us when we hit the ground. Before I could shout, the demon king's large hand closed around the back of my neck and yanked it to the side, ripping off the collar and exposing my neck to him.

The arm around my waist was gone, and I felt something cold on my skin. It wasn't another collar. No, not this time. This time I could see the edges of holo-blade in his hand.

"I will kill you myself if you hurt her!" Leo yelled.

"I just want to know what her blood tastes like. I tried that sample the human brought me all those months ago. It was exquisite. You've already sampled her today, Leo. I can tell by the red glow that surrounds you."

In his hand I could see a holo-blade form. *No, no, no.* I needed all my magic for the Keeper Stone. I glanced up toward the stone, still high above my head and nestled into the wall of the cave. I didn't need this bastard to take even a drop of it.

"Don't touch me," I growled.

"Bold words for the position you're in right now. Have your pretty wings given you confidence? Have they increased your magic? Tell me what I'm about to experience."

"Fuck off," I spat back, and Leo lurched toward us.

"Stay where you are," his father demanded, backing up with me still pressed against him. We were at the very edge of the pool. Only a few more steps, and we'd be in the water.

Now that the collar was gone, once he cut me, it would only be a matter of time before the demon king would touch my blood and his own abilities would be boosted, just like Leo's.

"Vera. It's going to be okay," Leo said, and the confidence in his voice helped me relax, just a little.

"Don't lie to her. I'll bleed her dry just like all the fae before her. Just like all the fae of this cursed city."

"No. Your vision of a world without fae will never come to pass. Vera and I are proof of that. The world has changed, and there is no place for your views in it."

"That's where you're wrong. Without their precious veil, these self-righteous insects will be no more. Didn't you see how easy it was to take this one?" the demon king asked, nodding to me. "They don't stand a chance."

Despite the angle of my neck, I tried to look to Leo, and when I caught his eyes, I could see the fury inside them. Fury, but as he watched me, there was something else. Something akin to pride.

"They're stronger than you think."

Damn right I was.

Before his father had another chance to speak, I took advantage of no longer wearing the collar to create a barrier around me, and then used the heel of my foot to kick while at the same time slamming my hand against his face. The surprise attack knocked him back a step toward the water, enough for him to let go and for me to scramble away.

"Vera!" Leo yelled as I ran toward him.

He caught me in his arms, holding me tightly.

Enraged, the demon king's voice rumbled like thunder off the walls of the cave. "This is it then? This is your decision? To be one of them? Because you have to choose, Leo. Are you demon or are you fae?"

None of us saw the flash of swirling blue and white zipping through the air until he was right above us. None of us saw the sharp arrows in Laurie's hands until they were pointed right at the old demon's throat, until Laurie was right there, yelling.

"He's both, asshole!"

The world around us seemed to move in slow motion as the mist of the cave parted, allowing us to see the arrows sink into the flesh of the old demon's neck. He staggered back, with Laurie tumbling over him, both of them falling into the pool behind him. As I shouted Laurie's name, Leo leaped into the water as well, a giant splash of black wings, only to emerge seconds later, shooting up and out with Laurie draped over his shoulder.

"Is he okay?" I ran to his side as he placed Laurie down on the ground. "And your father..." I looked back at the pool.

Laurie coughed, water and blood spitting out of his mouth. He tried sitting up but fell back on the ground.

My eyes quickly scanned his body. "Laurie, you... you are..." I yanked up his shirt, gasping when I saw several gaping wounds, blood pooling in each. It looked bad. Really bad. He was a mess of blood and ripped skin, obvious tears from the arrows the hunters had brought with them, but I couldn't tell how deep any of his injuries were. I had no way of knowing if they'd punctured any organs. "What did they do to you?"

"You should see the other guys." He groaned under my touch before his whole body was racked with coughs. "Leo—"

When I turned to Leo, he was staring at the pool; the small ripples from the waterfall were the only movement we could see. It was true. The demon king was dead. I reached over, taking Leo's hand in mine.

"There was no other end," Leo said.

"I saw the blade..." Laurie coughed. "He hurt... so many. Including both... of you."

"Don't talk." I put my hands on the biggest gash on his stomach. "I'll link with you."

"No." He shook his head and coughed again. "Don't. If you link with me, you won't have enough power to revive the Stone."

"Then you heal him, Leo." I looked over my shoulder and up at him, but Leo's expression was unreadable as he stared down at Laurie. "I'll go to the Stone, and you stay here with Laurie."

"No." Leo placed a hand on my shoulder. "Vera, if you try to fix the stone on your own, you could be killed. That's why I came here with you."

"I'll just have to do it on my own then."

"Vera..." Laurie closed his eyes and took a deep breath. "Stop being you for like... a second."

"What?"

"I love your stubbornness, but... right now..." He took another deep breath. "Go fix the damn stone."

I heard shouts near the entrance of the cave. More hunters. When I looked back to Laurie, he hadn't opened his eyes.

"Vera." This time it was Leo, his hand gripping my shoulder.

"Laurie?"

He didn't answer.

"Laurie?"

No.

No.

No.

"Laurie." I called his name again, but he didn't move. "Laurie!"

"We'll come back as soon as we do this." Leo's voice was calm but firm.

Unable to take my eyes off Laurie, I didn't realize what was happening as Leo took my arm and guided me to my feet. Was he breathing? Was he asleep?

"But Leo—"

Leo spun me to face him. "We have a job to do. You're going to save this city, and then we'll save him. Together. Okay?" He didn't wait for my answer. "I need you to focus," Leo said as he held me close.

Wrapping his arms around me, we soared into the air, Laurie lying on the floor of the cave, becoming smaller and smaller until he disappeared entirely in the steam.

The ledge beside the Stone hadn't broken away, and Leo landed there, turning me around in his arms to face the rock in front of us.

"You can do this," he said. "I know you can."

I had to. And I had to do it quickly.

I stared at the rock, my mind blank. Now that it wasn't glowing, it just looked like a regular rock. What the hell was I supposed to do? Using my magic was one thing, but putting magic into something was completely different.

"Do you know what you're doing?" Leo asked, as if he knew what I was thinking.

"Not at all."

When the Keeper had first brought me here, the lady in my vision had said to protect them, but how? I hadn't been able to protect Laurie, so could I really protect a whole city?

With one hand on the stone, I grabbed Leo's hand with my other. Maybe I could do both at once. Closing my eyes, my heart started to thrash against my chest. I tried to focus on all of it. The cold stone beneath my hand, the pulse of Leo's heartbeat. She said to protect them, and didn't that include Leo? Leo was who I wanted to protect the most, so I closed my eyes and thought about mint and campfire, leather and wood, dragons and unicorns.

No matter what I did or what I thought or how hard I pressed, the stone was still gray and dull.

"I don't feel so good." My voice shook as I took my hand away. My hand looked gray too. My whole arm looked pale, and my head was starting to feel heavy. It didn't look like I had done anything, but I obviously had used some, if not almost all, of my magic. Maybe this had been a mistake.

"If I do more... Leo, I don't know if I can. It wants to take everything; I can feel it. What I have, it isn't enough. It needs all of me, but if I let it, I'll burn out, but... I'm scared."

"Hey." Leo's voice was steady. "I brought a backup plan." He held up the crown in his other hand and put it near the stone.

The crown.

That sad, sad crown.

My heart clenched at the sight of all those rubies, made from the hearts of thousands of fae.

"Listen, fuckers, I know you can hear me in there," Leo shouted. "Wake up and help us out here!"

Was I hallucinating? Was Leo really yelling at the crown?

"Who... What? What are you doing?" Words were becoming difficult to say.

"These jerks," he yelled, pointing to one of the rubies on the crown. "All the dead fae that made these rubies. I know they're in there because they've talked to me before, but I don't hear anything! We can use their power so we don't have to use all of yours!"

Maybe I *was* hallucinating. I leaned my head against the wall of the cave to steady myself. "Maybe... Don't call them assholes...?"

Leo made a face but took a deep breath before trying again. "Oh ye amazing fairies of yore," he intoned.

Seriously?

"Stop," I managed to say. "Put it on... Let me try."

Leo put the crown on his head, and I squeezed his hand. The red glow he'd had earlier seemed to slowly surround him again like a faint mist. As seconds passed, I could feel something, something small, smaller than small, like the tiniest tingle of a flame barely touching my skin. It wasn't much, but it was there, and it was coming from Leo.

"Do you feel it?" Leo asked, and I nodded.

I swallowed, unsure what to do next. We both closed our eyes, and I tried to concentrate. What was there to say to the ghosts of dead fae? I said the only thing I could think to say.

"I'm... sorry."

My eyes shot open at the sudden jolt of electricity that coursed into my veins. I looked to Leo, and the glow around him burned slightly brighter.

"I'm sorry," I repeated. "We are sorry about what happened to you."

Leo paused and then nodded. "Keep going, they like you."

I didn't let go of Leo, but with my other hand, I touched the Keeper Stone again.

"We... need... your help. To protect. Please?"

Nothing happened, and I thought that must be it, that this was all for nothing, but then Leo squeezed my hand tighter, and it came to me all at once. The light on the stone was very, very dim, but what I was feeling was anything but.

My body jerked with a sudden surge of power, and I had to force myself to keep my hand connected to the stone. It was like a tsunami of electricity was flowing from Leo to me and then into the stone. More power than I'd ever experienced. It was dangerous, and frightening, and I wondered if it would drown me as well.

More, more, more. The stone demanded *more*.

Did I have more to give?

The light around the stone began pulsing in time with my own heartbeat, and my chest felt tight like a rubber band that could snap at any second. Leo held on to me, and I kept my hand on the stone, even as my fingers went numb.

How long could I hold on?

My vision was darkening around the edges. I didn't have much time. This was working, *damn it*, but where I had worried at first about not having magic to pour into the stone, now I wondered if the Hellfire rubies were giving me too much.

How long did I have until this stone took everything?

"Vera!" Leo was shouting, but he sounded far away. "Vera!"

If Leo hadn't had the crown, I would have burned out a long time ago, but now, with him next to me, with the help of these poor dead fae who came before me, we stood a chance to protect the living.

If I could just hang on for a little bit longer, I could do it. My heart was beating faster and faster, each thump of my heart building and racing in time with the growing light from the Stone. The light was so beautiful, so clean and pure and bright, dizzying and enchanting, overwhelming everything in sight.

Leo was yelling something, but he wasn't letting go. He was right there with me.

We were doing this together, and all around us the world was white—no, not white.

Silver.

25

VERA

White, fluffy clouds shifted by me.

And two eyes, watching me intently.

Was this heaven?

Then I heard a snarl, and I had to wonder if maybe this was hell.

"Down, Zeus!"

"Get your damn dog off her." A familiar voice yelled, and when I looked over, there was Rand, in my room, standing in front of my mirror.

With a crown on his head.

"Did I die?" I asked out loud.

Rand turned to me just as I felt a hand squeeze mine. Leo was there, sitting on my bed. It wasn't a dream.

But Rand still had a crown on.

Leo brought my hand to his lips and planted a kiss. "You are very much alive," he said. His face fell, and I could tell he was still shaken. "If we hadn't had that crown with us, if we hadn't been able to use that power... Vera..." His voice broke.

I swallowed and nodded. "Thank you, Leo. What about—"

"Does this mean we get to go home now?" Zell said, yawning. "Because my girl is waiting on me."

"Can you shut up? They're clearly having a moment," Rand yelled at him.

I looked at Rand again. "Yeah, what he said. Wait, what's that on your head?"

"Oh, this old thing?" Rand yanked the gold crown off his head and threw it at Leo. He caught it before it hit him and threw it back. "That lunatic is making *me* accept it."

"You can always get a new one made." Leo shrugged. "One without those rubies."

I tried to prop myself up to see better and squinted up at Rand, noticing something underneath the collar of his shirt. "Rand. Do you have a new tattoo?"

A loud bark and a ball of white fur jumping on me interrupted him. "Zeus," I chuckled. "Are we still not friends?"

"That's his happy bark, princess," Zell said, and for the first time I saw him sitting across the room at my new table. "Little guy has been in here all day waiting for you to wake up. I think he was worried about you."

Zeus snarled at me again, and I wasn't as sure.

"Lie down," Leo commanded, and the dog and I both immediately obeyed, with Zeus padding over to the end of my bed and dutifully curling into a little white ball without complaint. "I meant the dog, not you."

"Right. Help me up?" Leo shifted me in the bed, propping me up with some pillows so I could see everyone. Marcus was on his tablet, furiously typing away.

My heart sank. "We didn't do it. Technology still works. The veil is still down."

Marcus lifted his head. "That's about sixty percent true."

"Huh?"

"The veil has returned."

"That's wonderful!"

"But."

"But?"

"The Gate is operational again, meaning it still requires fae to open it. But invisibility is gone, and technology still works here. I'd say that's a fair compromise. With the security lessons they've learned recently, I'd say that this is probably the best outcome."

"The old dude quit too," Zell called out.

"He means the fae king," Leo clarified. "He's decided to step aside. It seems he's realized that it's time for the younger generation to take the reins."

"I thought his head was going to explode when you showed him how to use a holo-watch." Zell snickered.

"He'll have some help figuring it out."

As if she knew we were speaking about her family, Mia burst through the door. Her pale face was red, as if she'd been crying, and she flew straight for my bed, ignoring both Leo and the little growling dog.

"Vera!" she said, leaping onto me.

"Mia!" Once our arms were around each other, I never wanted to let go. Mia sobbed on my shoulder, and I squeezed her tight against me. Tears were freely running down my face too as I remembered what I'd seen.

"I'm sorry. I'm so, so sorry, Mia. I didn't mean for this to happen, for any of this to happen. I'm so sorry. Please forgive me. I never wanted—"

"I know." Mia backed up and took my hand in hers. "Come on," she said, nodding to the door. "I want to show you something."

"She needs to rest," Leo protested as I got up. I gave him a kiss on the cheek and then followed Mia with Leo close behind.

Mia opened the door, and I gasped.

I'd never seen him like this. Laurie was normally the embodiment of life and light and energy, yet here he was, lying in bed, his hair a mess. Someone must have linked with him and healed his wounds, but he still looked more tired than I'd ever seen him.

"I'm not dying, you know. Everyone keeps crying around me like I'm dying, but I'm not. Mia's being dramatic. I'm just exhausted, that's all."

"When I last saw you..." I didn't even want to think about the last time we'd been together.

"Come on, Vera. You had that little faith in me?"

"That's not it. I saw... I saw what happened. I was there. You..."

"I know I don't have whatever crazy magic you have going on, but I am still the crowned prince of Rowan, Vera. It takes more than you think to kill me. I also had a little trick up my sleeve that your guy gave me. If your blood is what made Syn, then I'm not surprised you have the cool wings. That stuff is crazy powerful. If Leo hadn't given a vial of it to me, I might not be here."

"You used Syn to boost your abilities?"

"I did. I took out the hunters, who were all pathetic cowards when faced with a fae that wasn't raised in their little labs. Leo..." His voice trailed off as he looked behind me.

When I turned around to see if Leo was okay, he was doing something I'd never seen him do.

He was bowing. Deeply.

"I am sorry for what my father did to you and the others," he said. "He organized all of this, from the dissolution of the veil to the tainted Dust that took away fae powers. I don't know how to repay this debt, but—"

"Will you shut up? I didn't know what to say to you, Leo. I know he was a bastard, but he was your father."

Leo stood up, his face grim. "He lost the right to be called that a long time ago. Still. I am sorry. For everything."

"I'm going to commit these apologies to memory. Did you hear that they're giving me an award? I'm like a war hero. Look around this room and tell me what you think popular opinion of me is right now."

The room smelled sweet, overly sweet, like a perfume that had been sprayed too many times in a small space. The windows were open to let in fresh air, but there was no escaping the sheer volume of flowers that threatened to take over the bedroom. Everywhere I looked I saw bouquets of flowers, and though most of the blooms were hues of blue, I saw all shapes, sizes, and colors in the vases that were on the table, on the floor, by the window, everywhere. It seemed like every single household in Rowan had sent a bouquet of flowers to wish their prince a speedy recovery.

"The smell...," I said, trying not to breathe it in. Leo coughed behind me.

Laurie grimaced. "I know. It has me wishing I was unconscious again, but it comes with the territory." He adjusted his body so that he was sitting more straight up in the bed. "I have something to tell you that will be... difficult... for you to hear."

"Oh?" A million scenarios racing through my head, and I scooted forward, straightening up and bracing for the bad news. Judging by the look on his face, it had to be serious. He said he wasn't dying, but was his condition worse than I had expected?

"What is it?"

"So you see." He cleared his throat, his chin jutting out slightly. "I have decided that I'm going to give up on you."

"You... huh?"

"I wanted to inform you that I will no longer be engaging in regular daydreams about you, and you will have to rely on Leo to flirt with you from now on because I no longer have time for it. I know this will be difficult for you, Vera, but it is for the best."

"You daydream about her?" Leo asked from behind me, and I heard Mia giggle.

Laurie waved his hand in the air. "That's beside the point. The point is that my life is simply going to be too busy to focus all day on how beautiful you are. I need to focus on my recovery and then every-thing with Rowan. I'm sure you understand."

"I..." I had no idea how to finish that sentence. Not one clue. None. Zip, zero, zilch. As relieved as I was that his awful, terrible news wasn't awful or terrible at all, my brain couldn't form a response.

"You can't convince me otherwise, Vera, so don't try. Even tears won't make me change my mind. The decision has been made, and I am sticking to it no matter how much you beg me to reconsider."

He was... serious? *He was serious.* It was taking every ounce of control that I possessed to hold back the giggle that was threatening to break through at any moment. The serious look in Laurie's blue eyes and his formal tone made me think twice about laughing out loud.

"Well." I nodded solemnly to match his energy. "Okay then. I won't try to change your mind."

"Good. And no tears," he reminded me. "I won't be swayed by tears."

"No tears, I promise."

"Good."

"Good."

"You see, my father…" From the way his fingers gripped the sheets, I could tell that he was struggling with what to say. He sighed and stared up at the ceiling. "After everything that's happened, he's stepping down."

"This blue-winged idiot is apparently going to be their next king," said Leo, and when I looked up at him, I thought I might die of shock when Leo actually smiled.

"Too bad I'll have to deal with some other king of Vestia since you couldn't handle it," Laurie shot back.

"You guys being friends is weird," I told them. "But I like it."

"Good, because Leo said I can stay with you guys whenever I want a vacation from this place."

"I never said that."

Looking back at Laurie, I tried to judge by his reaction if this was a happy announcement or not. Noticing in the tension in his face, I assumed that Laurie wasn't excited about this decision.

"When?" I asked.

"Soon. It will be a quick coronation."

"I see. And how do you feel about this?"

"Honestly? I'm not sure. There's so much I want to do. Now I'll be able to do it."

"Then I'm happy for you," I told him.

"And you'll be happy too? I had hoped that you could find happiness with me, but that isn't the hand we've been dealt. As much as I hate to admit it, that demon over there has proven himself worthy of you, and I won't get in the way of your happiness."

"Laurie..."

"And anyway, I'm going to be a little busy, you know, being king and all."

"Is that all?" I tapped my chin and pretended to contemplate. "From what I hear, it seems like they're letting anybody be a king these days."

In an instant the tension seemed to vanish from his face, his blue eyes twinkling once again. Laurie laughed. "You're right."

26

VERA

Hundreds of fae hovered in the air underneath and around the sweeping branches of the colossal Darach Tor, the sacred tree of Rowan. The tree was easily as tall as the palace itself, its thick branches twisting and turning into the sky.

The small rays of the afternoon sunlight that sneaked through the tree's branches reflected off the bright colors of their wings. Pink and periwinkle, honey and pumpkin, their wings created a kaleidoscope of vibrant shades, like a tapestry hanging in the air. Their long dresses and cloaks swayed in the breeze beneath them, and the air buzzed with the fluttering of wings and the whispers of their conversations.

At the sound of a trumpet, all the fae dipped toward the ground, their wings moving in sync, their feet landing softly in the grass.

Mia and Victor were the first to appear under the tree. The other fae seemed to step aside, giving the princess and her lieutenant turned boyfriend the space to be the first couple to dance.

At first glance, Mia looked perfectly composed, her white hair, worn long and wavy down her back, complementing the soft lilac of her dress. But I knew better. The twittering of her blue wings told me everything I needed to know about how excited she was, especially when her wings stilled as Victor brought her close and the music began.

"It's sickening how romantic all this is, isn't it?"

I couldn't help but snicker. "I'm sure Zell would dance with you, if you asked him," I told Elise, but when I looked around, I didn't see her boyfriend anywhere.

As she stood beside me, watching more fae join Mia and Victor under the tree, the tall, blond demon didn't seem to care. She flicked her hair back over her shoulder and rolled her eyes. "He's not here. That idiot has been working with the engineers I brought with me from Vestia all day. I can't believe these fae have existed all this time without basic technology."

"Judging by all the young fae I've seen flying around with cell phones, I have a feeling they're going to adjust very, very quickly. It was a genius move to bring a bunch with you."

"I'm a business woman after all. When I see an opportunity, I seize it. Vestia has every piece of tech the fae of Rowan might want, and I'm going to be the first to sell it to them. I'm not the only one who knows how to seize a moment, you know."

"Oh?"

"As much as I loathe to remember back then, I wanted to be the one to buy you at the auction that day."

"No way, really?"

"Really. A certain hothead beat me to it. The same hothead who is flying this way." Elise pointed in front of us. There was Leo, the silver tips of his black wings shining in the fading sun. "Leo," she said as he approached.

"Elise."

She smiled sweetly. "Hurt her and you die."

"Hello to you as well."

Elise's smile didn't break. "Now that we understand each other, I'll leave you two alone. Vera, I'm sure I'll see you again soon."

"Of course." I watched her wings expand as she flew back toward the palace. I turned to Leo and fingered the lapel of his jacket, admiring the black suit he'd chosen for the evening.

"I'm glad you came tonight. I know it's been busy here."

"Did you think I would miss..." Leo gestured around to the fae dancing under the tree. "...this?"

"Do you even know what *this* is?"

"I..." Leo opened his mouth to answer but then promptly closed his lips. "No. Actually, yes. It's an opportunity to see you in this incredible dress." He held my hand up, giving me a quick twirl, my long black dress spinning with me. "And was it made by..."

"Elise brought it with her from Vestia," I told him.

"Ah. I like it even more now. The black fabric makes the colors of your wings stand out."

"It's part of the tradition of the Darach Tor. Mia told me that it's custom for fae to wear the colors of the wings of the one they love. So I thought..."

Leo nodded slowly but then reached into the pocket of his jacket, taking out a small handkerchief.

"A rainbow-colored suit isn't exactly my style," he said, "but I had a friend show me how to sew together a few fabrics and—"

"Leo..."

As I watched with wide eyes, he adjusted the handkerchief in his upper pocket so that just a hint of the many colors of fabric poked out the top.

"You knew," I said, hardly able to believe what I was seeing. "You knew about the tradition, and you... Did you say you made that? You... you... *sewed* it?"

"I'm an inventor. I'm good with my hands. It wasn't hard."

"Wait, did you say a *friend* helped you? That friend wouldn't happen to have blue wings and white hair?"

"We'll use the term friend loosely, but he's growing on me."

I couldn't help but chuckle as I imagined the insane amount of patience Laurie must have had to try to teach Leo how to sew anything.

My fingers grazed over the fabric now resting against Leo's chest, but then his own hand found mine and wrapped around it, keeping me close.

"Now," he said, "may we dance?"

As Leo secured an arm around my waist, we rose into the air, our wings guiding us under the massive tree to join the other fae.

And then it was just the two of us.

AFTER WEEKS PASSED and we rested and recovered, I moved back to the place that felt the most like home. Our home. My home. My home with Leo.

Rob joined Rand in Vestia, and Marcus had moved into his own place with Lydia, but we kept in contact and made plans to see each other at Elise and Zell's wedding in the spring. It was going to be the society event of the year for Vestia, and I even heard a rumor that Zeus would be the ring bearer.

Occasionally we'd get news from Rowan that a team would be passing through on an undercover mission to free more fae, and more than once they used our house as a place to stay before going back to Rowan. Since we never knew when we'd be needed, Leo busied himself with new inventions and I spent most of my time expanding the garden behind the house. We planted flowers of every imaginable variety, eventually adding in vegetables and fruits to share with everyone who worked at the house. One summer morning we buried Leo's ring under the prettiest rose bush in the yard. I helped him build a small bench that we put nearby, so the two of us could watch the sunsets together in what had become our special place.

Sometimes, often, it didn't feel real. It didn't feel right that we could be this happy after everything that had happened. But we were, and I tried to let myself indulge in this new reality with the man I loved.

One night it was almost dark, and Leo and I had been sitting on the bench in the back garden for at least an hour, listening to crickets and watching fireflies dance, when I suggested that we should go back inside.

Leo stood up and stretched, and I was about join him when I realized he was no longer standing.

My breath caught in my throat at the sight of this demon, this *prince*, with his bare chest and broad shoulders and dark wings, kneeling in front of me.

Me.

A fae.

I swallowed, unable to speak.

My eyes widened as Leo took my hand in his and smiled. My heart thumped in my chest as I realized what was happening.

"Before we do that, I think it is past time for me to say something to you, Vera."

"Say it anyway."

"I will. You already know this, but I'm yours, Vera. Everything of mine is yours. My life, my heart, my soul. Everything about me is yours to command."

My heart was thrashing so loudly against my chest that I wondered if he could hear it. Unlike me, Leo's face was completely calm, with no hint of the insane anxiety bubbling up inside me.

"Leo..."

"I know I'm not worthy of you, but—"

I fell to my knees in the dirt in front of him. "No."

"What?"

"No— I mean no, that's not true." I grabbed his other hand and held both up to his chest. No way was I letting go. "You are amazing, Leo. You've done amazing things that have changed the world. You saved me more times than I can count."

He chuckled. "You saved me too. You can command me as you wish, just please allow me to always love you and always be by your side. Will you be my wife?"

How could I speak with tears rolling down my cheeks? Lips quivering, I mumbled something, and Leo's silver eyes searched mine.

"Is that a yes?" he asked.

"Of course it is!" I muttered, letting go of his hands and flinging my arms around him. I almost knocked him over in the dirt, but he caught me, just like he always did. If he wanted me, I'd never leave his side again. I knew without a doubt that I'd be damned if I ever let him leave mine either.

Leo wrapped his wings around us to keep us in place, and it felt like a warm blanket was covering us both. With the touch of his finger, he tilted my head up to him. "Don't you want to see the ring?"

He helped me stand up, and then he reached into his pocket, taking out a small black box covered in velvet. He opened it, and inside was a silver ring with one of the prettiest diamonds I'd ever seen.

"I made it actually. I had a friend send me gemstones from Rowan and then I combined them to make this stone. A silversmith there made the band. They might not know a lot about science, but they do know art. I thought the little princess was going to lose her mind when I called her about it."

"Mia already knows?" I asked him, eyes wide as he nodded and gently slipped the ring on my finger. I couldn't help but stare at the way the fading sunlight reflected off the clear stone.

"I have one more thing for you. Come here." He didn't wait for me though, scooping me into his arms before he leaped into the air.

"I can fly myself, you know."

"No need."

We soared into the air, for longer than I had expected, and it was dark when we finally landed somewhere I hadn't expected to ever go again. Leo put me down atop the hill on the other side of the bridge leading out of Alliance.

I'd spent so many years just on the other side of that bridge. I'd grown up in the dorms there, knowing that one day I'd be sold to someone, never knowing who that might be or what terrors awaited me. I thought of the lazy days in the yard, the stressful days waiting for the monthly blood draws, the secret conversations with Henry. A lump formed in my stomach.

On such a happy day, why were we here?

My arms began to tremble, and my fingers felt numb. That was until Leo's hand found mine. "Leo? What's going on?"

"This is my second gift to you. We're here to watch."

"Watch what? It's too dark to see anything."

"That's because the whole island is empty."

"Empty? Why?"

Leo didn't answer, but squeezed my hand, his thumb rubbing on my new ring. The small gesture reassured me, even though I didn't know why we were there. With his other hand, Leo reached into the backpack beside him, took out his phone, and pressed a button to make a call.

"Go time?" I heard Rand say.

"You give the orders, Your Majesty."

"Not this time. I'll let you take this one."

"Then yes." Leo looked at me and smiled. "Go time."

I heard it before I saw it, loud pops and cracks that seemed to come from every direction on the island. Then they became louder, and I saw orange and yellow flames rising up here and there, their light casting shadows on the empty buildings. The auction house. The dorms. The labs.

Together we watched the island burn. Every building. Every blade of grass. Every inch of history and terror and pain, all burned away in a fiery inferno that sizzled and crackled. Smoke rose into the air in tall plumes visible even in the night sky.

Leo was beside me through it all.

"How?" I whispered. "How did you do this?"

"First, I bought the island."

"What?"

"I bought it. The whole thing. Every building, every home. All of it."

"How?"

"I sold my shares of Syn."

"You did?"

He shrugged. "I didn't need them. The whole thing was a hassle anyway. Elise can manage it just fine. After I sold them, I bought the island. I closed everything down and bought all the slaves and had Rob help me bring them to Rowan. No fae will be sold here ever again. No fae will grow up here like you did."

I couldn't believe it. Syn had been his life's work, and he'd sold it.

And the island... I didn't even have words to describe how I felt. I felt a lot of things, all of them at once, but more than anything I felt relief.

"I know it's not enough," he said. "There are still fae that need to be rescued. But I had to do something."

"You've done so much already."

"It's not enough. It will never be enough." Leo turned to me. "The fire will erase the buildings, but I know it won't erase everything that happened. We can build something new here, if you want, or leave it to rot. I don't care. Whatever you want to do, I just want to do it together."

I couldn't imagine anything better.

EPILOGUE

"That's enough for tonight," Leo said, clapping the book shut.

"Again! Again!"

"Yeah, again!" I added my voice to the pleas coming from our son. "Read it just one more time? Please?"

"I have a feeling you both could recite the story yourselves without the book at all," Leo said, replacing the book on the shelf near Aaron's bed.

"But it's better when you read it," the boy whined. "You do the dragon voice better than Mama. She doesn't roar as loud as you."

Aaron stretched his little arms above his head and yawned, the light on the bedside table shining through his black wings. Aaron's wings were much thinner than Leo's, more like fae wings than a demon's. Where the tips of Leo's wings were silver, the color of Aaron's changed depending on the light. I'd spent many hours simply staring at him, marveling at the fact that he had been created, that we created such a perfect being. In those hours I spent holding him, letting my fingers caress his wings, I saw silver, sometimes I saw a hint of red or yellow, or some mysterious mix that seemed beyond understanding.

When it was obvious that his father was not moved by our pleas,

Aaron clutched his tiny stuffed dragon and sank down into the bed. With me snuggled next to him, Aaron's silver eyes stared up at his father.

"It's late, little one," Leo said, leaning down to kiss his head. "Even dragons and unicorns need their sleep."

Leo extended a hand, and I took it, letting him help me up and out of the bed. It was getting harder to get up on my own with each passing day. The twins growing inside me were happily kicking away like they did every night, making sure I was always aware of their presence, especially at night during Aaron's bedtime story.

We stayed in the doorway after I turned off Aaron's light. He was asleep before we even made it out of the room, and then the house was quiet. I knew our days of silence were numbered. Once the twins were born, we'd be grateful for any amount of peace and quiet.

Back in our room, I went into the bathroom to get ready for bed, and Leo followed me in. He'd already taken his shirt off and came and stood behind me at the sink. Leo reached his big hands around my waist, rubbing them on my ever-growing belly. The movement felt good over my itchy, stretched skin.

"Tell me what you see," he said, nodding to the mirror.

"I see a tired pregnant lady."

"Try again."

"I see an extremely handsome demon."

"I see the love of my life." Leo leaned down and whispered in my ear. "You've never looked prettier." He pressed a kiss to my neck as his fingers tickled up my sides, making me squirm.

"You know, a really hot demon once told me that pretty things are a pain in the ass."

"The things that matter in life usually are."

The End

· · ·

WANT to read more about Leo, Vera, Laurie, and friends? Join my newsletter at http://www.laurencrowne.com where I regularly share side stories, fan art, and character interviews.

All of my books take place in this same world, so if you want more stories about the demons and fae of Vestia and Rowan, be sure to check them out. Thanks for reading!

ACKNOWLEDGMENTS

THANK YOU, readers! Thank you for taking a chance on this story of Leo and Vera, and thank you for all of the amazing reviews and emails you've sent me! I love hearing from you, and I'm excited to hear what you thought of the end of this series.

Of course, this page would not be complete with out a huge thank you to my husband. He's my biggest cheerleader, and without him I never would have been able to chase my dream of being an author.

This book would not be possible without Anne, Abigail, Linda, and Crystalle at Victory Editing and Heather at Book Cover Artistry. They're an amazing team, and I couldn't do this without them.

ABOUT THE AUTHOR

Lauren Crowne writes sexy, funny, action-packed fantasy and paranormal romance, transporting readers into a world of fae, demons, wolf shifters, and more. She always dreamed of being an author, and she is delighted and honored to share the stories that have been bouncing around in her head for years. When she isn't writing, Lauren is addicted to drinking iced coffee and traveling with her husband and kids. You can find out more about her on Facebook, Instagram, and TikTok.